WOLF

SENTINEL SECURITY #1

ANNA HACKETT

Wolf

Published by Anna Hackett

Copyright 2022 by Anna Hackett

Cover by Mayhem Cover Creations

Cover image by ADB Imagery

Edits by Tanya Saari

ISBN (ebook): 978-1-922414-60-1

ISBN (paperback): 978-1-922414-61-8

Heart of Eon - Romantic Book of the Year (Ruby) winner 2020

Cyborg - PRISM Award Winner 2019

Edge of Eon and Mission: Her Protection - Romantic Book of the Year (Ruby) finalists 2019

Unfathomed and Unmapped - Romantic Book of the Year (Ruby) finalists 2018

Unexplored – Romantic Book of the Year (Ruby) Novella Winner 2017

Return to Dark Earth – One of Library Journal's Best E-Original Books for 2015 and two-time SFR Galaxy Awards winner

At Star's End – One of Library Journal's Best E-Original Romances for 2014

The Phoenix Adventures – SFR Galaxy Award Winner for Most Fun New Series and "Why Isn't This a Movie?" Series

Beneath a Trojan Moon – SFR Galaxy Award Winner and RWAus Ella Award Winner

Hell Squad – SFR Galaxy Award for best Post-Apocalypse for Readers who don't like Post-Apocalypse

"Like Indiana Jones meets Star Wars. A treasure hunt with a steamy romance." – SFF Dragon, review of *Among Galactic Ruins*

"Action, danger, aliens, romance – yup, it's another great book from Anna Hackett!" – Book Gannet Reviews, review of *Hell Squad: Marcus*

Sign up for my VIP mailing list and get your *free box set* containing three action-packed romances.

Visit here to get started: www.annahackett.com

CHAPTER ONE

As Nick "Wolf" Garrick exited his Aston Martin DB11, he narrowly resisted the urge to slam the door.

A valet raced over. "Evening, sir. I'll take good care of her."

Nick just grunted and handed over the keys. He glared at the entrance to the Plaza Hotel. He wasn't in the mood—to be polite, to attend this shindig, or to socialize.

Scratch that. He was never in the mood to socialize.

Anger churned inside him, and he straightened his tuxedo jacket and headed for the red-carpeted stairs into the building.

He had a job to do, and he'd do it. He and the Sentinel Security team had gotten word, last-minute, that the target of one of their ongoing investigations was going to be at this charity dinner tonight.

A bunch of New York's wealthiest would be in attendance including Michael Denning. On the outside,

Denning was a wealthy businessman...who also happened to be doing lucrative arms deals on the side with several rebel groups in South America.

Nick and two others from Sentinel Security were in charge of planting a near-microscopic bug on the man.

"God, I love a hot guy in a suit," a female voice said in his earpiece. "The beard is an added bonus."

He flicked a glance up at the security camera above the hotel doors. He snorted.

"You're hot, Wolf, especially when you're grumpy," Jet "Hex" Adler said.

The tech whiz was running comms from the Sentinel Security office in Chelsea. Knowing her, she'd hacked into the hotel security feeds in under a minute and had full control of the hotel's computer system. The woman could hack anything.

He didn't deny he was feeling pissed off. He'd flown in from San Francisco today after a successful job to help his boss' sister. While Nick had been away, he'd gotten a panicked call from his little sister, Nola. Technically, half-sister, but he didn't bother with the half. From the day she'd been born, Magnolia had been his family in every sense of the word.

She'd called, worried because her best friend was getting death threats.

He strode into the Plaza's lobby. It was all cream marble and gold accents, a giant chandelier hanging overhead. Once, he'd felt uncomfortable in places like this. Like a bull in a china shop. But his work had taught him how to blend into all kinds of different settings and situations. Fancy hotel or arid, desert battlefield—he could do either.

His thoughts didn't linger on the grandiose decor as he made his way to the Grand Ballroom. Instead, they turned to threats of death to one Elaine Madden.

They were pretty fucking ugly threats. Nola and Lainie had been best friends since middle school, joined at the hip since they were twelve. Being six years older, he hadn't paid too much attention to his sister's slightly awkward, geeky friend. He'd been too busy counting down the days to getting out of the house and away from his overbearing, asshole stepfather. The day Nick had graduated, he'd joined the Navy, and was gone. He'd been obliged to go home when he could, to see Nola, but that was it.

The less time Nick and Charles Newhouse spent in the same room, the better.

Then on one vacation, he'd discovered his sister's sweet friend had morphed into a beauty. A smiling, smart, gorgeous young woman.

His hand flexed.

Then he'd fucked up and kissed an eighteen-year-old Lainie Madden by the pool.

It had been wrong. She was too young for him. He was the son of an ex-con, something his stepfather never let him forget. At the time, he'd also been a SEAL, doing some pretty tough, shitty missions.

And Lainie was Nola's best and closest friend.

That was something he could never let himself forget.

He'd spent the years since keeping a lock on the

highly inappropriate attraction he felt for Lainie. Mostly by not spending too much time with her.

After his stint as a Navy SEAL, followed by several years in SAC—the CIA special activities center, he hadn't seen much of her. Lainie had gone on to become the successful CEO of a billion-dollar online graphic design company, Pintura.

He'd seen her beautiful face and velvet-brown eyes on the covers of a bunch of business magazines. He'd even kept a couple.

Lainie was off-limits. He'd never, ever do anything to hurt his little sister. Nola was the only person who'd always loved him unconditionally. Hell, he didn't want to hurt Lainie, either, and Nick knew he wasn't built for relationships. Lainie had candlelit dinners and white-picket fences written all over her.

Still, he sure as fuck would keep her safe.

He gritted his teeth and stepped into the Grand Ballroom.

The charity event was in full swing. The ballroom had an ornate, curved ceiling, and was flanked by fancy columns. It all looked overblown to him. There were circular tables set up at one end, overflowing with flowers, and a dance floor at the other end. People, in their glittering best, mingled and laughed politely.

After Nola had called him, panicked about Lainie's death threats, he'd raced back from San Francisco, only to be unable to get a hold of Lainie all day. She hadn't answered her phone. Hadn't returned his messages. She wasn't at her fancy apartment in Tribeca. Or at the Pintura office.

Her assistant had assured him that she was in meetings, but Nick didn't think Lainie was taking these threats seriously.

Now Killian, Nick's boss, had pulled him in for tonight's job.

Nick blew out a breath. His first priority for tomorrow would be to track Lainie down.

He nabbed a drink that he would pretend to sip and studied the crowd. He spotted the mayor of New York, a famous actor, and several billionaires.

He also saw Denning.

The older man laughed heartily, his second wife—a much younger, glamorous blonde—stood beside him, decked out in a clinging, designer gown. From the intense investigation Sentinel Security had completed, Nick knew the man also funded a twenty-two-year-old bikini-designer mistress in Miami and a twenty-eight-year-old opera singer in London.

Not to mention the lucrative, illegal arms deals. Denning kept himself very busy. No, looking at the wide, congenial smile, no one in this crowd would guess what Michael Denning did in his free time.

A new couple swept into the room. A few people turned to look and whispered.

They made a striking pair. The man was tall, well-built, with a hawkish face and dark hair. He looked like he'd been born wearing the tailored tuxedo.

But Nick was well aware Killian "Steel" Hawke, the owner of Sentinel Security, looked just as comfortable in mud-splattered fatigues, cradling an M-4. Nick knew because they'd fought side-by-side too many times to count.

And it didn't take more than one look into Killian's black eyes to know he was dangerous.

Nick let his gaze skate over Killian, like they were strangers. All part of the plan.

The woman on Killian's arm was elegant. Her brown hair was streaked with strands of blonde, and upswept, accenting her stunning face. Her black dress encased her curved, feminine form. She had a faint smile on her face, her blue eyes taking in the crowd. She looked like a beautiful society woman.

In truth, she was Hadley "Striker" Lockwood. Hadley was former British Intelligence—MI6. The elegant façade hid a sharp mind and a strategic genius. She was an impressive sniper, and an expert in close-quarter combat.

She also had a sexy, British accent, and fought dirty.

He watched her take a glass of champagne, smiling sweetly at the waiter.

Nick circled the room, away from Killian and Hadley. A woman in a formfitting, red dress spun, bumping into him.

"Oh, sorry." Her gaze latched onto his face and her smile turned sultry. "Hi, there."

Nick lifted his chin and sidestepped her. He didn't have time for any fluttering eyelashes. He needed to get this job done, then get back to his apartment and do some more research on Lainie's death threats.

Some had arrived in the mail—printed on generic, untraceable paper—and a slew had come electronically, via fake email accounts. The ones Nick had seen so far were vile and sickening in their sadistic detail.

He'd seen some of the worst of what humanity could do to other people, and the thought of anything like that happening to Lainie...

Anger burned. He knew her success made her a target. He was just angry that she hadn't returned his calls.

And pissed she hadn't come to him sooner.

Shit. Get your head in the game, Garrick.

He was here to ensure they planted this damn bug on Denning. Nick knew better than anyone, that if you got distracted on a mission, people died. His gut curled into knots.

Focus. On. The. Job.

He moved through the crowd, and spotted Killian and Hadley moving in on the target.

A bright, beautiful smile broke out on Hadley's face. If anyone could charm the dirty businessman and get the tiny tracker on the man's skin, it was Striker.

Nick pretended to sip his drink, alert in case the plan went FUBAR. If Hadley didn't succeed, she'd hand off the tracker to Nick and he'd accidentally stumble into Denning.

He had no doubt Killian and Hadley would get the job done, but Killian didn't just plan a backup plan B. He planned C through Z, as well.

The music from the band swelled, and he let his gaze skim over the dance floor.

A flash of green caught his eye, but it was the wickedly feminine curves inside the green dress that kept his gaze riveted. The dress made him think of Greek goddesses. It skimmed over a mouthwatering body, and he tried not to stare at the amazing cleavage like a pervert.

Then he took in the loose fall of deep-brown hair and the pretty face as she smiled at her dance partner.

Nick's gut clenched.

Lainie.

OKAY, so this party wasn't so bad.

As her handsome dance partner spun her, then pulled her close and dipped her, Lainie Madden laughed.

She'd always been a hopeless dancer. She'd been a geek at school, and took coding classes, not dance lessons.

But Brandon—or was it Brent?—was making her feel downright graceful. He was handsome. Sure, it was in that bland, boring, Ken-doll kind of way that had never done much for her, but still, he was prettier to look at than her keyboard and computer screen. Definitely a nice change from her overflowing email inbox.

Lainie kept her smile in place, enjoying the dance and the pleasant buzz from the glass of champagne she'd had. She didn't drink much and was a total lightweight.

Because you're always working.

Ah, there was her annoying, inner voice. Always trying to put a damper on things.

Busy CEOs of successful companies have a lot of work to do, she told herself.

She narrowly avoided stepping on Brandon/Brent's foot.

And I'm here tonight, not *working, so quit nagging.*

You didn't want to come, her inner voice countered. *You're here because it's for charity. And I know you're planning to do more work later. You have no personal life and you never let anyone get too close.*

Lainie resisted the urge to wrinkle her nose. *Shut up, inner voice.*

Her inner voice sniffed. *Well, at least you aren't worrying about the death threats.*

Annnd Lainie's good mood instantly plummeted.

No. No way. She absolutely was *not* thinking of those horrible messages and the increasing bombardment of cyber attacks on the Pintura website. She'd hired more security staff to help her overworked team.

She had no proof, but she was sure they were related. Whoever was fantasizing about killing her was also trying to hack her company's computer system.

She missed a step and bumped into her dance partner.

"Steady, there." He shot her a handsome smile.

"Sorry. I warned you that I wasn't great on the dance floor."

His hand curved around her hip. "You're doing fine."

She waited to feel some sparks or heat. Her best friend Nola was always nagging her about her nonexistent love life.

Lainie had sworn off love, and sex, and men.

She felt her inner voice stir and stomped on it. *Don't you start.*

She was too busy anyway. Pintura was her life and it left little time for anything else. And the sad reality was that she stunk at choosing men. Her college boyfriend had cheated on her, and her most recent boyfriend had cheated on her with a plump-lipped influencer. *Ugh.* She'd wised up and dumped Keenan six months ago.

Thankfully, she hadn't loved him. He'd been gorgeous, a model, and a few years younger than her, and...gorgeous. She was a little embarrassed to admit she'd only been with him for his looks. They'd had zilch in common, and she'd gotten pretty tired of posing for pretty social media photos every time they went out.

The sex had been okay. She'd been hoping for fireworks and got more of a gentle fizzle. It always felt like Keenan was performing when his clothes came off, more worried about looking and sounding good than ensuring she enjoyed herself.

So, no men. She didn't need any more self-absorbed cheaters.

The song ended. She stepped back, smiling. "Thank—"

"I'm cutting in," a deep voice said.

Brandon/Brent frowned, and Lainie's head shot up.

Her gaze met a deep blue one.

Nick Garrick.

Her body froze, then it came to spectacular life.

This was what sparks felt like.

Nick was about the same height as her dance partner, but that was where the similarities ended.

Lainie's heart pounded. Nick was broader and had more bulk. His tuxedo didn't hide any of it, as it was all muscle. His chestnut-brown hair needed a cut, and his beard suited him. He looked a little rough and a lot tough. He made Brent—she was sure it was Brent—look like he was twelve.

Brent straightened. "Sorry, we were just—"

Nick shouldered past the man and swept Lainie into his arms.

He moved across the dance floor astonishingly well. She was shocked that a big, bad former Navy SEAL could dance.

Her body brushed against his hard one, and tingles erupted everywhere. He'd always made her breath catch. She'd thought her major crush on her best friend's brother had dimmed over the years, but boy was she wrong. When she'd first met her new friend Nola's older brother, she'd been a gangly, awkward twelve-year-old, and he'd been a gorgeous, athletic, eighteen-year-old with a bad-boy edge. And throughout the years, when she'd caught glimpses of him, he'd matured into a handsome man, still with an edge.

But this Nick—this hard-eyed man—was nothing like that long-ago teenage boy.

"You get my messages?" His voice held a touch of gravel.

Lainie swallowed. "I've been busy—"

"Someone is trying to kill you, and that doesn't take precedence?"

That bossy, take-charge tone made her hackles rise. "Nola shouldn't have called you. I'm handling it."

"She's worried. She showed me photos of some of the messages. You should be worried, too."

Lainie dragged her gaze off his rugged face and looked over his wide shoulder. Really wide. Nick was big and powerful, and under her hand she could feel the flex of his muscles.

"I'm taking precautions, Nick. I have a security team at work—"

"Corporate security. You have a small, inexperienced team."

Her gaze flew straight back to him. His eyes were the color of cobalt. Such a deep, mysterious blue. "You looked into my company?"

"Yes. You're in danger. Nola's worried. I'm worried. You're...like a sister to me."

Ugh. She hated hearing that. Hated that the man who often starred in her most secret fantasies saw her as a sister. She hated even more that he'd always treated her like that. Nola's little friend.

Except for one time.

She'd been eighteen. Nick had been home from the Navy on R&R. He'd filled out, had been fit and strong. It was the first time she'd seen him with the sexy beard.

He'd had a huge fight with his stepdad. Lainie had very little time for Nola's stern, snobby father. Mr. Newhouse always took every chance to rub Nick's face in the fact that his father had been a criminal. Like a child had anything to do with that.

She'd heard them fight, seen Nick sitting by the pool on a lounger, shoulders hunched.

She'd ended up sitting with him. They'd talked, and she'd even managed to make him laugh.

Then, he'd kissed her.

Sadly, for Lainie, it was still the hottest, sexiest kiss she'd ever had.

Unfortunately, Nick had pulled back like he'd been burned, and taken off like she was toxic. She hadn't seen him much since then. Glimpses of him at Nola's parties, the odd dinner with Nola and their group of friends. He was always scrupulously polite.

That decade had hardened him.

Nola said he'd been part of the CIA. Whatever he'd done, it clearly hadn't been easy.

Lainie lifted her chin. She wasn't eighteen anymore, and she wasn't stupid. She was a smart, successful businesswoman. She was a CEO, and she was used to giving orders, not taking them.

"I'm not your sister," she said.

Something flickered in his eyes, and he leaned closer. "No, you're not."

Dammit. Butterflies were dancing in her belly. His hand clenched on her hip, and she felt the press of those strong fingers burning through her dress. Her gaze dropped to his lips.

"You're coming with me," he announced.

What? "Nick, I'll call you tomorrow. I need—"

"No." He pulled them to a stop in the center of the dance floor.

"What do you mean no?" She'd been running her own company for several years and didn't hear no very often. "I agreed to attend this event tonight. I'll—"

"I said no. It's too dangerous. Whoever is after you could be here."

Lainie felt a cold shiver skitter down her spine. Her

gaze ran over the laughing crowd. "No one's going to do anything in the middle of a crowd."

"It's the perfect place to do something." He wrapped a hand around her bicep. The impact of his fingers on her bare skin made her gasp.

Don't get distracted, Lainie.

"I'm not leaving." She put a hand on her hip.

"You are," he growled.

"God, you're annoyingly bossy. It's not an attractive trait, Nick."

"I don't give a fuck. I care about you being safe."

Her heart did a weird flip-flop. She ignored it. "What are you going to do, carry me out of here?"

His blue eyes narrowed. "If I have to."

She gasped, her mouth dropping open.

Now his gaze dropped to her lips.

"You can't," she said. "People will stop you, or—"

"I'll make it look credible. I guarantee, no one will get in my way."

Lainie made a scoffing noise. "I'm adding arrogant and overconfident to bossy."

"Thank you."

She rolled her eyes. "They weren't compliments, Nick."

"Enough arguing."

She waved a hand. "All right then, let's see your grand plan. I won't be bailing you out with hotel security."

He yanked her close and kissed her.

Lainie's brain short-circuited.

Her lips parted, then Nick's tongue was in her mouth.

Oh. *God.* The man tasted so good, like the best chocolate—rich, dark, delicious.

He made a low sound that vibrated through her. She kissed him back. She met him stroke for stroke, plastering herself against him.

In that moment, she wasn't Lainie Madden. She wasn't a workaholic CEO with a bad track record in men. She wasn't at a mostly boring charity party.

She wasn't receiving nasty death threats.

She was pure feeling.

And Nick Garrett was holding her and kissing her.

Then he lifted his head and muttered a curse.

Lainie blinked, dazed. She licked her lips.

He cursed again.

Then he grabbed her arm and dragged her across the dance floor, through the crowd, and out of the ballroom.

And dammit, he was right, no one stopped him.

CHAPTER TWO

Nick took the key for his Aston Martin from the valet, handed over a tip, then shoved Lainie in the passenger seat.

He rounded the car, cursing himself.

Why the hell had he kissed her? He could still taste her on his lips. *What part of "off-limits" didn't you comprehend, Garrick?*

He muttered another curse and locked down every single emotion churning inside him.

"Wolf, where are you going?" Hex said in his ear. "Killian said you stormed out."

"I'll be in touch soon." He shut off his earpiece.

He slid into the driver's seat. Beside him, Lainie crossed her arms, staring ahead.

All that did was push her breasts up against the low neckline of her dress.

Nick yanked his gaze off her cleavage and started the car. With a roar of the engine, he pulled out onto the street.

"In case you hadn't realized, I'm pissed at you and your high-handed bullshit," Lainie snapped.

He grunted. "Noted."

She turned to face him. "You don't sound worried, or apologetic."

"Because I'm not."

She made a very feminine, enraged sound.

Nick felt it in his cock. *Fuck.* His hands clenched on the wheel. She looked gorgeous in her green dress. Those damn curves. His hands flexed. Her perfume filled his car, and he pulled it in with each breath. It was sweet and spicy.

Just like Lainie.

"Whether you like it or not, Lainie, I'm keeping you safe. I promised Nola, and it's what I do."

He felt her looking at him.

"I can look after myself," she said.

He glanced at her. "Nola's really worried." *He* was worried.

Her face changed, worry creeping in. "I told her it would be all right. Between my security team and the police—"

"It's been a month. They found anything yet?"

She sagged against the seat. "No." She fidgeted.

God, for a second, he was young again, watching a guilty Nola and Lainie trying not to lie about something they'd done wrong. Neither of them could lie worth a damn.

"Something you haven't shared?" he asked.

She cleared her throat. "I really didn't want Nola to worry."

His brows drew together. "Go on."

Lainie turned in her seat to face him. "Don't get mad..."

"People usually only say that when they know the other person is going to get mad."

She toyed with some of her hair, her fingers brushing across her collarbone.

Fuck. He was going to have the imprint of his zipper on his cock at this rate. He tried desperately to get a lock on his desire. "Spit it out, Lainie."

"I didn't show Nola all the letters. Just a few." She licked her lips. "The ones that were the least horrible."

Nick sucked in a breath. The ones Nola had shown him were horrible. "How bad?"

She swallowed, her voice a whisper. "Bad."

"I'm stepping in, Lainie. I don't care if that ruffles your feathers. Your safety comes first."

She just stared at him for a beat, then sighed. "I'd be foolish to turn down the assistance, but you didn't have to come in like a bulldozer."

"Then you should've answered my calls today."

She stiffened. "Ugh, you're annoying."

"Get used to it, babe. You're feistier than I remember." Like a kitten clawing at him.

She rolled her eyes. "Where are we going?"

"My office."

"Sentinel Security?" She sounded curious.

"Yes."

"I've heard a lot about them. A lot of whispers and rumors about the owner, but the company has a good reputation."

Nick grunted again. He drove them into the West Chelsea historic district. The Sentinel Security warehouse came into view.

The huge, brick warehouse had been built in the late 1800s and served as a storage and transfer point for cargo heading in and out of New York. A large, arched doorway was set in the center, and arched windows flanked by black shutters dotted the brick façade. On top perched a more modern addition made of glass and iron, with several green-filled terraces.

Lainie leaned forward. "The old Hudson warehouse?"

"Yeah."

"I watched them renovate this."

He touched the dash, and the garage doors opened. They drove down the ramp into the lower levels below the large building.

"This place is huge," Lainie breathed.

"Yeah, it was an old storage warehouse. Killian, my boss, purchased it years ago." It had sat in near ruin for almost a decade, and once Killian had left the CIA, he'd set about turning the place into his base of operations. "He had it completely remodeled and rents parts of it out." To fully vetted businesses who were all clients of Sentinel Security and needed secure premises. "It's mixed residential and business use. And there's a huge courtyard in the center. You can still see the old rail tracks from the 1800s."

Nick parked in his space and climbed out.

Lainie looked around, studying Hex's red Audi TT. He didn't see Killian's Ferrari SP 48 Unica, so he guessed he and Hadley hadn't returned yet. The other two members of Sentinel Security's elite Alpha team, Matteo "Hades" Mancini and Bram "Excalibur" O'Donovan were currently in Cuba on a job.

Nick led Lainie to the elevator. He touched his palm to the screen, and it beeped. Thankfully, they were only going one level because that damn perfume of hers was taunting him.

Little sister's best friend. Little sister's best friend. He needed the words tattooed on his damn head.

The doors opened. They were still underground. Several levels of the Sentinel Security office were built beneath the warehouse.

"The upper levels are where we meet with clients, and where the admin staff work," he told her. "The cyber security team have a level to themselves, with their fancy computers and servers. Another level is for the security specialists who take care of the more mundane work, like security background checks and standard corporate security."

"And this level?" she asked.

Where Alpha team took care of more complicated cases. "Where my team does their work."

Lainie took in the brick walls and arched doorways. The old-world brickwork contrasted with the sleek, modern lights and furniture. A green wall, filled with lush plants, covered the end of the space.

He strode through the open plan area and under an archway into the command center.

One wall was covered in a huge, seamless, interactive computer screen. Hex sat on her chair at her long desk, drinking a huge soda. Her pink-tipped dark hair brushed her jaw line, and her tiny body was clad in her usual jeans and T-shirt.

"Hey," Nick said.

"Wolf! Where have you been?" Hex swiveled. "Killian said you bailed—" Hex's blue-green gaze snagged on Lainie. The hacker had one blue eye and one green. "Oh."

"Hex, this is Elaine Madden. My sister's best friend—"

"The head of Pintura," Hex breathed. "I use your website all the time." The hacker leaped up.

"Lainie, this is Jet Adler."

"Call me Hex."

Lainie smiled. "Nice to meet you."

"You, too. So, you knew Wolf when he was young? I need *all* the goss."

Nick tugged on Hex's pink-tinged hair. "Behave."

"Never." The tech whiz elbowed him. He shook his head and saw Lainie watching them, her face expressionless but something working in her eyes.

"You work for Sentinel Security, Hex?" Lainie asked.

"Yup." Hex waved a hand at the screen. "I'm the goddess of all things tech. They wouldn't survive without me."

Nick snorted. She was mostly right. Lainie was watching him and Hex carefully. He couldn't get a read on her expression.

"So, what was Wolf like as a teenager? Tell me he was a dork with braces."

"Wolf?" Lainie asked.

He cleared his throat. "My codename from the military."

Lainie's eyes widened at Hex. "You were in the military, too?"

Hex shook her head. "Not exactly. I'm a hacker."

At the surprise on Lainie's face, Nick tugged Hex's hair again. "A legal one. Who used to work for the Agency."

"The CIA," Lainie said quietly.

Hex winked. "Now Killian pays me a buttload to keep the Sentinel guys on track. So? Wolf in high school?"

"He was tall, handsome, the quarterback of the football team, with a total bad-boy vibe, and every girl at school had a crush on him."

Hex's nose wrinkled. "Figures."

"Including you?" The words slipped out before Nick could stop them.

Lainie gave a strangled laugh. "Nick, I was twelve when I met you. And I was dorky and geeky. I thought you were a young god. I would have sold my soul to have you smile at me."

Some strange sensation moved through him. He'd spent a lifetime reminding himself that his sister's smart, beautiful, accomplished friend was off-limits. For so many different reasons.

You're trash, boy. Not worthy to breathe the same air.

Your father was an ex-con. We all know what blood flows in your veins.

Nick's lips flattened. He'd learned a long time ago to

ignore his stepfather's voice. The man was a prejudiced, bigoted asshole.

"But from what I remember, he was far less bossy and annoying back then." Lainie crossed her arms again.

Damn, again with the soft, beautiful breasts. It was impossible to ignore them when they were right there, accentuated by that damn dress.

He kept his gaze locked on her face. "I'm only bossy when people don't listen to reason."

"*Your* version of reason," Lainie countered.

Hex scoffed. "Wolf, you're bossy all the time."

Now he crossed his arms. "Well, I know better than to be dancing the night away at a party when some madman is gunning for me."

Lainie gasped. "It was a charity event I'd committed to six months ago. Raising money for research into rare cancers. And my team already looked into the security. A madman is hardly going to attack me in the middle of a crowded room."

"You don't know that."

Heat filled her cheeks and she stalked up to him. "It was a party, Nick." She poked him in the chest. "You might be out of practice, but parties are generally a place to have fun. Where you smile and socialize."

"Not really in Wolf's skill set," Hex said.

He glared at his friend.

"There were dangerous people there," he said.

Lainie was smart, and he saw something move behind her eyes. "Why were you there?"

"That's not important."

Now her eyes widened. "You were on some sort of mission..."

At that moment, Killian and Hadley strode in.

"Where did you go?" Killian demanded.

Lainie looked at the elegantly dressed couple, blinking.

"God, Killian, you rock a tux." Hex looked back at Nick. "You're no slouch, Wolf, but the tux looks like it's trying to tame you and failing. Killian looks like he wears his all the time. Hadley, you're gorgeous as always. Bitch."

"My feet are killing me," Hadley said, in her cultured British accent. She slipped her heels off and sighed in relief.

"Everything went okay?" Nick asked.

Killian nodded, which meant they got the bug planted on Denning. Then Killian's dark gaze zeroed in on Lainie.

"Ms. Madden, welcome to Sentinel Security. I'm Killian Hawke."

"Hi." Lainie pushed a strand of hair back behind her ear, looking a little dazed.

Nick scowled. He knew Killian had that effect on women, but it still annoyed him.

"Wolf is extremely concerned for your safety," Killian said.

She seemed to break out of her stupor. "I know, but I assure you—"

"I've seen some of the threats. I'm concerned, too."

"She tells me those are only a few of them," Nick said unhappily. "The least nasty of the bunch."

"All the more reason to take this very seriously," Killian said.

Obviously, having the owner of Sentinel Security mention his concern made an impact. She bit her lip, worry filling her face.

Nick didn't let himself look at her lip, but he felt a violent need to comfort her, reassure her. He couldn't help himself. He reached out and touched her back.

"We're going to make sure you're safe, Lainie. No matter what."

"THANKS." Lainie accepted the cup of tea from the beautiful woman who introduced herself as Hadley Lockwood.

"Trust me, with Wolf on the case, he'll have whoever is threatening you behind bars before you know it," the woman said.

Smiling, Lainie fiddled with the cup, trying not to be jealous of the woman's lovely accent. The cup had the Sentinel Security logo on it. A gold shield with a stylized S in the center of it.

"You were an agent, too?" she asked Hadley.

The woman gave her a faint smile. "Something like that. I moved from London and joined Sentinel Security just over a year ago. I love New York. And we have a great team."

Hex blew the woman a kiss from her chair. "Love you too, baby."

Killian and Nick strode back in. Both had ditched

their jackets and bowties. Lainie's heart skipped a beat. Somehow, that made them both look more attractive. If that was even possible.

Killian was the more classically handsome of the two. A little leaner, his hair and eyes like black ink. He radiated a dangerous intensity that made her feel like she was being sucked into a black hole.

Nick was broader and tougher looking, with his shaggier, brown hair and beard. He looked dangerous, too, like he'd leap in front of a speeding truck and stop it with a glare.

Both were heart-stoppingly hot.

Nick's blue gaze met hers. "Now, let's discuss who the hell is sending you these threats."

Lainie knew it wouldn't be smart to turn away their help. Nick and his team were experts.

She set the tea down. "I've received threats before, but my security team deals with them." She sighed. "The downside of success is that some people want a slice of it. People I've never met claim they had a similar idea, that they're entitled to a part of my company. They want money, they want me beaten up, they want me dead—" She felt the throb of a headache forming and rubbed her forehead.

Nick sat in the chair beside her. He gripped her knee and squeezed. "*Nothing* is going to happen to you. I won't let anyone close."

Her throat tightened. She reminded herself that he was doing this because he'd promised Nola, and he loved his sister.

Lainie had lost her brother, Elliott, years ago to

cancer. She missed him every day. She loved her parents and saw them at Christmas. They were so normal. Content to work, raise a family, then retire. They didn't like to travel, didn't want fancy things. She knew this all too well, as she'd tried to buy them trips and gifts. Her dad had finally sold his hardware store two years ago, and Lainie had helped them buy a condo in Florida.

They were happily retired. Her father played golf, badly, and her mom knitted and crocheted.

They had no understanding of her business or technology. And they had no interest in knowing anything about it. They hated New York winters, and never visited her. They'd been good parents, maybe not the most effusive or demonstrative, but they fully expected Lainie to take care of herself.

And she could. One hundred percent. But knowing someone—especially this strong man—was determined to keep her safe did something to her.

Gah. It must be some old, latent instincts left over from caveman days. The woman drawn to the strong protector. She knew better than anyone that leaning on a man was a big mistake. At first, they seemed great, but it didn't take long for them to get bored or decide the grass was much greener somewhere else.

Killian sat on the edge of a long desk and crossed his ankles. She glanced at his sharp face, and her gut tightened. There was something about him. Something in her hindbrain warning her not to make any sudden moves.

"Go on," Killian said.

"The threats started a month ago. Just a few at first. Some came in the mail, and some via email. Then they turned into a daily deluge over the last week." She clasped her hands together. "The police were notified but haven't made any headway. We've also seen a large increase in attempted cyber attacks on the Pintura website."

Hex straightened. "Really?"

Lainie nodded.

"And you think the two are related?" Nick asked.

Lainie nodded again. "They escalated at the same time."

Hex popped up and walked over to the huge, interactive screen, tapping on it. Windows popped up in front of the woman as she tapped in commands. Then the Pintura site filled the screen, the familiar, hot-pink and turquoise logo in the corner.

Hex muttered and kept tapping on her small square of screen. "Can you give me access to the email threats?"

"Sure." Lainie gestured to the laptop on the desk. "Can I use your computer?"

"Go ahead."

Lainie accessed her site and signed into her emails. Her stomach tightened just thinking about them.

"I've messaged you," Hex said. "Just send them my way."

"Done." Lainie hit a key.

Hex tapped on the huge screen, then lifted a heavy-duty tablet and swiped on it.

"If there's something to find, Hex will find it," Nick said.

Lainie admired the sense of respect the Sentinel Security team shared. It was clear they all trusted each other. They had an easy camaraderie. Her gaze flicked to Nick, then to Hex, then to Hadley. She wondered just how deep his relationship went with them. Was he dating one of the women? They were really comfortable with each other.

The ugly twist in her belly did not feel good.

Focus on the person out to kill you, Laine. She cleared her throat. "At first, I just thought this was another crazy person. The threats were all about me deserving to die—" she winced "—and the various ways they'd do it."

She saw a muscle tick in Nick's jaw.

"I'm analyzing now," Hex said. "I'm pulling apart the writing pattern, the words used, the grammar."

Hadley rose and stood beside Hex. "Hmm, this guy is...creative."

Lainie looked away and Nick squeezed her knee again. She felt that small touch all the way up her leg. It made her feel better, even if her inner voice was yelling at her to pull away.

"I'm fine. I've made myself read them all."

Hadley made a sound. "These are pretty over the top and gory. It feels intentional." Her beautiful face turned considering.

"Hadley's had a lot of psychological training." Nick turned to look at his colleague. "To scare her?"

"That's my take," Hadley said.

"I'm looking at your cyber attacks," Hex said.

Lainie straightened. "What? You're in the Pintura system?"

"She hacked it," Killian said.

"That's what I do." Hex winked. "Don't worry. I

won't mess anything up, and no one will even know I've been here."

"Why do I bother paying a small fortune for my system security?" Lainie tried not to sound disgruntled.

Nick's teeth flashed white. For a second, Lainie's gaze dropped to his smile.

No men, remember? Especially bossy ones related to your best friend.

"Nothing can keep Hex out," he said.

"Lainie's right," Hex announced. "The emails and cyber attacks are linked."

Lainie gasped. "How do you know?"

"The proxy server of some of the email accounts matches those that initiated the cyber attacks."

"What? My security team couldn't find that information."

Hex nodded. "The guy's good and has some skills, but I managed to dive deeper and uncover it."

"Can you pinpoint the attacker's location?" Nick asked.

Hex shook her head. "No luck with that. He's bounced things all over the place. There's a small chance I could trace him, during a live hack, but not from this info."

"God." Lainie sagged in her chair. "What the hell does this asshole want?"

"There haven't been any demands?" Killian asked.

She shook her head.

"But he has you and your company in his sights," Nick said, voice grim.

"We don't know it's a him," Hadley said, eyeing the emails again. "But it's likely."

"Pintura is in the middle of planning a crucial acquisition of another company, Bloom. The timing of these threats is really bad." Lainie pulled a face. "If there is ever a good time to get death threats. It's vital that this acquisition goes off without a hitch. The market and investors are watching."

Nick shifted closer. "Don't worry, Lainie, I promise I'll find whoever is doing this."

She didn't doubt him for a second. "I'm going to be involved in this."

His brow creased. "There's no need—"

"This is *my* life, my company. If the acquisition doesn't go ahead, people will lose their jobs. I'm giving a crucial keynote presentation at the FutureTech conference this weekend. I can't miss it."

Nick looked at his shoes, glaring, then he looked up. "Where?"

"The conference is in Las Vegas."

His brow creased. "I hate Vegas." He paused. "It would be safer for you to lay low."

She shook her head. "No way. I'm not letting this asshole control my life any more than he already does."

"Lainie—"

"No." She looked at Hex. "I know my site better than anyone. I can help Hex."

The hacker nodded. "That could help speed things up."

Nick's frown deepened. "You have a company to run."

"And I have a very good management team. My life and my life's work are under threat. No one is stealing those from me."

Nick looked like he was gnashing his teeth.

Lainie felt a spurt of satisfaction. "Did you think I'd sit by, like a sweet, incompetent damsel and let you rescue me?"

He crossed his muscular arms. Her gaze wanted to trace the thick lines of them.

Don't get distracted, Lainie. "I don't need rescuing, Nick. I can rescue myself." She looked at all of them. "But I'm smart enough not to turn down help from you all. But I will be involved, and I'll pay—"

He growled. A full-on growl.

She put her hands on her hips. "Don't growl at me, Nick Garrick."

"I really like her," Hex stage whispered.

"Me too," Hadley agreed.

Killian cocked his head. "No one will cut you out, but understand, if you're in danger, Wolf is the one to trust. And the one in charge."

She looked at Nick.

"Understand?" Nick said.

Lainie lifted her chin. "Fine."

"I'll make security arrangements for Las Vegas," he said. "And in the meantime, you and I are going to be attached at the hip. I'll take you to and from the office and your apartment. If you need to go anywhere, I'm with you. If I can't be with you, someone else from my team will be."

Her mouth dropped open. "I don't want my

employees to get upset or panic. Only a select few and my security team know about the threats. And if word gets out to the market, it could impact the Bloom purchase. Nick, I can't have a bodyguard following me around."

"It could also tip this guy over the edge." Hadley was looking at the threats on the screen. "If he sees she has a bodyguard, an expert security person with her constantly, it could force him to escalate."

Lainie's belly clenched. She didn't want that. At all.

Nick rose, a hard look crossing his rugged face.

She wasn't sure she liked or trusted that look. "So where does that leave us?"

"In love," he said.

Her eyes bugged out of her head. She couldn't breathe. She was damn glad she was sitting down. "Ah...what?"

"Or in lust at least," he said. "You'll introduce me to everyone as your new lover."

She heard one of the women make an amused sound.

Okay, Lainie had a sharp mind, but it wasn't firing at this moment. "Lover?"

"Yep. Boyfriend. Significant other. Man sharing your bed."

Nick was suggesting they fake being lovers?

Oh, God.

Killian nodded his head. "A fake relationship is the perfect cover."

No, no, no. Pretend to be lovey-dovey with Nick Garrick? It wasn't that she couldn't do it. It was that it might be too easy to do it.

Nick put his hands on the arms of Lainie's chair and leaned over her. "To the world, you'll be mine."

Those words trickled inside her, making her belly curl. "Um, I'm not sure this is a good idea..."

"It's the only way I'm letting you out of here. The only way you can go to the office and Las Vegas."

She swallowed against her dry throat. "I want my objection to this plan recognized."

"Noted."

She blew out a breath, feeling like she was making a deal with the devil. Or a wolf. "Fine."

CHAPTER THREE

Nick drove toward Lainie's Tribeca apartment.

He didn't like that she'd demanded to be a part of the investigation. He wanted her far away from whoever this sick fuck was.

He wanted her safe.

So that's why you volunteered to play her lover? A muscle ticked in his jaw. He'd do whatever the hell he needed to in order to ensure her safety.

"Are you going to brood and glower all the way there?" she asked.

"Yes." He heard a stifled giggle and glanced her way. "Nothing about this is funny."

"I know."

She smiled at him, and his gut clenched. Why did she have to be so damn pretty?

"I'll remind you that this fake relationship idea was all yours," she added.

He grunted.

"I have to keep my sense of humor, or I'll be curled up in a frightened ball, crying."

He snagged a parking space across the street from her building and turned off the engine. "Then don't get involved. Let me handle it."

She shook her head. "That's not the kind of woman I am, Nick. I'm used to being independent."

"Damn." And he admired her for it. He'd always liked that smart brain of hers. Nola was always gushing about the amazing things Lainie did.

"Sorry if that makes things harder for you," she said.

"Don't be. None of this is your fault. Come on. I'll walk you up."

She huffed out a breath. "The doorman is right there. I can—"

Nick gripped her arm. "I'm not arguing on this one, Lainie. And I'm the kind of man to walk his woman to her door."

Her gaze traced over his face. "Fine."

"And I'm checking your apartment and security system."

She rolled her eyes. It made him think of her and Nola, up to mischief. *That's right. Remember she's your sister's best friend and off-limits.*

"How about you install five new locks on my door while we're up there?" she said sassily.

"Not a bad idea."

"No." She wagged her finger at him, then opened the car door.

They crossed the street toward the large pre-war

building. It made Nick think of Batman and Gotham City.

Lainie greeted the doorman warmly by name.

The man beamed at her. "Have a great evening, Ms. Madden."

Nick followed Lainie inside and nearly did a double take. "Jesus."

She smiled back over her shoulder. "I know. Isn't it great?"

The lobby was decorated in ostentatious art deco style. There were gold and bronze accents everywhere, along with acres of marble and travertine. As Lainie led him to an elevator, he spared the richly painted vaulted ceiling a quick glance.

While the elevators were all surrounded by ornate cast bronze and looked old, he was relieved to see her hold a keycard up to a very modern card reader.

"I'm on the twentieth floor," she told him.

"Nice." And more secure. "And everyone needs a card to access your floor?"

"Yes. My cleaning service has a card and building management."

Nick grunted. The elevator slowed.

The doors opened, and they made their way down a short hallway. Lainie unlocked her door, and Nick shouldered his way inside first.

There was no art deco up here. Lainie's apartment was decorated in a clean, modern style.

The place was wide open, with a pale, herringbone-patterned oak floor, and contemporary lines. The black-framed, tall, arched windows probably had good views.

Right now, he just saw the glitter of city lights. The furniture and rugs were stylish, but still looked comfortable. The kitchen had a huge slab of marble for an island, and rich, wood accents. A large, green plant provided a pop of color against the white walls.

"Damn. Nice place, Lainie."

"Thanks." She dropped her evening bag down on the entry table and kicked off her heels. "It was the first expensive thing I purchased, after Pintura became a success."

"You earned it." He looked at the view of the city lights out the nearest window. "Nola's always saying how hard you work."

Her place was modern, but had feminine touches, and it smelled like Lainie. She'd made it her home. A vase of pretty pink flowers rested on the table, and there were some interesting pieces of art on the wall.

Her cheeks pinkened. "Thanks."

"Your folks must be proud."

Her smile slipped a bit. "They are. In their own way." She shrugged a shoulder. "They don't really understand how a website can be successful. My dad owned a hardware store. He thinks building something useful involves nails, screws, and sweat equity."

She sounded matter of fact about it, but under it, he thought he detected something.

"I'm going to check out the place," he told her.

"Go ahead." She yawned.

Nick kept it quick. He checked all the rooms. Her bedroom was last, and he stopped, staring at the bed.

It was large, with an intricate metal headboard that

consisted of curls, twists, and spirals. Romantic and sensual. Perfect for slim hands to hold onto while her man went down on her.

He looked away, muttering a curse. She had a huge, walk-in closet, and when he turned, he saw a few scraps of pink lace tossed over a chair and his gut tightened.

He needed to get out of there.

He strode back to the living room. She was checking her phone, her tiredness obvious.

"Security system?"

She nodded at a panel set discreetly in the wall by the front door.

"You use it?"

She licked her lips. "Um..."

"You use it now. Every night."

She pinched the bridge of her nose. "All right."

He looked at the panel and tapped. "Your system is decent, but there are some upgrades we can do. I'll arrange for our guy to stop by tomorrow and do the install."

Lainie sighed. "I'm too tired to argue with you."

"I'll let you get to bed. I've already programmed my number, and the Sentinel Security office's into your phone."

"You did?" She whipped out her phone and touched the screen, swiping madly. "Nick, you need to use your words and ask first."

"My way was faster."

"How did you even get into my phone?"

He didn't bother to answer.

"Argh," she growled.

"If anything worries you, call me. Anything. Any time."

She kept her gaze on his. "Dammit, you make it hard to stay angry with you."

He touched her chin. "I'll be here to pick you up in the morning."

"Nick! I really can get myself to work."

"I'm not arguing."

"I'm letting you get away with being bossy because I need sleep. That's the only reason."

His lips quirked. "Get to bed." He couldn't stop himself tracing her jaw. Her skin was so soft.

He saw her chest hitch. Her gaze ran over his face.

"You wear the same perfume," he said.

She blinked. "What?"

"The same perfume you wore when you were eighteen. Something with vanilla."

Her cheeks went pink. "Jean Paul Gaultier Classique. It's my favorite." Then she went up on her toes and kissed his cheek. "Thank you, Nick. Bossiness aside, I'm grateful for your help."

Shit. He dropped his hand. He'd never, ever had any problem controlling his desire before.

Except around this woman.

He stepped back. "Good night, Lainie."

"Night, Nick."

With a nod, he headed back to the elevator. As it moved downward, he leaned against the wall and closed his eyes.

Lainie was a beautiful, appealing woman. He was attracted to her, but nothing had changed. Even though pretending to be her lover would probably just about kill him, he wasn't touching her for real. There were a lot of reasons he couldn't.

She was his sister's best friend. She meant the world to Nola, and he wouldn't mess with that. Nola would never forgive him if he hurt Lainie.

Lainie was so good, kind, fresh. Meanwhile, his father had gone to jail for robbery, and then drank himself to death. Added to that, Nick had done some dark, bloody things during his career, things that would shock her. Things he never wanted her to know.

She was way too good for him. She was only six years younger than him, but he felt a lifetime older.

And most importantly, he was here to keep her safe. He knew he needed to focus on that. If he got distracted, he could get her hurt or killed.

Old memories rose up, clawing at his gut. *The echo of childish laughter and a gap-toothed smile. Then body bags.*

Lives lost, all because Nick had been distracted.

His gut rebelled at the thought of Lainie's bright light extinguished.

Fuck, no. Not on his watch.

Nick exited the building and headed for his car.

He'd keep his sister's friend safe, and keep his hands off her.

"ALL RIGHT, that's a wrap. Thanks, everyone."

At the head of the conference table, Lainie dropped back in her chair, trying to beat back her tiredness.

After the long meeting, her team happily filed out.

Nick had dropped her off at the office building that morning, with strict instructions to stay inside. Thankfully, he hadn't come up to the Pintura office level, so they hadn't needed to pretend or field a bunch of nosy questions from her staff. After seeing her safely to the elevator, he'd sped off in his sexy James Bond car.

She hadn't had enough sleep. If she got less than seven hours, she was always sluggish.

Her assistant bustled in. "You look like you need this." The woman held out a large coffee cup done in the Pintura colors of hot pink and turquoise.

"Deva, you are a goddess." Lainie took the latte gratefully and gulped.

Deva Chopra was of medium height, with a slim-hipped body and brown skin. Her black hair was cut off in a stylish bob with straight bangs. Her dark eyes studied Lainie. "Late night?"

"I had that charity thing at the Plaza."

"Followed by hot sex with a hot guy?" Deva asked hopefully.

Lainie choked on her coffee. "Um, no."

"Bummer."

"Are you and Nola conspiring? I told you both, no men. Keenan has cured me."

"Keenan doesn't classify as a man. More like a man-baby." Deva pulled a face. "He's pretty, but that's about it."

Lainie lifted her cup in a salute and sipped again. That was a very apt description of Keenan Jonas.

Deva dropped a few files on the table. "Some things

for you to look at. Budget approvals, draft of your conference speech, and some final paperwork for you to sign off on regarding the Hall dismissal."

"Ugh, that woman never goes away." It was no fun dealing with firing disruptive, toxic employees.

"Sign the papers and that should be it," Deva said.

Lainie took a large gulp of coffee. "Are the contracts from Legal ready? On the Bloom acquisition?"

"Not yet. There was a glitch from one of the hacks, and it's delayed them."

Lainie frowned, setting the cup down on the table. "Nothing serious, I hope."

"No. This hacker isn't getting far into the system. It's just causing delays."

Damn. Pintura needed the Bloom acquisition to go off seamlessly. It was important for the next steps of her company and its expansion. Bloom was a fantastic image library that she wanted to include in Pintura's offerings.

She rubbed her temple. Between the acquisition, the upcoming conference, the death threats, and now Nick... Her plate was full.

"Okay, tell Legal to get me the paperwork as soon as they can. I want to go over it with a fine-toothed comb."

Deva arched a brow. "You never miss anything. I've never met anyone with a brain like yours."

"It's only because I put the work in." She lifted the cup again. "And caffeinate."

Deva smiled. "And have brilliant staff."

"That too. Keep the coffee coming."

"Sure thing, boss."

Work consumed Lainie. The morning slipped away

as she got on calls, met with staff members, scrutinized contracts, and attacked her emails. But thankfully, she got loads done.

She'd just finished another meeting when her phone rang. She smiled when she saw her best friend's name.

"Nola. Have you sold any gazillion-dollar real estate today?"

"In fact—" her best friend drawled "—a penthouse on Central Park to a French couple. My commission will be big. I'm buying the pair of sexy Louboutins I saw in Nordstrom the other day to celebrate."

"You rock." Nola was like the sister Lainie had never had. They just clicked. They had fun, propped each other up when they needed a hug, and could call each other out if the other was screwing up.

Nola had made no bones about the fact that she'd hated Keenan.

"Did Nick get in touch?" Nola asked.

Lainie hitched her butt on the corner of her desk. "You could say that."

Nola groaned. "Did he bust his way in, grumpily saying 'I'm not arguing' a lot?"

"Oh, my God, yes."

"I know my brother. It is his most annoying, yet strangely comforting trait."

"Yes, well, he had some things to say."

And he kissed me senseless. And now he's pretending to be my lover.

Not that she'd ever tell Nola that.

"I want you safe, Lainie. These threats..."

Lainie heard the worry in Nola's voice. "It's going to

be okay, Nola. I have my security guys working on it, and now Nick is involved too. I promise you, and I'll be careful."

"You have that conference in Las Vegas coming up."

"I can't miss it. I'm giving the keynote speech, and all eyes will be on Pintura as we acquire Bloom. But I'm sure the casino security will—"

"Take Nick."

Lainie's heart thumped. "He said he'd sort it out for me." A long weekend away with Nick in Las Vegas sounded like a very bad idea.

"Good," Nola said.

Deva appeared in the doorway, files in hand.

"I have to run," Lainie said.

"Okay, stay sparkly."

Lainie smiled. It was a saying they'd used as glitter-polish-obsessed pre-teens. "Stay sparkly." She rose. "Those the Bloom contracts?"

"Yes. They're in your inbox as well. And I bought you a muffin. White chocolate and raspberry." Deva held up the paper bag.

Lainie moaned. "You deserve a raise."

"Why, yes I do," Deva agreed, with a wink.

Lainie got busy with the contracts, munching on the muffin and frowning as she noted parts on the paperwork with sticky notes to check with the lawyers.

She noticed a few things missing and rose, wandering out to Deva's desk. Her assistant was busy on her computer.

"Deva, can you pull the file on Bloom for me, please? I need the early memos. And tell Darren from

Legal that I need thirty minutes when he has a chance."

Ever efficient, Deva nodded, her hands already on her keyboard.

Then her assistant's dark eyes went wide. "Oh, wow. Tell me that he's here for me."

Lainie looked up...and spotted Nick striding through the open-plan Pintura office.

He looked like a wolf on the prowl. Half her staff—the female and gay half, plus maybe a few of the straight guys as well—all stopped and watched him.

Her belly did something weird—a hot, tingly dance. "Um, no, he's here for me."

Deva's eyebrows disappeared into her dark hair. "You've been holding out on me."

"No. I... He's Nola's brother."

"Really?"

"He works in security. He's helping me with my issues."

"I know you mean the threats, but I wish you meant your lack of orgasms."

Lainie hissed. "Quiet. Nola's *brother*." She enunciated the words carefully. She wasn't sure if she was emphasizing it for herself or for Deva.

"Did you see him?" Deva said. "I wouldn't care who he was related to."

"Quiet." Lainie pasted on a smile. "Nick."

He didn't look cheery, but he stepped in close and slid an arm around her. "Lainie."

She barely hid her squeak of surprise.

His lips brushed her cheek. "You smell good."

Heat filled her cheeks. She could feel everyone watching them.

"We need to talk," he murmured quietly.

All pretend, Lainie. Fake. False. Phony. Her belly clenched. "Sure. Nick, this is my assistant, Deva. Deva, Nick Garrick."

"A pleasure." Deva smiled, giving Lainie huge eyes.

Nick responded with a nod.

Lainie grabbed Nick's hand and dragged him into her office. Far away from prying eyes. When she glanced back, Deva fanned her face dramatically behind him.

She shot her assistant a look, then closed the door.

Nick studied her office.

Lainie loved her space. It was filled with bright light. She had a glossy, white desk, and on the wall behind it were three long canvases depicting cherry blossoms.

"Did something happen?" She clutched her hands in front of herself.

He whirled. "Why didn't you tell me about Joseph Greene?"

She blinked. "I honestly didn't think about him."

Nick stalked toward her. She felt hunted.

"You didn't think of the man who stalked you, sent you threats, and frightened you out in front of your office building?"

"It was over a year ago, and he's in jail, right?" Her pulse skittered. "God, he's out, isn't he?"

Nick's gaze moved over her face, and he released a breath. "No. But he could still be involved."

"He's not well, Nick. He believed we were in love,

and he created this whole fantasy. Including that he and I had created Pintura together." She grimaced.

The man had scared her.

"I read the report," Nick said. "Building security pulled him off you."

She shuddered. "Yes." She rubbed her arms. "He jumped me when I left for the day. I seem to attract less-desirable men."

Nick cocked his head. "Now you're talking about Keenan Jonas."

She felt a burn of embarrassment. Of course, Nick knew about Keenan. "Yes. Call him an early midlife crisis. He cheated on me."

"Then he's an idiot."

She blinked. "My college boyfriend cheated on me, too. I seem to attract the type. Disloyal."

Nick moved closer, and she bumped into the desk behind her.

"That's on them, not you," he said.

They stared at each other.

"If they couldn't see what they had, then they weren't good enough for you." He reached up and tucked her hair back behind her ear.

She smelled his scent. Not cologne. No, it was probably just his soap or shower gel, but it had some woodsy scent that teased her nose.

His gaze dropped to her mouth.

Lainie felt like the air around them was heating up. All she could see was Nick, and the silvery flecks in his dark blue eyes.

There was a sudden sound of papers slapping the floor.

They jerked apart and Nick spun.

Deva crouched and picked up some dropped files.

"Sorry. I tried clearing my throat, three times, but clearly you couldn't hear me over that sexual tension thick enough to cut with a knife, or maybe a machete." Deva made a chopping motion with her hand.

Lainie closed her eyes for a second.

Nick just stared at Deva for a beat, then his gaze sliced back to Lainie. "You need self-defense training."

"What?" Her brain wasn't quite firing quick enough to keep up with the change of subject.

"When you finish work today, I'll have someone from my team pick you up. Come to the office and we'll train. You can't rely on a guard or a good Samaritan to save you if someone corners you. I'll show you some moves."

Before she could answer one way or another, he nodded and strode out.

"God, that man's ass deserves a medal." Deva grinned. "And he's going to show you some *moves*."

"Self-defense," Lainie said.

"Sure. Just Nola's brother, huh?"

"Look, he's helping me out, and just between you and me, he's pretending to..." God, why was it so hard to get the words out?

"Eat you up with his eyes?" Deva offered. "Undress you mentally?"

"Deva! We're pretending to be in a relationship. As a cover."

Her assistant arched a brow. "You're really buying that?"

"It's true. Besides, I've sworn off men, remember? I'm all work. I have no interest in anyone with a Y chromosome or an overabundance of testosterone."

Deva grinned. "Uh-huh. Or muscular bodies, tight butts, or sexy beards?"

"Shut up, Deva."

CHAPTER FOUR

Nick paced beside his desk, too edgy to sit down.

He'd spent the day organizing the Sentinel Security hardware guy to install upgrades at Lainie's place, planning their trip to Las Vegas for the FutureTech Conference, and looking into Joseph Greene. After some calls, he'd determined that the guy was still behind bars at Rikers and had no visitors and no calls.

It burned him that the guy had terrorized Lainie for several weeks, and that Nick had never known about it. He blew out a breath, his hands on his hips.

The man had touched her, frightened her, had convinced himself they were a couple in love.

Nick had gone over Greene's notes. They were love letters with a desperate, threatening undertone, but nothing explicit. And they hadn't contained death threats.

Greene hadn't written the latest notes.

Nick tapped the keyboard. A headshot of the model Keenan Jonas appeared.

Nick's lip curled. Is this what Lainie was attracted to? A pretty boy?

The man had soft hands, a smooth face, and a perfect smile.

There was a picture of the pair of them together. They looked good. They were at some event, with Lainie in a sexy, blue dress. Her ex was hogging the limelight, partly blocking her in most of the shots.

Nick's stepfather would love the guy.

He grunted. Lucky for Lainie, the idiot only had one brain cell and had cheated on her with a plastic blonde. Nick tapped his fingers on the desk. Still, he'd check Jonas out. The guy could be nursing a grudge after losing his wealthy girlfriend.

Nick would hunt down whoever was after her and wouldn't stop until he did.

His thoughts turned to her. Today, she'd been wearing a fitted, gray business dress, outlining those killer curves. Her office at Pintura had suited her. The place had a good vibe, and he could see that her employees enjoyed working there.

Then, that moment in her office...

Heat filled his gut. He'd been seconds away from grabbing her.

Fuck. *Get a grip on it, Garrick. You're not touching her, no matter how much you want to explore that curvy body.*

But he hadn't even been around her for twenty-four hours and he realized keeping his hands off her was going to be hard, especially when they were supposed to convince everyone they were lovers.

His phone rang and he saw it was an international call from France. He pressed it to his ear.

"Garrick."

"Wolf," an accented female voice purred. "It's always nice to hear your growl."

"Gisele."

Gisele Aubert was an Interpol agent who sometimes fed him information. When he could, he returned the favor. They'd fucked a few times, as well. Gisele enjoyed expensive champagne, hot sex, and no attachments.

"I have some intel for you, Wolf. Out of French Guiana." There was a pause. "The Cardoza Cartel."

Nick stiffened, and his hand clenched on the phone.

"I know you keep track of them," Gisele continued.

"Yeah. Email it to me."

"*Oui.* Are you in Europe anytime soon?"

"No."

"A shame, *mon ami.* I enjoy our times together. Stay in touch."

He saw Gisele's email appear on his screen and clicked it.

The Cardoza Cartel was running deals with links to US crime groups in Florida. He'd pass the information onto Killian. His boss would make sure the right people got it.

Then he saw a name in the text. *Carlos Andres Martinez.*

Every muscle in his body strung tight.

He closed his eyes, and in that moment, he was back in Colombia. He'd been with the CIA then, on his last mission. They'd been evacuating the US Embassy in Bogotá, after credible threats from the Cardoza Cartel.

Threats spearheaded by the ruthless, ambitious, second-in-command of the cartel, Carlos Martinez.

Nick had been in charge of the mission to evacuate the ambassador and his wife and child. And also to destroy sensitive data. On top of all of that, his superiors had wanted to catch Martinez.

In those frantic hours before the evac plane landed, Nick had been juggling trying to keep the ambassador and his family calm, destroying the embassy's classified data, and tapping his contacts in the city.

Only Madison had been unaffected. The ambassador's daughter had been cute as hell. A precocious six-year-old with pigtails and a missing front tooth. She'd followed Nick around, peppering him with questions.

Then Nick had gotten a lead on Martinez. His hands flexed. He'd desperately wanted to take the asshole down.

But Martinez had been smarter than Nick had given him credit for.

A beautiful, pregnant woman had turned up at the embassy, crying, saying that she was pregnant with the child of the ambassador's right-hand aide. The guy had sworn he hadn't known her, but he had a playboy reputation, and had cut a wide swath through both the embassy females and the locals.

Nick had been trying to get to the bottom of it, and desperate to track down Martinez, and he'd delayed the evacuation.

The woman had been a cartel member sent by Martinez.

She'd murdered the ambassador's wife, Jennifer, and Madison before Nick had worked it out. He'd only managed to save the heartbroken ambassador.

He'd never forget holding Madison's blood-splattered body as it went cold.

He'd been distracted. He'd been focused on comforting a pregnant woman and getting the bad guy. He'd taken his eye off his official charges, and they'd paid the price.

He unlocked his jaw. He wasn't going to see Lainie splattered in blood because he was too distracted by her tempting curves.

"Wolf?"

He looked up and saw Killian in the doorway.

"You okay?" Killian cocked a brow. "I said your name three times."

"Sorry. Busy. I got some intel from Gisele at Interpol. I forwarded it to you."

Killian tilted his head. "On?"

"The Cardoza Cartel. They're making inroads in Florida."

His boss' gaze sharpened. "Martinez involved?"

"Yeah."

"You okay?"

"I'm fine."

Killian eyed him, but thankfully didn't press. Killian knew all about Colombia, and he'd sat with Nick too many times to count on the anniversary of Jennifer and Madison's deaths and drank bourbon with him.

"Any luck with Lainie's attacker?"

Nick shook his head. "I'm combing through her past.

She's got an asshole ex, and a stalker in jail. Both look to be a bust."

"Your emotions are involved with this one," Killian said.

Nick jerked. "She's my little sister's best friend. And I'm keeping her safe. And..."

Killian raised a brow.

"She has no idea what I've done, Killian. She's good, kind, smart..."

He saw understanding in Killian's eyes. His friend got it. Understood how it felt to put your hands on something clean, and worry you'd sully it.

"Okay, keep me updated." As Killian stepped through the arched doorway, he paused. "In our work, we do the jobs others don't want to know about in order to protect our country and our people. We both know things aren't black or white. And we lose people, Wolf. It's the nature of the job. Use it to make you better at what you do." He strode out.

That's what he did. Madison's gap-toothed smile motivated him every day to ensure he did his job well and didn't fuck up again. And he'd use it to ensure Lainie didn't get hurt.

He tried to focus back on the screen, but his edginess got worse and worse. He decided to hit the gym and burn off some energy before Lainie arrived. He'd asked Hadley to pick her up. He needed to work off this tension.

In the locker room, he changed into black workout shorts and a T-shirt. He hit the treadmill first. Killian kept a state-of-the-art gym for the Sentinel Security employees. After he'd warmed up, he headed for the weights.

He hit the bench press, grunting as he lifted the loaded bar.

But with every push he saw Lainie in that green goddess dress, the tops of her creamy breasts spilling everywhere.

Fuck. His cock twitched. That wasn't what he was supposed to be thinking about.

Gritting his teeth, he sat up. He felt hot and stripped his shirt off. Then he dropped down and did some push-ups.

Soon, sweat was pouring off him. Thankfully, his mind had gone blissfully blank.

He did some more push-ups. Then he heard a noise and lifted his head.

All the blood went straight to his cock, and his head filled with Lainie.

Shit. He rose.

She stood in the doorway, under the arch of brick. She was wearing pink leggings that hugged her like a lover, and a tiny, pink top that left a strip of skin bare across her belly.

"Hi." She fiddled with her ponytail. "Am I early?"

"You're right on time."

Her gaze went to his chest and stayed there.

Nick felt like the temperature was rising in the gym.

"Lainie?" His voice sounded like gravel.

Her gaze jerked up. "What?"

"You ready?"

She shifted her feet and ran her hands down the sides of her leggings. "Yes, where do you want me?"

Flat on your back with my cock inside you. Shit.

What the hell was she doing to him?

"On the mats. Let's get to work."

OKAY, Lainie knew she'd sworn off men, but come on. The freaking universe had put one of the best chests and sets of abs she'd ever seen in her entire life on display in front of her.

She was being tortured.

Nick was shirtless and a little sweaty, which strangely added to the appeal. His tanned skin was stretched over taut muscles of all different kinds.

She snuck another peek. She was human, after all. She nearly whimpered.

He had a six pack, and sculpted pecs. His chest was covered in a light dusting of dark hair.

"Okay, we'll start with some basic moves," he said. "Remember that most attackers are bigger and stronger than you."

"Great."

"If someone grabs you, you need to react fast, break their hold, and run for help."

She dragged in a breath. "React, break, run for help. Got it."

Nick moved fast and gripped her wrist with one big hand. "Try to get free."

She tried not to focus on those rough hands wrapped

around her skin. She wriggled her arm, then yanked and jerked, but he was too strong.

"Try this. Put your hand on mine." He grabbed her hand and pressed it over his. "Push down, then swing your arm around this way, then grab my wrist and push down."

They followed through the move, and Nick bent over toward the floor.

"Good," he said, straightening. "Again."

They kept practicing until the move felt more fluid.

"Oh yeah." She grinned, bouncing on the balls of her feet. "I'm a badass."

He gave her a faint smile. "Okay, She-Hulk, stay focused." They shifted back into the center of the mats. "Now, let's practice if someone grabs you from behind."

He circled around and threw an arm around her neck. Lainie found herself pulled back against that hard, bare chest.

Her mind went blank. She smelled healthy, male sweat, and that woodsy scent that she now associated with Nick. Heat poured off him.

"Lainie? Are you listening?"

"Sorry." She shook her head. "Show me."

"Grip my arm with your hands, and keep me from choking you. Then drop your body weight down, be heavy. I want you to target the knees, try to knock me off balance."

He went through the move slowly.

"Again."

Again, that muscular arm wrapped around her. She

felt heat throb through her. Why did he have to feel so good?

"This time, move quicker," he said.

She did as instructed and managed to knock him down...and herself in the process.

Nick fell on his back on the mats, and she fell on top of him with an *oof*.

"You're supposed to get free and run," he said dryly.

"That was what I was trying to do." Her face was only an inch from his.

"Remember, if you can't get free, target key areas. Eyes, nose, throat, balls, and knees."

She blinked. "Okay."

"Poke the eyes, ram a palm to the nose, chop to the throat, and a kick to the knee."

She swallowed. "And the balls?"

Something flickered in his eyes. "Knee them, kick them, pull them."

She felt heat in her cheeks. Okay, maybe she shouldn't be talking about pulling balls when she was lying on top of Nick.

"But we aren't going to practice that bit." He sat up with the flex of those impressive abs, bringing her with him. "Let's go again."

Her next couple of attempts were not quite as successful. But on the third one, she sent Nick down again, but she tripped and landed on him again.

"Sorry." She shifted, and her knee pressed between his legs.

He made a sound and gripped her hips.

"Sorry. *Sorry*." She shifted and pressed her palms to

his chest. Damn, he was hard. His skin was covered in a sheen of perspiration, and her hand slipped. She dropped down, her chest pressed to his, their faces so close that their noses brushed.

She sucked in a breath, desperately trying to ignore the fact that her panties were growing damp.

"Well, I'm not sure if I'll get picked up for the wrestling team." She tried for a casual laugh, but her throat was tight. "My technique needs some polishing."

He rolled and dumped her beside him. He cleared his throat. "Let's keep going, but don't try to unman me."

"I didn't do it on *purpose.*"

They kept practicing until Lainie felt a lot more like a badass. A slightly sweaty, uncoordinated badass.

"Good work." He nodded.

"I did do well, didn't I?" She buffed her nails on her shirt.

Nick smiled.

That smile softened the rugged lines of his face. Not much, but a little. For a second, she got a glimpse of the handsome teen he'd been.

Suddenly, she was so grateful that he was helping her. That she wasn't alone dealing with all of this.

Lainie acted on instinct and hugged him.

Her cheek pressed to his bare chest. He froze, but she held on for a second. He was so strong and solid. And he cared.

Damn, sometimes she missed her brother Elliott so damn much. Not that her feelings for Nick were even remotely brotherly, but it was nice to have someone looking out for her.

Nick pressed a hand to her spine, on her bare skin.

She gasped and looked up.

His blue eyes were scorching hot, and she couldn't breathe. She'd been trying to avoid this, and her inner voice kept telling her to step back and stop touching him.

But she couldn't.

Instead, she went up on her toes. That big, strong hand on her back pushed her closer.

Then she kissed him.

She half expected him to curse and push her back.

Instead, his lips opened, his arms closing around her and yanking her closer.

Oh, boy.

They grabbed at each other. His tongue was in her mouth, and she moaned. His big palm covered half of her butt.

Suddenly, the room was spinning. He lifted her up and she found herself flat on the mat, with a growling Nick on top of her. His mouth slanted over hers, the kiss going deep.

Yes. Oh, yes.

As his tongue delved deeper, she pushed up into his hard body. She felt his hard cock grind against the juncture of her thighs.

He felt so good, tasted so good. Smelled so good.

Then he pulled back.

Lainie sucked in a shaky breath, her body still humming with need.

She looked up into his conflicted face. She saw desire —so much desire—but it was mixed with less-pleasant, turbulent emotions.

Crap, it hurt. The thing was, her desire was underscored with other, warmer things. This wasn't just lust for her.

Nick felt...like a recognition. A click of the right things sliding into place.

And that scared the hell out of her.

He sat, and she did, too.

It took a moment to steady herself. Her gaze dropped to the really large bulge in his shorts. She barely held back a whimper.

"Lainie."

She jerked her gaze up. Right, she shouldn't be eyeing his erection. Large, very hard erection.

"Should I apologize?" She wrinkled her nose. "Or maybe you should apologize?"

Nick rubbed the back of his neck. "That shouldn't have happened."

Why did his words feel like a blow? She agreed with him, after all.

"It was..." He paused, like he couldn't find the right words.

It was everything. Achingly perfect, exciting, passionate, felt so right.

"Wrong," he finished.

Lainie sucked in a sharp breath. Clearly, he didn't feel the same as her. God, she felt like she was eighteen again.

His heavy gaze hit hers. "There are reasons this is a bad idea."

She nodded. "I have a few of those too. Nola."

"Nola," he agreed. "You're my sister's best friend. This has messy written all over it, if things go badly."

Lainie couldn't argue with that. She'd had messy once. Her college boyfriend, who'd been involved in the early ideas for Pintura, had been messy with a capital *M*. In the end, it had been a nightmare. Trent had cheated on her, betrayed her trust. She'd been glad to see the back of him.

"Nola means the world to me," Lainie said quietly.

"Me too. My job is to protect you. I can't let my focus split. A distraction could get you killed."

There was a dark undertone to his voice. She cocked her head. "You lost someone."

He blew out a harsh breath. "On a mission. With the CIA."

His tone said he wouldn't talk about it.

His gaze hit hers. Direct. "I'm not what you need."

She held up a hand. "I decide what I need, no one else."

"I'm not the right guy for a woman like you."

"Wait? A woman like me? What does that mean?"

"You're younger, sweeter, nicer..."

She frowned. "I'm six years younger than you, Nick. That's hardly an age gap."

He scraped a hand through his hair. "My father was an ex-con."

Anger fired through her. "That's Nola's father talking. Mr. Newhouse took every chance to rub your face in that because he's an asshole."

"No, it's just a fact." Nick pushed to his feet and held out a hand to help her up.

"For the record," she said. "Who your father was is a non-issue. He made his choices, and you make yours."

He shook his head. "You don't know me. The things I've seen, done—" A muscle ticked in his jaw.

She stilled. "As a SEAL?"

He nodded. "And after...when I worked for the CIA."

There were dark, dangerous shadows in his eyes.

"Nick—" She had to stop herself taking a step toward him.

Lainie had taken risks in business. She knew to win big, sometimes you had to put everything on the line. She knew she should let this drop, but a part of her just couldn't leave it like this.

"I like you." She lifted her chin. "I'm really, really attracted to you."

His hands balled into fists. "It's a crush—"

She felt a spurt of anger. "I'm not a teenager anymore, Nick. I'm a woman." She lifted her chin. "I know a lot of shit is swirling around my life right now—" she dragged in a breath "—but to me, you'd be worth the risk. This is worth it."

He made a noise and spun away. His big body was tense, every muscle taut.

Her heart sank. If he felt the same way, if he really wanted her, he wouldn't be this...conflicted.

"It's not worth it to me," he said.

Oh, *God*. She pressed a hand to her stomach. That really, really hurt.

Nick turned back to her. Regret was written all over his rugged face.

"I don't do relationships. I want to fuck you, but I don't think that's enough for you. And more than that, I want to keep you safe. I promised you, I promised Nola."

Lainie shot him a sad smile. "And you always keep your promises."

He gave her a curt nod. "It's the only thing I know."

"Okay, Nick. We'll forget this ever happened." Somehow, she'd scrape her pride up off the floor. "It's fine. I've sworn off men anyway." She tried to lighten her tone.

His eyebrows rose. "You're trying women now?"

"Ha ha. No." Although she narrowed her gaze. "Maybe I should?" But that kiss, and the fact that she really liked him rubbing what she guessed was a very generous cock against her, probably negated that idea.

Suddenly a figure flew into the gym.

"Lainie!" Hex cried. "There's a massive hack in progress on the Pintura site."

"What?" Panic hit Lainie.

"Come," the hacker said. "Quick!"

CHAPTER FIVE

H ex and Lainie rushed out of the gym.

Nick took a second to compose himself—which meant get his cock under control.

To me, you'd be worth the risk. This is worth it.

Fuck. He wanted Lainie so damn much. Fighting this pull was tearing him up inside.

And he'd hurt her. He'd seen it on her face. Lainie Madden couldn't lie and should never play poker.

The last thing he'd wanted to do was hurt her.

He shoved a hand through his hair. When he said it wasn't worth it, he'd meant risking her life. But he didn't think she'd taken it that way.

It's for the best. He'd meant what he'd said. He wasn't going to let her get hurt, he had to stay focused.

He strode toward the command center.

Inside, the women were standing at the interactive screen, their fingers flying.

They looked like they were conducting a very tense orchestra.

"They're getting in deeper," Lainie bit out. "He's already passed several layers of security. *Dammit.*"

"I'm initiating the trace." Hex frowned. "Shit. He's trying to be sneaky."

Hex was far shorter than Lanie, the lights shining off her pink-tipped hair. Lainie was taller, curvier, and clad in figure-hugging Lycra, with her ponytail bobbing.

The women looked so different, but were both in sync. They fired words at each other, hands moving fast.

Nick didn't think they even knew he was there.

"What's going on?" Killian stepped up beside him.

"There's a large hack on the Pintura site."

"Shit."

"They're trying to keep the fucker out and track him."

"I'm on their trail!" Hex cried.

"Stay on them," Lainie said. "I've messaged my cyber guys. They're helping me shore things up and keep this guy out of our central data." Lainie's face was fierce. "He's not taking down my site or threatening my customers."

Matteo "Hades" Mancini strode in. His dark hair was shaggy, with a touch of a curl, and his shirt was white against his bronze skin. He always looked like he'd just rolled out of some woman's bed. Nick had heard Hades described as a fallen angel come to life by more than one woman.

The man paused and eyed Lainie and Hex. "I have to admit; those two look strangely attractive doing this."

Nick shot his friend an annoyed look. The man might have worked in Italy's elite anti-Mafia unit for years and then Interpol, but Nick wouldn't hesitate to take him on. "When did you get back?"

"An hour ago. I left Bram to clean up." Hades grinned. "The lovely, curvy brunette looks especially attractive in that outfit."

"Shut up, Hades," Nick growled.

The man's grin just widened.

"She's Nick's," Killian said.

Those words hit Nick somewhere deep. *His*. For a shining moment, he wondered just how it would feel if Lainie was his. For real.

"So I see," Hades murmured.

"She's getting death threats," Nick said. "I'm protecting her."

"The signal is narrowing," Hex said.

"I'm switching back to you," Lainie said. "My team is holding him out of our servers."

"The asshole is bouncing everything all over the place," Hex complained.

A world map appeared on the corner of the screen, and red, gold, and green lines pinged all over it.

"I'm not letting him hide like a coward," Lainie said.

"I'm running a little program of mine." Hex tapped. An image of an animated woman with pink-tipped hair and large eyes appeared on the screen. The cartoon woman was tapping on a tablet.

"Love your avatar," Lainie said.

"Hex has a cartoon picture of herself?" Hades snorted.

"Hex, update?" Killian said.

The hacker didn't turn around. "Working on it, but

I'm a little busy right now, boss man."

Lainie glanced at Hex. "Hex, can we amplify the—?"

Nick didn't pay attention to the tech speak as the women worked. He wasn't quite sure what half the things they were talking about were.

He had to admit, though, watching Lainie work was hot.

"Narrowing the field," Lainie cried.

He saw the lines on the map narrowing and changing color. Some turned green and disappeared, others flashed gold or red. They were mostly centered around the North and South America region. His gut tightened.

The lines thinned out, more of them turning green.

North America.

He sensed Killian tense as well.

USA.

Dammit.

The lines were attached to a red dot that formed on the map.

Over New York City.

"Fuck," Killian muttered.

Fuck was right.

Lainie stepped back, her face white. "The hacker is in New York." She turned. "They're here."

Hex gripped her arm. "We'd already guessed as much. It'll be okay, Lainie."

Nick watched the emotions cross her face. Fear was front and center.

There was a ping on the screen.

Another nasty email appeared.

I'll find you. I'll get you alone. I'll slice you open, cut you deep, and paint the walls with your blood, you thieving bitch. I'll listen to your screams and smile. You can't escape me. I'm always watching. Always waiting.

Soon you will die, Lainie Madden.

Soon.

Lainie let out a small cry.

Nick crossed the room. "Lainie—"

"It'll never stop," she said shakily.

He watched her face crumple.

"Whoever this is wants me to suffer, and I have no idea why. I try to live a good life. I work hard, make a good product for my users, treat my employees well, donate to charity, be nice. What did I do to deserve this?" She threw a hand at the screen.

"Kitten." He cupped both her cheeks. "Look at me."

Her brown eyes were panicked, boiling with emotions.

"Just breathe," he said.

"I can't."

"You can." He pressed a palm to her belly. "Just breathe. In. Out."

"You should run, Nick. Get far, far away. Don't take on my mess."

"I'm not going anywhere." He loved the feel of her soft belly under his palm. "We're going to sort this shit out. You just have to hang in there a little while longer. You're *not* alone, Lainie."

She swallowed, then looked around at the others, pausing on Hades to blink a few times. Then she looked back at Nick.

"You with me?" he asked.

"I think so," she whispered.

God, he liked holding her too damn much. He made himself pull back. "Come on, I'll drop you home."

She was quiet on the drive. He didn't like seeing her so subdued.

He found a parking space near her building. When she got out of the car, she shivered.

"Hey, it's okay," he said.

She nodded. "You're coming up, I assume."

He gave her a nod and she looked relieved.

Then she tossed her head back. "I *hate* that this person has me afraid."

"Remember I'm watching your back." His lips twitched. "And you have your self-defense moves, too."

Her jaw tightened. "That's right. I'll be kicking and scratching and yanking balls, if I need to." She sounded fierce.

Nick winced. "There you go."

She led the way into the lobby of her building. "Hi, Evan."

"Evening, Ms. Madden." The older African-American doorman smiled at her. "There was some maintenance on your level today. Someone working on your security system, and some plumbers for building work. It's all finished, but if there are any problems, just let me know."

"Thank you." She smiled at the man.

After a short elevator ride, she unlocked her door and he watched as she put the code into her security system.

"I'm going to make it an early night," she said. "After the late one yesterday, it's all catching up on me."

Nick wandered over and checked the new sensors installed on her windows. "Your new sensors are in, and they're all linked up to your system."

He didn't tell her that he was also linked up to her system. If anything went off, it would register on his phone.

"Great." She yawned. "Now I'm safe in case someone decides to scale twenty floors."

He shot her a look.

Their gazes met, and her face changed.

Shit. He knew she was remembering that kiss in the gym.

"I know I shouldn't, but I really want to kiss you," she said quietly.

Nick sucked in a breath and looked at the floor. She was so damn hard to resist. "We can't. You know it's a bad idea."

"I know. It's hard though." She fiddled with her ear, a nervous move. "The best kiss I ever had was when I was eighteen, sitting by a moonlit pool."

His body locked.

"It finally got surpassed. Tonight, in the gym."

His hands curled into fists. He wanted to close the distance between them. Desperately.

He made himself think of Nola. Of Madison.

"I'm not touching you. Except for keeping up the appearance that we're together, that's it." He forced the words out, even as a voice inside him howled at him to touch her, kiss her, claim her. "That's all it can ever be."

She sucked in a breath and turned her head, looking at the windows.

"I'm sorry." His voice was thick and husky. "Good night, Lainie."

Emotion rippled across her face. "Good night, Nick."

On the walk back to his car, Nick tried not to think about what Lainie felt like under him. Her taste was still on his lips, dammit.

He slid back into his car and moved his seat back. He'd stay and keep an eye on things for a while. She was shaken up after the latest message from the asshole stalking her.

He trained his gaze on her building. Thankfully, they'd had no snow yet this winter, but the night was cool. He had his coat in the back if he needed it. Later, he'd get a coffee.

He pulled out his phone and sent a few emails. He was no stranger to a stakeout. It was a necessary evil on some investigations.

When his phone lit up with a call and he saw the name, he hesitated. Then he answered. "James."

"Nick. It's been too long since you called."

Former Ambassador James Meehan retired after the death of his wife and daughter in Colombia. He'd never remarried and had purchased a small horse farm in Tennessee. He lived a quiet life and called Nick regularly.

For some damn reason, James had never blamed Nick for the death of his family.

"How are you?" Nick asked.

"Good. Busy with the horses. Got a real spitfire of a filly that I'm working with. Thinking about growing some grapes, maybe make my own wine."

Nick laughed. "Wine, huh?"

"Think I'd be good at it." A pause. "You get some time off, you should come for a visit."

Nick rubbed the back of his neck. "I'll see what I can do."

"I know Sentinel Security keeps you busy."

"Yeah."

"Too busy. You taken a vacation lately?"

"You're starting to sound like my sister," Nick grumbled.

James laughed. "You got a woman you spend time with who you aren't related to?"

Nick snorted, although velvet-brown eyes and lush curves flashed through his head. "I know where to go if I want some female company."

"I don't mean a hook-up, Nick."

"There's no one special." His voice sounded off, even to him.

James was quiet a moment. "Who is she?"

"Who?"

"Whoever has you tied up in knots and lying to yourself?"

"There's no one. I'm just helping one of my sister's friends. She's in trouble."

"Ah. Did I ever tell you that Jennifer was my sister's friend?"

Nick's fingers tightened on the phone. "No."

"Tried to ignore her for nearly a year. She was still in college and so damn beautiful. She finally cornered me in the boat house at a party, and uh, persuaded me to see reason." There was love and amusement in his voice.

No sadness, no anger, no accusation. How could James not blame Nick? "James, hell, I'm sorry you don't still have her."

James sighed. "I'm sorry too, but it wasn't your fault, Nick. I wish you'd believe me when I say that. The fault for Jenn and Madison's death falls squarely on Martinez and the Cardoza Cartel." The man's voice had firmed. "I know my girls will get justice one day."

Fuck, yeah. Nick did everything he could to mess with the Cardoza Cartel's plans. One day, Martinez would end up dead or rotting in a prison cell.

"Anyway, listen to me," James continued. "If you find a woman, a good, beautiful one who lights you up, you grab onto her. A woman who you think about when you go to sleep at night, and one who's the first thing on your mind when you wake up, then you hold on, and you don't let go."

Nick's muscles went tight. "What if she deserves better?"

"No better man than you, Nick Garrick." A long, gusty sigh came down the line. "Wish you could see it."

"I'll try and get to Tennessee when I can, James. Better have a bottle of Angel's Envy Cask Strength bourbon waiting for me."

James snorted. "That stuff costs a fortune."

"And I'll claim a woman when you start dating again."

A beat of silence. "Touché." Warmth trickled into the other man's voice. "Take care of your girl, Nick."

"Bye." After ending the call, he stared out the windshield blindly. He heard Madison's infectious laugh, remembered the way she'd followed him around, declaring that she'd like to join the CIA one day. For the first time in a long time, the memory made him smile.

The hours ticked by. No one suspicious entered Lainie's building. He knew Hex had hacked into the video feed in the lobby. He'd get an alert if facial recognition picked up anyone entering who shouldn't be there.

He raised his gaze toward Lainie's floor. There were no lights on in her's apartment. She'd be tucked up in that big, romantic bed, asleep. Would she wear cute pajamas, or a sexy nightgown?

"Fuck, Garrick, seriously." He had several worried texts from Nola. He could just imagine what she'd have to say if she knew he was obsessing over Lainie.

He looked up at the darkened windows again. *No.* He wasn't going to touch her.

That's when it happened.

The windows of Lainie's apartment blew outward, sending glass raining downward. Like a shower of diamond shards.

What the fuck?

He was out of the car in the blink of an eye. Flames were flickering in the windows above. His heart thundered in his chest.

Lainie.

Body on high alert, he slipped into mission mode. His senses flared to life, energy flooding his system.

As he sprinted for her building, alarms started blaring. Lights were coming on all over the building.

Nick's focus narrowed. He ignored the shouting

doorman as the man opened the door, and Nick charged inside.

He had to get to Lainie.

LAINIE COUGHED AT THE SMOKE. In shock, she held up her hands. Bits of glass were stuck in them from the explosion.

God, had there been a gas leak?

She coughed again.

She was only wearing her navy-blue, slinky night-gown with a touch of lace, a matching, tiny robe, and her favorite fluffy, gray slippers. Cold air rushed in through the broken windows, icy on her skin. Her hands stung from the glass and cuts. Her heart pounded.

She coughed again. Fire was flickering by the windows. Her head felt stuffed with wool, and she couldn't think. Somewhere, fire alarms were ringing.

She had to get out.

She stumbled to the emergency door to the stairwell. Glass crunched under her slippers. God, she'd been going to get a glass of milk from the kitchen when the blast had happened. She hadn't been able to sleep. There had been too many thoughts of Nick's commanding, overbearing presence in her head. Not to mention his body, that rugged face, that sexy beard.

That kiss in the gym.

She'd almost reached the kitchen when she was knocked off her feet. She'd thrown her hands up to protect her face from the flying glass.

Lainie reached the stairwell door and shoved it open. A sob broke free.

Behind her, she heard the fire-suppression sprinklers come on, dosing her apartment. The heavy door closed behind her, closing her in the empty stairwell. Shouts echoed from below.

She felt a little dizzy, but she couldn't hold the railing because of her bleeding hands. She felt glass pricking through the thin soles of her slippers, so she kicked them off. Carefully, she headed down the stairs, the concrete cool on her bare feet.

Dizziness hit and she spun into the railing. Pain burst in her hip, and she bit her lip.

"Keep going, Lainie." What if the fire got out of control? What if she was trapped in here and burned to death?

God, her beautiful apartment, her things. It was on fire.

They're just things. She sucked in a breath and kept going. She rounded the landing, trying to focus on where she put her feet so she didn't take a tumble down the stairs.

She was almost at the next floor when her foot slipped. She grabbed the railing by instinct and pain exploded in her hand, glass cutting deep.

"Ow, ow, ow." She pressed her arm to her chest, tears welling.

She hobbled on. The smoke smell grew stronger.

Oh, no.

She picked up speed. There was the sound of pounding footsteps that echoed in the stairwell.

She rounded another corner and slammed into a hard chest.

"Lainie, thank God." Nick pulled her into his arms.

"Nick?" She pressed into him. Her edgy panic changed to relief. "Oh, God, Nick."

"I've got you, kitten. Hold on." He looked her over, saw her hands, and his face darkened. "Come here." He swept her into his arms and started down the stairs.

She blinked. She wasn't tiny by any means, but he showed no apparent effort in holding her.

"Watch your hands," he warned.

She pressed her face to his neck and held on.

The lobby was filled with the chaos of panicked people. Outside, sirens wailed.

"Come on." He headed outside, shouldering through the door.

"Why were you here?" Her teeth chattered. It was freezing outside.

"I never left."

She saw his car, where he'd parked it earlier. He opened the passenger side door and set her inside, then grabbed a coat from the back seat. He wrapped it around her shoulders.

It enveloped her, as did the rich scent of Nick. She breathed it in and felt some of her jitters calm.

A fire truck screamed to a stop in front of her building. She saw firefighters in all their gear leap out.

Nick closed the car door, rounded the hood, and got in.

He started the car and cranked up the heat, then he pulled out.

"We can't leave," she said. "I'll need to talk to the fire-fighters. My place is on fire. Oh, God."

"Lainie, this was no accident."

Everything in her froze.

No. That couldn't be right.

A cold shiver ran through her, and her blood turned to ice. "You think whoever's threatening me did this?"

"I don't believe in coincidences."

She curled in on herself. "Why would somebody do this? How can you murder someone you don't even know?"

He reached over, his big hand on her knee. Warmth pumped off him.

"It's going to be all right."

"How? Whoever this fucked-up asshole is, they just blew up my apartment. They could have hurt other people." A horrible thought hit her. "God, other people could be hurt." And it was indirectly her fault.

"The blast seemed targeted to your place."

He said it so calmly. Her chest was tight, and it hurt to breathe. "Can you check for me? If anyone was hurt?"

He glanced at her. "Yeah, kitten, I'll check."

"Thank you."

"God, your hands are a mess."

"I won't lie, they're really starting to hurt."

Nick growled. "I'm going to make whoever did this pay."

The dark, deadly promise in his voice made her shiver. "I'm fine, Nick." At least she would be. She leaned back in the seat. There was no way she'd let some nameless, faceless person terrorize her and destroy her life.

"Where are we going?" she asked.

"My place. And I'll arrange for a doctor to look at your hands."

She raised a brow. "You have a doctor that you can call out in the middle of the night?"

"Yes."

Tiredness and pain mixed together, draining her energy. She huddled there, her brain floating.

Then, she jolted, and realized he was driving back into the Sentinel Security warehouse.

Lainie frowned. "Wait. You live at your office?"

"It's a big building. The lower level is all offices, but the upper levels are apartments. Killian gives us a good deal."

"And a short commute."

"We all travel a lot, so having a secure apartment in the building makes sense."

She let him lead her into an elevator and she huddled in his jacket. Her bare feet were freezing and she was trying not to focus on the fact that she wasn't wearing a bra.

This time, the elevator took them higher. The doors opened into a small vestibule. Nick touched a fancy pin pad to open his front door.

With a gentle hand on her back, Nick nudged her inside.

The large space had a modern, industrial vibe. Outside the floor-to-ceiling windows, the lights of the city glowed, and a small terrace was covered in plants. Inside, the polished-concrete floor, rich, wood accents, exposed brick walls, and heavy furniture screamed "man lives here."

The place suited him. She wandered toward the large windows and took in the great view of the river. The giant, black-leather couch looked comfortable and masculine.

Nick had pulled out his cell phone and was talking to someone. Or barking orders at someone.

Tiredly, she dropped down on the couch, staring blindly at his huge television. She held her hands carefully on her lap.

"Lainie?" Nick knelt in front of her. "Dr. Chu is on his way." Nick's gaze dropped, rage igniting in his eyes. He gently stroked her wrists. "Your hands."

She found it shocking that such a big, powerful man could be so gentle.

"Nick..." Her voice was a low whisper.

"Yeah?"

"Could you please hold me? It's been a rough night, a rough few weeks really, and—"

He moved, sitting beside her. His arms wrapped around her carefully, and he pulled her against him. He pressed his face to her hair.

Lainie let out a shaky breath and relaxed against him.

"I've got you, Lainie."

She closed her eyes. He did. And she liked it. Too much.

Nick Garrick was like the animal he was named after —a lone wolf. If she got too used to him being here, he'd break her heart when he left.

CHAPTER SIX

The knock at the door had Nick reluctantly pulling away from Lainie's curvy body.

He opened the door to Dr. Daniel Chu.

The slim man was wearing pajamas with ducks on them. Rubber ducks. Some were yellow and smiling, and some were red with devil horns.

"Really?" Nick asked, quirking an eyebrow at the good doctor.

"Wolf, my friend, it's 2:00 AM. You call me when I'm in my ducky pajamas, I'm coming in my ducky pajamas." The man was also carrying a black bag.

"Over here." Nick's gut was still churning. Panic was an ugly choking emotion inside him.

Lainie was hurt. He hated it.

"Daniel Chu, this is Lainie Madden."

The doctor strode to the couch and dropped the bag on Nick's coffee table.

"Hello Lainie, I'm Daniel." He made a clucking

sound as he looked at her hands. "You've done a number on your poor hands."

"There was an explosion." Fury vibrated through Nick. "She's being targeted." He'd already called in the explosion to Killian. He and Hex would pull all the info on what had happened and deal with the police.

"You poor thing." The doctor opened his bag and pulled out some gear. He sat beside her. "Don't worry. We'll get you fixed up. Luckily, your robe stopped anything getting on your arms. Let's start by pulling the glass out of your palms. Wolf, can you move that lamp over here? I need more light."

Jaw tight, Nick dragged the tall, black-iron lamp closer to the couch and flicked it on. *Fuck.* It made her hands look worse.

Daniel held up some large tweezers. "Wolf, get some water. I'll give you some pain meds, Lainie."

"Thanks," she whispered.

Once she'd taken the pills, Daniel got to work on her hands. Nick paced beside the couch.

"I'm sorry you had to get out of bed," she said.

"Oh, don't be." Daniel pulled a small shard out and dropped it in a bowl. Lainie winced. "I'll send Killian a nice, big bill." The doctor smiled. "And my husband loves to hog the bed when I'm out of it. He'll keep it warm."

She smiled. "I like your pajamas."

"Thank you. You have excellent taste."

Nick rolled his eyes. He watched every move Daniel made. "Make sure you get everything."

Daniel made a sound. "Who's the doctor here? Quit hovering, Wolf."

Nick couldn't help it. Seeing her hurt had short-circuited something in his head. He strode across his rug.

It could have been worse. She could be in the hospital.

He could have lost her.

"Wolf," Daniel snapped. "Take a chill pill. She's fine. Her hands look a lot worse than they are because of the blood. The glass fragments are small."

Lifting her head, Lainie looked at Nick. Her dark eyes looked huge and tired. "I'm okay, Nick. It doesn't even hurt anymore."

He was enraged that she was hurt at all.

Something shifted inside him, tightening his chest.

He was done.

He was done denying everything he felt inside for Lainie Madden. Her life was in danger, and he was the best person to keep her safe. She was a distraction to him just being beside him. If she was in his bed, in his arms, he could protect her even better.

Hell, he wondered if everything he'd done had brought him to this. All his training, all his combat experience, had all been so he could keep Lainie safe.

Daniel cleaned her hands, then bandaged them.

The doctor looked at Nick. "Have you caught the asshole who hurt her yet?"

"Not yet, but I will."

"Good." He finished bandaging her hands. "Lainie, I'm going to leave you some extra meds and bandages. I'll check on you tomorrow."

"Thanks, Doc."

"It's Daniel. And I've always got time for beautiful

ladies." The man winked. "And beautiful men. And grumpy, bearded hotties too, even when they drive me crazy."

Lainie smiled.

"Get some sleep. With Wolf looking after you, you'll be fine."

She nodded.

Nick showed Daniel to the door.

"She'll be all right?" he asked Daniel quietly. He knew the doctor never dodged or lied.

"Yes, Nick. Take a breath. She has a few cuts, but she's fine."

Nick released a breath. "She could've been killed."

"She wasn't." Daniel cocked his head. "I love this."

Nick frowned. "What?"

"You. All churned up over a woman."

Nick's scowl deepened.

Meanwhile, Daniel's grin widened. "Yep, love it."

"Go, before I kick your ass."

"Oh, you've been checking out my ass, Wolf?"

"Out." He closed the door hard behind the pain-in-the-ass doctor.

On the couch, Lainie looked disheveled, a little bit lost, and a lot tired.

"Bed," he said.

She looked at him. "How about you try a full sentence?"

His heart squeezed. At least everything that had happened hadn't dulled that feisty spark of hers. "Waste of words." He held a hand out to her. "You need some rest."

She sighed. "I'm too tired to argue with you."

"Good." He helped her up.

"Asshole," she muttered, but there was no heat in her voice.

"I often am." He led her down the hall.

"I'm making it my mission to teach you some manners."

He grunted. "I spent years doing some fucking dirty missions, Lainie. I'm pretty sure that ship has sailed...or sunk."

"I know a good guy when I see one, Nick."

His gut clenched. "I'm not a good guy."

"Bullshit." Her mouth moved into a bone-cracking yawn.

"Come on." He led her into his bedroom. He had a guest room, but it wasn't made up.

That was his excuse.

"You really sat outside my place?" she murmured quietly.

"Yes." He was damned glad he had.

His room was drenched in shadows. He grabbed a fresh T-shirt from his drawers. "The bathroom is through there. I'm guessing you want something clean to wear."

"Thanks. My nightgown does smell like smoke." Her nose screwed up, and she set his jacket down. "And I think it has blood on it."

He'd been studiously ignoring the filmy slip of blue, and he didn't need any more reminders that she'd bled.

With a nod, she took the T-shirt, headed into the bathroom, and closed the door.

Nick ran a hand through his hair. He tried not to

think about the fact that Lainie was in his bathroom and his bedroom. She was hurt. She needed rest.

She came out, and his body wanted to drink in every detail of Lainie wearing his T-shirt. Savage satisfaction rocketed through him. But when he saw that her face creased with tiredness, his protective instincts took over.

"Into bed," he ordered.

She didn't argue. He pulled the covers back and she climbed in.

Fuck. Lainie Madden in his bed.

Nick pulled the covers over her, his gaze snagging on her dark brown hair spilling over his pillow.

"Sleep well, Lainie."

She made a sleepy sound.

"No one is getting to you here."

He'd make sure no one disturbed her sleep.

He moved to shift away, but she reached, out and he carefully took her wrist. He was extra careful not to bump her injured hands.

"Nick, thank you."

Something twisted in his chest. "You're welcome, kitten." The hand by his side clenched. He wanted to lean over and press his lips to hers.

He forced himself to let her go and step back.

She was hurt.

But tomorrow, things were changing.

Yes, she'd been off limits for a long time, but now, Nick was staking his claim.

He let himself stroke a hand over her hair. "Sleep well."

"Will..." Her voice was slowed by sleep. "Safe now."

That twinge in his chest again.

He backed out and headed for the living room. Nick stood at the windows, staring out at the night-soaked city.

Someone out there was gunning for Lainie.

Where are you, you fucker?

He hoped Hex would uncover the person responsible. If not, it was up to Nick to hunt him down. He was good at that. He'd hunt the asshole down or lure him out.

Spinning, he headed for the couch. He was the best person to keep her safe. Fuck all the excuses he'd used before.

Lainie was his.

His to protect.

He grabbed a blanket off the back. He'd doze and get a few hours rest. The military had taught him to sleep lightly, and to come awake at the slightest noise.

Tomorrow, he'd ask Lainie some questions. His gut instincts said that this wasn't some random crazy. It felt personal.

Whoever it was, they were extremely motivated to hurt her.

"I'm going to find you, and you're going to regret it."

COFFEE.

She needed coffee.

Freshly showered, but bleary-eyed, Lainie stumbled into Nick's kitchen. She'd showered—the most awkward shower in her life. She'd kept her left hand mostly out of the water, since it had the most bandages. She'd taken the bandages off her other hand and braved the sting to wash her smoky hair.

She'd been so relieved to see the cuts on her hands weren't anywhere near as bad as she'd feared. Afterward, she'd rebandaged her hands and raided Nick's closet. She was wearing one of his white business shirts. She really needed some clothes.

God, did she still have clothes? Her heart clenched painfully.

Coffee. After coffee, everything should seem better.

There was no sign of Nick in the living area, or the glossy kitchen. She took a second to admire the black countertops and cabinets against the exposed brick wall. She heard water running somewhere, so she guessed he was in the guest bathroom.

Her mind happily tried to imagine Nick naked in the shower.

No. Lainie found the coffee machine and got to work. She breathed in the glorious scent of the brewing coffee with anticipation. Next, she popped a few painkillers Daniel had left for her to dull the sting on her hands. Her belly rumbled.

She found Nick's fridge fully stocked and pulled out eggs. Maybe she'd whip up an omelet for them.

After taking her first sip of coffee—oh, God, so good— she started mixing the eggs in a bowl. It was slightly uncoordinated with her bandaged hands but doable. She found salt and pepper, and chopped up some onion and ham.

She was humming to herself when Nick appeared.

"Morning," she said brightly, looking up. Then she nearly swallowed her tongue.

He was in suit trousers, but no shirt, his dark hair damp. It looked shades darker than normal.

There was that chest again.

She couldn't drag her gaze off him. He was built. Hard pecs, a faint covering of dark hair. Her gaze went lower. Carved ridges covered his abs. Her fingers flexed.

"Morning."

His gravelly voice jerked her out of her daze. "What?"

He shot her a faint smile. "I said morning."

"Right. It is morning. The sun is shining. The birds are singing."

Oh, crap. Shut up, Lainie.

Nick's lips twitched. "Did you sleep okay?"

She sighed. "I got a few hours. Your bed is very comfortable."

"And your hands?" He scowled as he eyed the bandages.

"Actually feeling much better. I popped a pill and I also braved a look under the bandages. The cuts aren't too bad." She poured a coffee and put one sugar in it. "Black coffee with one, right?" She pushed it toward him.

His eyebrows rose. "Yes." He took the mug. "How did you know?"

"That raging crush I had on you when I was a teenager. I knew everything about you. That you like to listen to rock music, especially Velvet Revolver. I learned all about football because you played. And I hated Mary-Ellen Richards."

"Mary-Ellen Richards?" He looked confused.

"You took her to prom. Blonde. Big boobs. I hated her."

His gaze dropped to her chest and jerked back up. "Um..."

"I was twelve. I didn't have any boobs at the time."

"Well, you made up for it, and I barely remember Mary-Ellen. That shirt looks far better on you than me."

Lainie eyed his chest again. "Do you need it?"

"No. I'll grab one from—" His cell phone rang. "It's Nola."

"Oh." Lainie kept mixing.

He put the phone on speaker. "Hey, No—"

"Nick! Oh, my fucking God. Lainie's apartment is a wreck. There was some sort of explosion—" Nola's voice was going more and more high-pitched.

Crap. Lainie's heart sank. She hadn't even thought to call her bestie in all the chaos.

"I can't reach her. No one knows where she is. My God, what if she's hurt? She could be in the hospital, with amnesia and in a coma."

Lainie blinked. Nola really needed to lay off the soap operas. She was addicted to them.

"Nola," Nick said.

"Nick! You have to help find her. She might—"

"Magnolia," he barked.

His sister finally went quiet.

"She's fine. She's here with me."

"Hey, Nola," Lainie said.

"Oh my God!" Nola screeched. "Why didn't you call? Are you all right? What the hell happened?"

"Okay, slow down," Nick said.

"I'm so sorry, Nola," Lainie said. "It was late. I was shaken up and wasn't thinking—"

"What happened?" Nola asked more calmly.

"I'm not exactly sure—"

"There was a bomb blast in her apartment," Nick said. "Likely set by the person who's threatening her."

Nola's gasp was clear on the line.

Lainie shot Nick a look. *Don't scare her*, she mouthed.

Nick scowled at her.

"Nick is taking care of me," Lainie said.

"I knew he would," Nola said.

"I'll keep her safe," he said. "We'll be at the Sentinel Security office, and Lainie will stay with me for now."

"Wait, what?" Stay with Nick? *No, no, no.* She was barely holding back from trying to lick his chest as it was. Living with him was a whole new level of temptation. "I can't stay here, and I have to go to the Pintura office."

"No."

"I have an important meeting today, Nick."

He crossed his big arms. Big, muscular arms. Her gaze traced a vein in his bicep.

No, Lainie. Focus.

"Well." Nola sounded pleased. "It sounds like everything's under control."

"No, it's not," Lainie said.

"I'll call you later, Lainie." Then Nola was gone.

"It's too dangerous to go to your office," he said.

"Nick, I have a business to run." She set the bowl of eggs down and circled the island. She faced off with him.

"And I have to be in Las Vegas for a conference in a few days."

"Your safety is my first priority." He stepped closer.

"I'm not letting whoever is doing this ruin my life or control my every move. If I do that, they've already won."

"They win if you're dead. I'm not going to let that happen."

Lainie growled. "Nick, please. Pintura is my life."

He looked away.

"It's important to me. I have the big acquisition coming up. I have to give the keynote at the FutureTech conference. All my employees are depending on me."

He looked back and gripped her chin. She felt an electrifying tingle shoot through her. His blue eyes met hers.

"You ever do anything just for you?" he muttered.

"Nick..."

"Fine."

She let out a relieved breath. "Thank you."

"But I'm coming with you and staying."

At her office? She blinked. "What?"

"From now on, I'm not letting you out of my sight."

"Nick—"

"Someone hasn't just threatened to kill you, Lainie, they've now *tried*." He held up her bandaged hands. "I'm not giving them a chance to try again."

Her heart thumped hard in her chest.

"You tell everyone that we're together to explain my presence," he said. "And it'll be fine. I'll stay out of your way."

Together. Her heart gave a solid thump against her ribs. "There's just one problem."

His brows drew together. "What?"

"I don't have anything to wear."

His gaze dropped, skimming over her body clothed only in his shirt. He took his time studying her bare legs and her nipples pebbled. Crap, she hoped he didn't notice.

"I think you look great." His gaze flicked up to hers.

Lainie froze. The heat she saw in his eyes ignited the simmering desire in her belly. *Oh, God.* She fought not to take a step toward him. There were reasons, lots of reasons, and she couldn't think of a single one of them right now.

"Don't look at me like that," she said breathlessly.

"Like what?" His voice was deep, gritty.

She swallowed. "Like you're thinking of—"

"Tearing that shirt off?"

Her belly spasmed and she felt herself go damp. "Nick, can you *not* talk about tearing clothes off, please?"

"Like I'm desperate to get my mouth on you and see how you taste?"

Her nails bit into her palm. "We discussed this. All the reasons this can't happen."

"I changed my mind."

She was pretty sure her eyes bugged out of her head. "What? You can't just change your mind." Because then it was all down to her self-control. Her very, very shaky self-control.

He took a step toward her, his rugged face laser-focused on her. She suddenly understood why they'd given him the code name Wolf. She certainly felt hunted. She took a step back and bumped into the island.

"Yes, I can. Running toward your burning building, not knowing if you were dead or alive—" He heaved in a breath. "Seeing you hurt and afraid, it changed everything."

"You said I wasn't worth the risk."

He gave a violent shake of his head. "Not what I fucking meant. I meant anything that risked your safety wasn't worth it. But this fucker attacked you. It's safer if I'm right beside you."

Lainie's chest was so tight she could barely breathe.

"I'm going to protect you, Lainie, and I can't fight how much I want you at the same time. You and me, it's going to happen."

She stared at him. She couldn't do this. Her heart clenched into a tight ball. Her parents loved her but in a distant way. Elliott hadn't wanted to, but he'd left her. And more than one ex-boyfriend had cheated or dumped her. People left her. She'd always wondered what the hell was wrong with her.

But what she felt for Nick... What it could turn into...

She wasn't sure she was strong enough to withstand him leaving her too.

"We can't," she breathed.

"We can." He took another step closer. "And we will."

Then there was a knock at the front door. "Wolf?"

It was Hadley's voice.

Nick stared at her for another endless second, heat

boiling in his blue eyes, then he spun and strode to the door.

Hadley waltzed in, her hands full of shopping bags.

"Wolf sent me an SOS this morning." Hadley held up the bags. "I did one of the things I am very good at, shopped and bought you clothes."

"Oh, thank you, Hadley." Lainie pressed a palm to her racing heart, trying to find her bearings after Nick's bombshell.

The other woman looked at Lainie's hands. "I'm so sorry you were hurt."

"I'm all right."

"Now, you totally rock Wolf's shirt, but I'm sure you don't want to wear that all day."

Lainie blushed. "Right."

"Come and see what I bought you. I got you all the essentials, including some toiletries and makeup. Oh, and Wolf told me to get you a bottle of Jean Paul Gaultier Classique."

Lainie's heart squeezed. She gave her fake boyfriend who thought he wasn't fake anymore one last look as she followed Hadley out of the room.

CHAPTER SEVEN

Nick followed Lainie into the Pintura office, trying to keep his gaze off her ass.

Damn, he'd have to give Hadley a bonus.

Lainie wore a fitted, gray skirt that lovingly hugged her curves, a black shirt, and black high heels that gave him ideas.

Right now, he didn't need more ideas where this woman was concerned.

"Morning, Dustin," she said to the young male receptionist at the front desk.

"Hi, Lainie." The young man's gaze hit Nick and widened.

"Ah, Dustin, this is Nick, my...boyfriend."

"Hi, Dustin," Nick said.

The man blinked. "Oh, hi."

"We'll be in my office. My Nickie-poo here wanted to see where I work."

Nickie-poo gripped her wrist and squeezed.

"Deva told me to remind you that the Kintore meeting is in thirty minutes," Dustin said.

With a nod, she wrapped her fingers around Nick's hand and tugged him toward her office.

The main office area was busy. The vibrant space, with all bright colors on the walls, had Lainie's essence stamped all over it. Her staff members were all busy at desks, or bustling toward the glass-walled meeting rooms, or seated on funky, soft furniture pieces, grouped in spaces for impromptu meetings.

She towed him into her office. Deva wasn't at her desk, so they didn't get waylaid.

"Call me Nickie-poo again and there will be consequences," he growled.

She poked her tongue out and dumped her handbag on the desk. "I'm not sure anyone will buy us as a couple."

He backed her against the desk. "Yes, they will, because we are."

She pressed a hand to his chest. "Nick—"

"Your perfume is driving me crazy." It filled his senses, made him think about finding all the places where she'd sprayed it on her skin.

She frowned. "You don't like it?"

"I like it too much."

She froze, her gaze locked on his mouth. He reached up and dragged a thumb across her luscious lips. She let out a small moan, then her tongue darted out and licked the pad of his thumb.

His cock throbbed in response. "Do you know how many fantasies I've had about you?"

Her lips parted. "No."

"Too many to count. Sweet ones, naughty ones—" his voice lowered "—dirty ones. I've pictured having you naked in so many different damn places. Imagined the sounds you'd make when I've got my mouth on you."

Her fingers clenched in his shirt, and she shifted against him.

"Sometimes, when I was deployed, thinking about you was the one thing that would get me through a rough night."

Her eyes flashed. "*Nick.*"

There was a knock at the door. Dragging in a breath, Nick forced himself to back up.

A woman of about fifty, with artfully gray-streaked black hair, breezed in. "Are you ready for the Kintore meeting, Lainie?"

Lainie straightened. "Ah, yes."

The woman paused and lifted her head. She wore a crisp white shirt tucked into wide-legged, emerald-green trousers. When she saw Nick and Lainie, her eyes widened. "Who is this?"

"Nick Garrick." He held out a hand.

"Hello, Nick Garrick, I'm Michelle McMahon, head of marketing for Pintura. And why are you here?"

"I'm Lainie's."

"Really?" Michelle managed to impressively turn the word into four syllables.

He put an arm around Lainie and squeezed. "Yes."

Lainie was tense, but she managed a smile. "Nick wanted to see where I worked."

"I didn't know you were seeing anyone." Michelle cocked her head. "And what do you do, Nick?"

"I work in the security industry."

"Mmm."

"Right." Lainie carefully her tablet off her desk.

Michelle gasped. "What happened to your hands?"

"Oh, I...had a little accident."

"At my place. She dropped a glass in my kitchen," Nick spoke, smoothly. "She should've just left it." He ran a hand down her back and felt her shiver.

How had he ever thought he could keep his hands off her? This attraction humming between them was too hot, too strong.

"It was silly. I grabbed for it." She held out her bandaged hands. "And cut myself."

"I hope it heals up quickly," Michelle said sympathetically.

"Me too," Lainie said. "Nick, make yourself at home in my office, and I'll—"

"I'm coming to the meeting." He smiled. "I won't say a thing or get in your way. I'm just excited to watch my kitten work."

Michelle sighed, hearts in her eyes. "Kitten. That's so cute."

Lainie turned to face him. "I don't think—"

He squeezed her hip.

She rolled her eyes and pasted on a smile. "Sure, sweetie. Let's go."

Nick sat in the corner of the conference room watching Lainie and her team prepare. Then a trio of suits from another company were shown in—two men and a woman.

As he promised, he sat quietly and didn't say anything. He was mesmerized by Lainie. She was personable but firm and ran the meeting with ease and experience. Her intelligence shone through, along with her passion for her product. It was hard to believe the sweet, geeky twelve-year-old had blossomed into the smart, tenacious CEO. She had a good team. Michelle and the other Pintura employees knew their stuff.

One guy from the other company, Kintore, was enamored too. He had a slick smile that widened every time Lainie looked at him. And when she turned to write on the whiteboard, the guy checked out her ass.

Damn that skirt.

Nick glared holes in the man and when he caught Nick's gaze, his face turned a little pale.

"I look forward to this marketing opportunity with your team." Lainie shook hands with the Kintore people.

Loverboy luckily kept it brief.

Nick followed Lainie back to her office.

Deva was busy at her desk. When she saw them, her lips tipped into a wide smile. "Hello, Nick."

"Deva."

"I hope the self-defense training went well."

Lainie frowned. "Ah, yes. I learned a lot."

Nick reached out and touched her hair. He could see she wanted to swat his hand away. "I wanted to come and see my woman in action at work."

"Your woman?" Deva said, smile getting wider.

Lainie glared at him. "Deva, hold my calls." She

yanked him into her office and slammed the door. "What was that?" She spun, hands on her hips.

Shit, she was cute. "What?"

"Intimidating my clients. This is my workplace, Nick."

"I didn't say a thing."

"You didn't need to. The Kintore CFO looked like he was going to puke from fear."

"He was staring at your ass."

She shook her head. "Men. They always have to prove who's bigger and tougher."

"I don't need to prove that."

She rolled her eyes.

There was a knock at the door, and she whirled and pulled it open. "What?"

Deva stood there, holding a vase of flowers.

"These arrived for you." The assistant frowned. "I think this must be some kind of joke."

Nick suddenly realized the flowers were dead.

Fuck.

He watched as shock hit Lainie's face.

Nick took the vase from Deva.

Lainie hurried forward. "Thanks, Deva." She closed the office door and leaned back against it. She looked at the dead roses with horror. The stems were filled with thorns. There was a card nestled amongst the sagging heads.

Nick set the vase on the desk, then snatched the card and opened it.

Lainie leaned into him, reading over his arm.

You will die, Lainie.

Like these roses.

Dead. Dead. Dead.

She sucked in a breath. "Well, he or she doesn't have a career in poetry ahead of them, but they are consistent." She strode to the windows, wrapping her arms around her middle.

Nick hated seeing the dejected set of her shoulders. He pulled out his phone.

"Hey, Wolfman." Hex's voice.

"Lainie just got a delivery of dead roses. The In Bloom Florist. Can you track it?"

"God. This sicko is sick. Leave it with me. How's she doing?"

He eyed Lainie. "She's hanging in there."

"Take care of your girl, Wolf."

"Thanks, Hex."

Your girl. He liked that way too much.

And if Lainie heard herself described as a girl, she'd have a fit.

He walked over to her. "You okay?"

She shook her head. "No. I... This isn't going to get better. It's only gonna get worse, isn't it?"

"Lainie—" he gripped her shoulders "—you're not alone. And it might get worse, but I'm going to be here. And I *will* stop this."

Her chest hitched. "Dammit, I don't want to cry. I hate crying."

"I hate it too." He pulled her into his arms.

She buried her face against his chest and wrapped her arms around him.

Damn, her curves fit perfectly against him. Lainie's

scent filled his senses. He pressed a kiss to her temple. Giving comfort wasn't something he was good at. He was the kind of guy to use his fists, shoot someone, or take action, but holding her close, he realized it wasn't too hard.

Share his strength. Help hold her up. Make the burden a little easier.

"You're going to be okay."

"Just hold me, Nick. Let me pretend this isn't happening. Just for a minute."

"Hold on for as long as you need."

HE FELT SO GOOD.

Strong. Solid. Hard.

Lainie hugged Nick harder, holding on tight. Like he could shield her from all the crap flying at her right now.

It was so, so tempting to lean on him.

"You believe me, right?" he asked.

"What?"

He pulled back, his blue eyes intense. "That I will sort this out. I'll find whoever is responsible and make them stop."

"I want to believe..."

He cupped her chin. She felt the rasp of the calluses on his skin and shivered.

"It's going to be okay." He brushed his hand down her back.

Oh, it felt so good.

She moved her hands to his chest and slid them

lower. She felt the flex of those glorious abs she'd ogled that morning.

He brushed her cheek. Her breath caught in her lungs and she went up on her toes.

Nick Garrick made her feel safe... And hot. The man lit up every single cell inside her. Hell, he had when she was a teenager, and now it was even worse.

It was getting harder and harder to remember all the reasons they weren't supposed to do this. Especially with him telling her that he'd changed his mind.

Their lips were close, and they stared at each other.

Instead of his usual hard, piercing look, his eyes were hot and stormy.

Nick slid an arm around her waist and yanked her up against him. Her breasts pressed against his chest. He groaned and she moaned.

Then his mouth hit hers.

Lainie threw her arms around his neck and kissed him back.

She felt surrounded by him and arched up, needing more.

She welcomed his tongue in her mouth and nipped his lip in return. She held on as he devoured her.

There was no coaxing or teasing, just pure hot demand.

Desire lit up her insides. Her panties were soaked.

He moved her two steps and lifted her off her feet. She clung to him, then her back hit her desk, and his delicious heavy weight was on top of her.

A hard cock pressed between her legs. *Yes.* On a

moan, she tried to wrap her legs around him, but was hindered by her tight skirt.

"I wanted to do this yesterday. When I saw this damn desk." One of his hands skimmed up her side, to her breast. His next kiss was even deeper.

Lainie was so aware of him. Of the hard press of his body, his woodsy scent, his rich taste. She sank her hands into his thick hair, writhing against him.

She needed him.

She needed Nick.

Then suddenly, he wrenched his mouth free, turning to look at the door. She liked the fact that he was breathing heavily.

A second later, there was a knock on her office door.

"Sorry, Lainie." Deva's muffled voice. "There's a call from management at Bloom. They said it was urgent."

Lainie let out a shaky breath. When Nick pushed off her and straightened, her inner voice got to work yelling at her.

No men, Lainie Madden. They can't be trusted. He'll hurt you.

"Just a minute." She straightened, smoothing down her skirt. "We can't do this, Nick. Nola, remember?"

"No more excuses, Lainie."

"I'm scared." She paused, pressing a hand to her cheek. "You're dangerous."

His eyes flashed. "I'd never hurt you."

"Not physically. You said you didn't do relationships. That you just wanted to fuck me—"

He moved fast, gripping her jaw. She gasped.

"I'm not gonna hurt you, Lainie. Yeah, I'm no expert at relationships, but for you, I'll do anything."

Her heart leaped into her throat.

His fingers smoothed along her jaw. "I'm going to treat you right, kitten. Give you everything you deserve."

"Lainie?" Deva called out. "I've put the call through to your phone. Line two."

"Take your call." He stepped back. "I have a few calls to make as well."

She nodded, couldn't quite look at him. "Okay."

She needed some time alone.

He paused in the doorway. "I get you need me to prove myself, and I will. I always keep my promises."

Watching him walk through the door, she released a shaky breath. She could still feel his touch on her jaw. So many emotions ricocheted around inside her.

She wanted to believe him so badly.

She dropped into her desk chair. Her gaze slid to the framed picture of her brother. Elliott was smiling his goofy smile.

"God, I miss you, El." She touched his face. "I think I'm in trouble." She let out a shaky breath.

She was crazy about Nick Garrick, and she wasn't sure she had the strength to stay away from him.

She made herself reach for the phone. She had work to do. It would help distract her.

Her heart already had a few dings and scratches, but she knew it wouldn't survive a pulverizing blow from Nick.

CHAPTER EIGHT

Nick strode into the Sentinel Security office in a bad mood.

He'd called Hadley, who was now with Lainie at the Pintura office.

Lainie was worried he'd hurt her.

A muscle ticked in his jaw. Hell, he'd pretty much tried to convince her of that a day ago.

No, fuck that. He was going to protect her, from the person hunting her and from herself. From what he could see, she worked too hard. She tried to take care of everyone else first—Nola, her employees, her Pintura customers. And her parents never put her first.

No one ever put Lainie first, but he would.

He blew out a breath and headed into the command center.

Killian and Hex were standing with Hades. The three of them looked up at him.

"Wolf, my friend, you look like a thundercloud," Hades drawled.

Nick grunted.

"Woman problems." Hex smiled. "One particular smart, sexy brunette."

"Quit it," Nick growled.

"Your feelings for her going to cause a problem?" Killian asked.

"No."

"I'm sensing more than this." Hades stroked his jaw.

"Way more," Hex added. "He gets hearts in his eyes when he looks at her. I've got video feed of him rushing up the stairwell at Lainie's place to get to her after the explosion."

Nick pinched the bridge of his nose and wondered why he put up with them all. "I'm claiming her. Lainie's mine."

That got him a beat of silence.

"Eek." Hex clapped her hands together. "I knew it. I can't wait to tell Hadley."

Hades shot him a knowing smile. "Happy for you, *amico mio*. Although, there are so many beautiful women in the world, that limiting myself to one—" He gave an elegant shrug.

Killian watched Nick steadily with assessing eyes. "You sure about this?"

"Yes. She's mine to protect. My feelings for her..." Hell, admitting his feelings still felt strange. "I'm going to use them to keep her safe."

Killian stared for another second, then nodded.

Hex grinned and gave Nick a wink.

"Yeah, well, I still need to convince Lainie that she's mine."

Hades laughed. "You need to use some charm."

Hex shook her head. "No, he doesn't. When you aren't looking, she watches you, Wolf. She likes you just fine."

"How about we focus on finding the asshole who's after Lainie?" Nick said. "What have you got on the blast?"

"Charges were set in the ceiling panels of her penthouse," Killian said.

"What? You're sure?"

His boss nodded. "Hex hacked the arson investigator's computer."

"How the hell did someone get explosives into her place?" Nick asked.

"I think I can answer that." Hex lifted her tablet and swiped.

The big screen on the wall flared to life. The feed showed the lobby of Lainie's building. It was clearly earlier in the day, and several overall-clad workers with ladders and toolboxes were heading toward the elevators.

"There was maintenance being carried out on her level," Hex said. "On the plumbing. They were legit and working in the ceiling."

Nick stared at the workers in the image. "But one of them wasn't legit." One of them was after Lainie.

"I'm running them all but nothing's popped so far."

"Our guy could've bribed a legitimate worker," Hades said.

Nick ran a hand through his hair. "What's this guy's angle? If he wants money, where are his demands?"

"Perhaps he's just cracked? A killer?" Hades suggested.

"It doesn't feel like that. He's making too much noise. He's enjoying taunting and terrifying her." Anger bubbled inside Nick. He would stop whoever it was.

"I'll keep looking for links," Hex said. "The damage to Lainie's place actually wasn't too bad. It had a top-notch fire suppression system. Her apartment is repairable, but it'll take a while to fix."

"She's staying with me until we catch this fucker," Nick said.

"Who wants to bet that she never moves out?" Hades murmured.

Nick ignored him. "Hex, can we arrange to get some of her clothes and personal items out?"

The woman nodded. "Sure thing."

"Thanks. Now, do you have anything more on the cyber attacks on the Pintura site?"

Frustration crossed her face, and the hacker screwed up her nose. "The guy has skills. I pulled in Remi to help me."

Remi Solano was a former Sentinel Security contractor. She was a talented hacker but had scaled back her work since she'd fallen in love with tech billionaire Maverick Rivera. Last Nick knew she was busy planning her wedding.

"Lainie and I traced him to NY, but after that, nothing." Hex blew out a breath. "I can't get any more detail than that. I'll keep trying, and see if Remi can shake anything new out, but he or she isn't making it easy."

Dammit. Nick restrained himself from kicking the

table.

"Keep the pressure on," Killian said. "This guy will miss a step eventually, and we'll be waiting." Killian's dark gaze met Nick's. "In the meantime, keep Lainie safe."

Nick nodded. "That's my plan. I'm going to go over the info some more," he said. "See if we missed anything."

He headed for his office and walked through the brick archway. His black desk was as neat as he'd left it. To be fair, he tried not to spend too much time sitting at it. The shelf on the wall held some hunks of polished rock that he'd collected from countries all around the world. There was also a framed picture of an oasis in the Sahara Desert. He'd spent a vacation there once after a brutal mission.

He dropped down and opened his laptop.

First of all, he messaged Lainie.

Okay?

I'm fine. Hadley seems frighteningly competent.

He could hear her sassy tone through the message.

Anyone have a grudge against you? Has anyone threatened you recently?

I'm a nice person, you know.

I know. But you're rich and successful.

And gorgeous. He didn't write that bit.

I have some business rivals.

Who?

They wouldn't do this.

Who?

So bossy. Shaun Hare at Graphite and Nora Jenkins at JenkTec.

Nick made a note. He'd check them out.

Any other unhappy exes apart from Jonas?

He hated the idea of any guy with the right to touch her.

Not lately. I've no time for relationships. Pintura keeps me busy.

Trying to warn him off.

Anyone else you can think of?

Honestly, I can't think of anyone who'd do anything like this...

I sense a but.

There have been a couple of disgruntled employees. Clara Hall. She was a great programmer, but felt she'd been unfairly treated and wanted a promotion. She was toxic. Bullied younger team members and caused discord. We caught her hacking into company documents.

This woman went on the top of his list.

And Chris Sweeney was let go for harassment. He kept making uncomfortable advances to several colleagues. We don't condone that kind of behavior.

Nick made another note. He'd check out Sweeney too.

Okay, stick close to Hadley.

Yes, sir.

Oh, he heard the sarcasm. He wanted to spank her.
Behave.

Nick got to work running the rivals and ex-employees.

The rivals all seemed aboveboard. The guy, Shaun Hare, liked the limelight. Did lots of interviews and podcasts. Hmm, he liked to badmouth Pintura and talk up his own design site.

It sounded like sour grapes. The online reviews said his site was harder to use, and less user-friendly than Pintura.

The ex-employees had disappeared. Chris Sweeney,

the harasser, had moved back to Ohio and was living in his parents' basement. Clara Hall had given up her condo and fallen off the radar.

Hmm, he'd need to dig a little deeper. His phone pinged, and he realized several hours had gotten away from him.

He had a message from Lainie.

> ***I have a business party to attend. Michelle and Deva both asked if my new boyfriend is coming with me.***

> ***Yes. Dress code?***

> ***Suit.***

> ***Get Hadley to take you back to her place. I'll pick you up from there. Time and address?***

> ***7 PM at a private penthouse. Central Park West.***

> ***Fine.***

Nick rapped his knuckles on the desk. He was excited to see her again. He missed her. Her smile. Her scent.

Focus on keeping her alive.

His jaw tightened. He needed to change for the party.

He needed to remember his mission.

LAINIE FLUFFED HER HAIR, then slicked red lipstick across her lips.

She stepped back. Okay, maybe this was wrong, but she'd dressed up for the party. A lot.

She wrinkled her nose. Okay, not for the party, but for Nick "Wolf" Garrick.

She wanted the man as worked up and confused as she was.

The dress was red and short. It hugged her body and had a deep *V* that made her boobs look bodacious.

Hadley had a killer eye.

Lainie was grateful the woman had given her a well-stocked, and stylish, emergency wardrobe. It sounded like her apartment hadn't been totally destroyed, so she was hoping to get some of her own clothes soon. She also needed to make some calls and organize for the repairs.

When she walked out of the bathroom, the woman in question was perched on a stool at the kitchen counter. Hadley's apartment was similar to Nick's, with a few extra touches. She had a collection of beautiful black-and-white photos from different parts of the world on the brick wall. A spider web in the desert. Traffic on Tower Bridge in London. A couple kissing by the Eiffel Tower. A lion crouched in long grass. Rain-soaked leaves in a jungle.

Hadley looked up from her phone. A beatific smile crossed her face. "Wolf is going to swallow his tongue."

"I love the dress, thank you." Lainie stroked the fabric. "I'm not sure it's right to torment him."

Hadley waved a hand. "All men need a little torment."

"He has to protect me."

Hadley crossed her long legs. "And he will. Wolf is very bull-headed when it comes to staying on target. A little too bull-headed sometimes."

Lainie paused. "He mentioned his final mission with the CIA. You know what happened."

"Not my story to tell," Hadley said gently.

And damn, Lainie was a little envious that this woman knew Wolf better than she did.

"I'd trust Wolf any day to do his job, no matter what," Hadley continued. "It's in the man's bone marrow to protect. When he looks at you... It gives me shivers. He wants you, Lainie. He really likes you."

Lainie bit her lip. "Really? At first, he made a compelling case for never touching me again. Now...he's being all demanding and growly and possessive, and saying the opposite."

"Mmm, Wolf's good at demanding and growly. I bet he looked good doing it."

Lainie sighed. "Yes." She cocked her head, a horrible thought hitting her. "Have you two ever...?"

Hadley held up a hand. "No. I don't have a brother, but I imagine this is what it would be like."

"I had a brother."

Hadley's head tipped to the side.

"His name was Elliott. He died of a rare cancer a few years ago. Rhabdomyosarcoma, or RMS." God, she hated those three letters.

Sympathy flooded the woman's face. "I'm sorry."

"Thanks. I miss him every day. He was an artist, and he inspired me to start Pintura."

"That's nice. A part of him will always be with you in your business."

"Exactly."

Hadley grabbed Lainie's arm. "Lainie, Nick can be pretty laser focused on his job, determined—"

"A bossy bulldozer."

Hadley smiled. "Often. Get him and Killian together..." She rolled her eyes, but then her smile faded. "He can be hard on himself. He hardly ever takes a break or a vacation. Fun isn't in his vocabulary."

"Okay." Lainie could see that.

"It should be. He's earned it. He never talks about his family much, except for his sister. But from what I've read between the lines, it wasn't great."

Lainie thought of Nola's parents. Her father was horrible, and her and Nick's mom had mostly checked out of her parenting responsibility years ago. She kept busy with luncheons and spa days.

"His stepfather is...harsh and judgmental."

Hadley nodded. "And I don't think Nick's had much soft. The careers he's chosen haven't offered much of that."

"Soft is not something I think of when I think of Nick."

"Doesn't mean that he doesn't need it sometimes."

There was a knock at the door.

"There he is." Hadley jumped up and headed over to let him in.

Dragging in a deep breath, Lainie slipped a sparkly

bag with her phone in it over her shoulder.

Then Nick came through the door. The man looked *way* too good in a suit. It did little to tame his rough edges, but it made her mouth water.

He saw her and jerked to a halt. Her belly coiled.

Oh, boy. Yes, this dress was so worth it.

His hot gaze ran over her, lingering on her breasts, before it took in her nipped-in waist and bare legs. Then it jerked back to her face.

The look on his features turned her insides hot and gooey.

"Let's go." His voice was husky.

"I'm ready. Bye, Hadley."

"Have fun." The woman winked at her.

In the hall, Lainie and Nick walked side-by-side toward the elevator.

"So, do you like the dress?" she asked.

Nick suddenly spun and backed her against the wall. She squeaked and gripped his shoulders.

"You're trouble." His rugged face was just an inch from hers.

"I'm not, I promise."

"I want to kiss you," he growled.

Her heart skipped a beat. *Oh yes, kiss me.*

He ran his nose along hers, inhaled, like he was drawing in her scent. "I want to do a lot more than kiss you."

"Nick—"

He stepped back and gently took her hand. "We have a party to get to. And what I want to do to you can't be rushed."

Oh, God. As he towed her to the elevator, she tried to wrestle her out-of-control hormones back under control.

He was quiet on the drive and Lainie tried not to fidget.

"Whose party is this again?" he asked.

"Don't pretend you haven't already investigated Jayson and his company within an inch of his life."

"Fine. Tell me what work Jayson Klein's company is doing with Pintura?"

"It's one of our big deals at the moment. He's created new, lightweight VR—virtual-reality—goggles."

He shot her a wry look. "I might have been a simple sailor, but I work for a security company that specializes in cyber security. I know what VR stands for."

"Sorry. I'm used to explaining all the techspeak to people. So, Pintura is doing a lot of the visuals for the program for the goggles. I have a team dedicated to it. Down the track, I'd like users to be able to use Pintura to customize their own VR experience."

"A win-win for both your companies."

She smiled. "Exactly. Jayson's a decent guy. Always has his fingers in a deal when he's not partying."

They pulled up at the building by Central Park.

After a short elevator ride to the penthouse, the doors opened into a large, stylish space with huge windows, showcasing a terrace overlooking the park. Music was pumping, and it was wall-to-wall people.

A robot holding a tray of drinks whirred over to them. Nick's eyebrows rose.

"Welcome," a computerized voice said. "Please take a drink and enjoy the party."

"Jayson also makes robots." Lainie took a glass of white wine.

Nick turned and scanned the crowd, then scowled.

"You know, parties are supposed to be fun," she told him.

He turned the scowl her way. "I don't find them fun."

She dusted a speck off the lapel of his jacket. "You need to relax a little. Look less bodyguard, and more besotted boyfriend."

He slid an arm around her and pulled her close. Her pulse spiked. *Traitorous body.*

"I hate that every man here will be drooling all over your beautiful breasts."

Oh. Her pulse did a crazy dance. "They won't. I saw a model here, and a hot, young actress."

Nick leaned in. His cologne hit her, making her think of the forest, and her belly clenched.

"They will," he said.

The desire in his eyes was so intense. He wanted her so badly, and she desperately wanted him to let go of that fierce control.

"Nick, please—"

"Lainie!" a voice called.

Frustrated, she turned and saw their host, the owner of KleinVR, weaving through the crowd toward them.

Nick let her go, and she missed his touch instantly.

"Jayson, hi," she said.

Jayson was slim and trim, with styled, blond hair. He reached her, smiling, then yanked her close and smacked a kiss right on her mouth.

CHAPTER NINE

Nick's body locked as he fought not to rip the guy away from Lainie.

With great restraint, he gripped her hips and pulled her back against him.

She was smiling. "Jayson, this is my boyfriend, Nick."

Again, Nick fought not to show his reaction. He hadn't been anyone's boyfriend for years, but he liked hearing Lainie say it. Liked it a lot.

She might not be on board yet, to believe it for real, but he'd get her there.

Jayson, the guy still lucky to have his arms attached, blinked. "Boyfriend? I didn't know you were seeing anyone?"

Nick frowned at the guy. They were business colleagues. Why would he know anything about her personal life? He pulled Lainie under his arm, plastering her to his side.

Jayson's face fell.

Ah, the guy liked Lainie in more ways than just business.

"Nick and I've known each other forever." She smiled up at him, and he was caught by the brightness of it. "I'm friends with his sister. I always had a giant crush on her older brother... But he never noticed me."

He ran his fingers across her cheekbone. "I always noticed you."

She blushed and his cock twitched.

Jayson's shoulders drooped even more. "Nice to meet you, Nick." His tone said it clearly wasn't. "Lainie, we've got the VR goggles set up in the living area. Just a prototype, but people are loving it."

Her face lit up. "I knew they would. The early versions were awesome."

"Enjoy my expensive wine and try out the goggles." He shot her a wistful look, nodded at Nick, then headed back into the crowd of partygoers.

"His romantic intentions are dashed," Nick said.

Her eyes widened. "Jayson? Romantic intentions? Hardly. The guy dates models. Young ones."

Nick was thankful she was clueless.

They circled through the crowd, and she sipped her wine. She introduced him to some people, and he kept a close eye on anyone paying her too much attention.

Damn, he hated parties. Too many people.

"Oh, there's my VR content team." She hurried over. Nick eyed the two young women and older man.

"Guys!" Lainie cried.

"Lainie." One woman was short, with blonde hair and a sparkling grin. "Have you tried the goggles yet?"

"Not yet. Jayson said people are loving them."

"They're *so* good." The other woman was Latina, with curly, dark hair. "The visuals are—" She kissed her fingers, her curls bouncing.

The man with them nodded. He was older, with dark skin, and a gray-tinged goatee and glasses. "I tried them. So. Awesome." The man eyed Nick curiously.

The tiny blonde waved at Nick. "Is this your man, Lainie? The office is abuzz about your hot guy."

Lainie swallowed. "Yes. Nick, this is Patrick, Chloe, and Isadora."

He nodded. "Nice to meet you."

Isadora, who had the dark curls, slapped a hand to her chest and winked at Lainie.

Chloe, the pixie blonde, beamed. "Nice work, boss."

"Stop it," Lainie admonished.

"You ladies need a refill?" Patrick asked.

"Yes," Isadora and Chloe chimed together.

Lainie's glass was almost empty. "Another Chardonnay for me."

"Nick, give me a hand?" Patrick asked.

Damn, Nick didn't want to leave her.

She made movements with her eyes, telling him to go.

Chloe grabbed Lainie's hand. "We'll go and try the VR goggles again. Meet us there, gents."

Nick pinned Lainie with a stare. "Don't go too far, kitten."

"Kitten." Isadora let out a wistful sigh.

The women towed Lainie off. He watched the flash of her red dress disappear into the throng of people.

"Can't take your eyes off her." Patrick nodded

approvingly. "She deserves that. She's worked hard to build her company, and has made it an awesome workplace, but she works too hard, makes sacrifices. We all want to see her happy." The man frowned. "And Keenan Jonas wasn't the man to do it."

They reached the bar and ordered the drinks. Jayson the douche had spared no expense.

Nick looked over the party. He spotted the VR area, with several people with sleek goggles over their eyes and gloves on their hands. They were holding their arms out, laughing and smiling.

He watched Lainie, Isadora, and Chloe slide goggles on.

She looked like she was enjoying herself. He suspected Patrick was right, and Lainie worked too hard. He knew her parents lived in Florida and didn't visit, and her brother had died. Nola had been heartbroken when the young man had died so young. So Lainie had no family close, no one to lean on. She had Nola, of course, but his little sister was a workaholic, too.

He and Patrick were just getting the drinks when a commotion broke out.

Nick spun.

Near the VR space, people were yelling. He heard a woman's shocked cry.

Lainie.

He abandoned the drinks and shoved through the crowd.

"My God." Lainie was wearing the goggles, her arms out. She staggered. "No. *No!*"

Chloe ripped the goggles off her. "Lainie?"

"What's wrong?" Nick pushed forward.

Chloe's pale blue eyes were wide. "I don't know. We had a fun dance program on."

Lainie's body was stiff, she was panting and then let out a sob.

Enough. Nick reached her and tossed the goggles aside.

Her eyes were wide, her face ashen.

"Nick—" Her face crumpled. "Oh, God." Tears rolled down her cheeks. People were staring.

He swept her into his arms. "Kitten, what happened? What's wrong?"

"I..." A sob broke free of her chest. "It was so horrible." She shuddered.

Jayson appeared. "Jesus, what happened? Lainie, are you okay?"

"We need somewhere private," Nick said. "Now."

Jayson nodded, worry on his face. "My study. This way."

Nick carried her down the quiet hall. Jayson reached a closed door, opened it, and flicked on a lamp on the desk.

Nick sat on a black-leather couch against the wall, settling Lainie on his lap. "Kitten, talk to me." He pushed her hair back.

She let out a gasping breath. "The images... On the VR. They were *horrible*." She closed her eyes and pressed her face to his chest.

In the doorway, Chloe, Isadora, and Patrick hovered, concern written all over them.

"The VR goggles she used," Nick barked. "Get them. Now."

Patrick nodded and hurried away.

Nick hugged Lainie closer.

Patrick didn't take long to return. Nick slid Lainie onto the couch, and her fingers tightened on him.

She didn't want to let him go. He liked that, but he had to see what she was afraid of. He stroked her arm and squeezed.

"I'm right here." He took the goggles.

"They're all fun, pleasant programs," Jayson said.

"Nick, don't put them on," she whispered.

He ignored her and settled them over his head. Suddenly, color washed over his vision, and he saw a packed dance floor. People laughing.

The dance club looked so realistic.

Then the music changed to something darker, and the images morphed.

He saw the dead body on the floor. Mutilated. The blood.

The body had Lainie's face.

Fuck. His gut clenched hard.

More images flicked through. Horrible ones. All of them showing dead and mutilated bodies. Each one had Lainie's face.

"Jesus." He tore the goggles off and shot to his feet. His gaze zeroed in on Jayson. "You did this." He took a step toward the man.

"What? No! I don't even know what you're talking about." Jayson held out a hand.

"These are your goggles."

The man spluttered.

"Nick, I'm sure it's not Jayson," Lainie said.

Nick held them out. "Put them on."

Jayson swallowed, then snatched the goggles and gingerly slid them over his head. A second later, he gasped. He shoved them off like they were a poisonous animal. "Hell. I had nothing to do with this, Lainie. I swear."

The guy was pale, and his shock looked genuine.

"I'll investigate," Nick said, not looking away from the man. "I'll find out who did this. If it is you, you'll regret it."

LAINIE CLUNG to Nick's hand as he strode into the Sentinel Security office. She almost had to jog to keep up with him.

Killian appeared, striding out of a brick archway. She almost did a double take. She'd never seen the owner of Sentinel Security in casual clothes. He was wearing a black turtleneck and black jeans.

"Lainie, are you okay?" Killian asked.

She nodded tightly.

Nick slapped the set of VR goggles on the long table. "Where's Hex?"

"Here." The woman skipped in, coffee in hand. Her hair was loose, and she was wearing leggings and an over-sized sweater.

"You were getting ready for bed," Lainie said.

"It's fine." Hex grabbed Lainie's arm and squeezed.

"I'm used to the odd hours, and this is important."

"The images on there..." Lainie looked away, stomach churning. "They're horrible."

She saw a muscle tick in Nick's jaw. "They're fucking disgusting."

Hex picked the goggles up and plugged them into her laptop.

"No one else saw those images," Lainie said. "Everyone else saw programs my team had put together."

"Lainie was targeted," Killian said.

A cold shiver ran through her.

Hex made a sound and tapped on her laptop. "The goggles were hacked."

Lainie gasped. "What?"

"Someone close by hacked the goggles, and fed in their own program. They had to be on the same wifi, then implanted a worm to put their own program into this particular set of goggles."

Lainie's heart thumped and she leaned into Nick. His arm tightened around her.

Right now, she leaned on him. She needed his strength to help her keep it together.

"Pull them apart, Hex," Nick ordered. "Find this asshole."

The hacker nodded. "I will. I'll analyze the goggles and the images."

Lainie winced. "The images are..."

"They're meant to knock you off balance," Nick said.

"They were real, weren't they?" Her voice cracked. "They were real dead bodies, not computer generated."

His jaw tightened. That was answer enough.

"Go and chill, Lainie. Try not to think about it." Hex looked at Nick. "If he's left his fingerprint, we'll find it."

Nick pulled her away. "Come on."

Lainie felt emotions bubbling inside her. "I'm tired of feeling hunted. Waiting for the sword to drop. This asshole is ruining my life, scaring me. I'm tired of it!" The words burst out of her.

In the elevator, Nick eyed her. "You're entitled to feel that way."

She kicked the wall.

He was watching her carefully.

"I'm not going to lose it." She tossed her head back. "Not completely."

He gripped her chin. "Lainie, I think you're coping really well. Your strength amazes me."

And just like that, her anger drained away.

Okay, that wasn't exactly true. It just changed to desire.

Tonight, she'd felt excited, terrified, disgusted, tired, weary, sad, and angry.

Now, the heat she felt was all focused on this tough, rugged man telling her she was strong and amazing.

They strode into his place and after he closed the door, she faced him.

"I want to kiss you."

Nick stiffened. "Lainie, you've had a rough night—"

"We're in your apartment. It's secure. In a secure building. I'll be safe here, right?"

"Yes, but there are never guarantees."

"There are no guarantees in life, Nick. I learned that when I lost my brother."

Silent tension pumped off him. "You've had a shock, you're shaken. You need to rest."

"I want to kiss you," she repeated.

"I'm doing this for your own good," he growled.

She angled her chin. "Maybe I'm sick of everything? Maybe I want to throw caution to the wind and take what I want for once?" Her voice ended up close to a shout.

He stalked toward her, and her heart stuttered. She fought not to back up. She knew he'd never hurt her.

He stopped just inches away. She saw his hands curl into fists.

"I'm trying to take care of you. You think I'm being an asshole?"

"Not exactly."

"I'm okay with you being angry at me, as long as you're safe."

Lainie swallowed. "I'm the safest I've ever been when I'm with you, Nick." She gently pressed her palms to his chest. "When I'm close to you." She closed the inches between them, pressing against him. "I'm the safest in your arms."

He made a low male sound. "Damn you, Lainie."

He yanked her against him. The kiss was hot, hungry, and soon she was moaning.

Nick's groan rumbled through him.

Then they were moving, not once taking their hands or lips off each other. The couch hit the back of her legs and she dropped down.

"One more kiss, Lainie." He knelt in front of her. "One kiss, then you're climbing into my bed, alone, to sleep."

"Nick..." she protested.

"One kiss. I'm not fucking you when you're still shaky and afraid. When I finally sink my cock inside you, I want both of us focused on that. I want the entire night to take my time worshipping every inch of that spectacular body of yours."

Her chest hitched. "You think I'm spectacular?"

"Every inch. Every curve."

Her heart did a funny little jig in her chest. The way he was looking at her...

If one more kiss was all she'd get from him tonight, she'd take it. "Okay. Now I want my kiss."

His hands skimmed up her legs, pushing her dress up.

Uh-oh. Any second he'd see...

"Fuck me, Lainie, no panties?" His gaze was scorching. "All night, you've been bare under here, standing beside me."

She licked her lips, saw more sparks flare in his eyes.

"Where's my kiss?" she demanded huskily.

"Oh, you'll get it, kitten." He pushed her dress up more.

She flushed. Her waxed pussy was on display. "Nick?"

His big hands slid up her inner thighs. God, it felt good. His fingers weren't smooth, and the slight calluses rasped against her skin.

"My mouth is up here," she said.

"I didn't say I was going to kiss your mouth." He gave her a sexy smile.

Oh. Her belly clenched.

He lowered his dark head; she felt the scrape of his beard on her inner thigh and jerked.

Then his mouth was on her. His tongue licked her, and she cried out.

Oh. Oh. *Oh.*

Pleasure was a hot and burning wave. Sensation flared between her legs, rushing all over her body.

Lainie sank her hands in his dark hair and pulled him closer. She spread her legs wider.

God, she was a shameless hussy.

His wicked, talented mouth set to work, and soon, Lainie was barely coherent.

"Nick, oh, don't stop." Her voice was desperate.

"I'm not going to, kitten." He said the words against her swollen flesh. "You taste like heaven. Always knew you would."

She felt a thick finger slide inside her, his tongue on her clit. That added to the sensation. She turned her head and bit her arm, trying to stifle the needy sounds she was making. Her hips lifted up to his hungry mouth.

"Let me hear you, Lainie."

She met his gaze. Her belly spasmed. She was so hot.

Nick's head between her legs, his mouth on her, her juices glistening on his lips.

"Say my name when you come," he ordered.

Bossy as ever. He went back to work. Soon, Lainie was rocking her hips up to him, her fingers clenched in his hair.

"Nick... I'm going to come." She needed to come.

Everything inside her was a hot, bright ball, the tension building.

He slid another finger inside her, stretching her, and sucked on her clit.

Lainie gasped. The orgasm tore through her—huge and relentless. She clamped her legs on his head, her body shuddering.

Nick held her as she finally cried out his name.

She closed her eyes. Pleasure from the best damn orgasm of her life made it pretty hard to think.

Her body was as limp as a cooked noodle. She opened her eyes and saw Nick looking at her.

That rugged face was filled with heat.

"You're beautiful, Lainie."

He leaned in and kissed her. She tasted herself on Nick Garrick's lips and shivered.

"Bed." He pulled her upright and pushed her dress down. "Alone."

Her gaze fell to the huge bulge in his pants. "Are you sure?"

"Yes." He cupped her cheek. "I'm not just going to keep you safe, kitten. I'm going to make sure you get everything you need. Now, time to sleep."

CHAPTER TEN

"Anything?" Nick asked.

Hex looked up a little blearily. "Good morning to you, too. I slept well, thanks, just not for long enough."

He tugged on her hair.

"How's Lainie?" she asked.

Still asleep in my bed, thanks to the long, hard orgasm I gave her last night. He cleared his throat. "Still sleeping. She'll be okay. She's tough."

"I like her. She's perfect for you. Helps loosen you up a little."

"Hex—"

"Don't mess it up, Nick. Don't let that gorgeous, smart woman, who totally watches you all the time, slip through your fingers. We all have a past and regrets, but we've all made a new start here. You don't have to be all work, all the time."

He dropped a kiss to the top of her head. "I'm not going to let her go."

Hex smiled. "Good. Now, do you want to know what I found?" She waved at the goggles on the bench. She'd dissected them into bits.

"Yes."

"I tried tracing the hack. No luck. The guy, unfortunately, is no novice."

Nick crossed his arms. He didn't care what the guy was good at. He was still going down.

"But, I ran through all the doctored images." She poked out her tongue. "So gross. Whoever did this is sick. Remi did a little work for me and tracked down some of them. Looks like most of them were sourced from some pretty sick sites on the dark web."

Shit, if billionaire Maverick Rivera got wind of his hacker fiancée poking around snuff sites on the dark web, the guy would storm in here, guns blazing.

"I don't want Lainie to have to see them again," Nick said.

"See what?" Lainie breezed in, looking fresh and sexy. She was wearing dark jeans, a gray shirt, and a black blazer.

All Nick could think about was the sweet sounds she made while he'd sucked on her clit.

She met his gaze, and heat filled her cheeks. She was thinking about it, too.

"Nick, are you being all overbearing and overprotective?" she asked. "And keeping stuff from me so I don't worry my pretty head?"

Hex snort laughed. "She has your number, Wolf."

He speared his friend with a look.

"I don't want you to see those fucked-up images again," he said.

Lainie's face softened. "I'd prefer not to see them again, either."

"So," Hex said. "I found something in the images."

Nick frowned. "What?"

"An image. Like a small logo. It's hidden in each of the images. Like a tag used by a graffiti artist, or something."

Lainie frowned. "Why would someone do that? They'd risk giving themselves away?"

"Because he wants to show how clever he is," Nick said darkly.

"It's kind of like a letter T with lightning at the bottom." Hex tapped on her tablet with her stylus, and an image appeared on the big screen.

Lainie gasped.

"Lainie?" Nick said.

She wavered and he reached for her.

He grabbed her arm. "Lainie?"

"I've seen this before." She shook her head. "It can't be."

"Where did you see it?" he asked.

"A long time ago. At college."

He helped her sit in a chair. "Hex, get her some water."

There wasn't a lick of color in Lainie's cheeks. He rubbed her wrists. She'd removed one of the bandages this morning, and he gently touched the healing nicks and cuts.

"Here." Hex handed her a glass.

Lainie gulped the water down.

"Talk to me." He crouched in front of her.

"I dated a guy at MIT. Trent. Trent Morton. We went out for almost two years. He was studying the same classes as me. I thought I loved him."

Nick hated the way his insides twisted when she said that.

"I was wrong. We had a lot in common. He was brash, confident, and thought he was destined to be the next Steve Jobs."

"He sounds like a douche," Nick gritted out.

"Turned out he was." She pressed a hand to her cheek. "I caught him in bed with the girl who worked at the computer store we went to all the time. Miss Tiny and Perky with a nose ring."

"He used this *T* logo?" Hex asked.

Lainie nodded. "It was his trademark. He doodled it on everything. We coded together a lot, and he was involved in some of my early ideas for Pintura. I didn't have a name for it back then, but my brother, Elliott, he was an artist and kept encouraging me to turn the idea into reality. Trent was actually a good sounding board for the technical stuff."

"But he wasn't in the picture when you started the company?" Nick asked.

"No. When I caught him naked with another woman, I kicked him out of my life. He spent the rest of our time at college trying to win me back." She sniffed. "As if. About a year after I graduated, I started the early version of Pintura." Her face clouded. "A few years after things really took off, he did try to contact me, and claimed he should be involved." She shrugged. "But lots of people did the same thing. Some people I didn't even know came out of the woodwork demanding chunks of my hard work, my blood, sweat and tears. I had my lawyers deal with it."

"And that was it?" Nick asked.

She nodded, her gaze moving back to the screen and the T logo. "I never heard from him again."

"Okay, I'm running everything on Trent Morton." Hex tapped wildly.

Killian walked in, looking impeccable in a dark-gray suit, his hair windblown.

"How was the meeting?" Hex asked.

"Fine." Although, he was scowling. "Did you have a breakthrough?"

"Maybe," Nick said. "An ex of Lainie's from college."

Killian nodded, but he seemed a little distracted.

"You okay?" Nick asked.

"Fine." He let out a sharp breath. "I just talked to Saskia."

"She okay?" His ballet dancer sister had recently been abducted by a Russian businessman. She was fine now and in love with the man who'd rescued her.

"She's already arranging to move her stuff to San Francisco," Killian said.

Nick raised his brows. "You thought she was going to change her mind?"

"Maybe."

Hex made a sound and leaned closer to Lainie. "Killian's sister fell in love with a hot guy in San Francisco.

Cam is former military, and now works private security. He is delish."

Killian gave Hex a flat stare. "I'm paying you to work, not to drool over Camden Morgan."

"The guy's in love with her," Nick said. "He's not going to let anything happen to her. And he makes her happy."

Killian sighed. "I know, but I still don't have to like it."

"All right, I have data coming in on the dastardly ex," Hex said. "He lives in New York." Images filled the screen.

The guy was medium height, pale skin with hazel eyes set a little too close together, but he had a charming smile. There were pictures of the guy all around New York.

Lainie stared. "It can't be him doing this. I mean, he's a cheating asshole, but not a stalker slash would-be murderer."

"Where is everyone?" a deep voice called out.

Hades swept in, wearing a three-quarter coat and scarf. The man's brown eyes hit Lainie, and a smile curved his lips. "We have a beautiful woman in the office, and no one told me?" There was a hint of an Italian accent in his voice.

Nick rolled his eyes. Matteo's father was Italian and his mother American. The guy could switch accents whenever it suited him. He always thickened the Italian when he was talking with a woman.

"What am I?" Hex asked dryly. "Chopped liver?"

"Hex, *bella*." He kissed her cheek.

"Lainie, you haven't officially been introduced," Killian said. "Matteo Mancini, Lainie Madden. Someone's sending her death threats."

"Lainie, a pleasure to meet you, even under such difficult circumstances." Hades took her hand and kissed her knuckles.

Lainie blinked, looking mesmerized.

Nick scowled at his friend. "Lay off, Hades."

"Lainie is Wolf's, remember?" Hex said.

Hades arched a brow. "Wolf never claims women."

Nick tugged Lainie up against him and wrapped his arm around her. "Lainie, this is Matteo 'Going to get his nose punched' Mancini."

Hades sketched a bow, looking unconcerned. "A pleasure, Lainie."

"Nice to meet you," she said with a small smile.

Hades' gaze dropped to Nick's possessive hold and his smile widened.

Hex's computer chimed.

"Have you got something?" Nick asked.

"Maybe. It seems that—" Hex grinned "—Trenty boy owns a VR bar in Brooklyn."

"VR?" Nick snapped.

"Yep, a whole bar called the VBar, where you can drink and watch whatever floats your boat on the goggles."

"That fuckhead," Lainie spat.

"It looks like the bar's very popular. It's all over social media. Some celebrities have visited."

"I think I'll pay VBar a visit," Nick said.

Hex giggled. "Sorry, I'm just trying to picture Wolf in VR goggles."

He ignored her.

Lainie straightened. "I'm coming."

"No."

"Yes."

"Lainie—"

"I'll get my coat." She spun and walked out, the heels of her boots clicking.

Hades looked at Nick. "You are going down."

"Fuck you, Hades."

"He's already half sunk," Hex said.

Nick looked at his friends. "She's mine, and I'll kill anyone who touches her."

Killian crossed his arms. "I think Wolf is happily down for the count."

THE SIGN for the VBar glowed in bright, neon pink.

Lainie tried not to glare.

Trent.

Trent was the one responsible for the threats? She shook her head. The asshole had cheated on her. They'd never have worked out long-term. Now he thought he had a right to do this to her?

"You okay?"

She glanced at Nick. He'd changed into jeans and a black leather jacket before they'd left Sentinel Security.

He looked hot, with a very large *H*. She'd changed, too. Her jeans were now tucked into knee-high boots.

She'd put on some heavier makeup, and Hex had pinned a cute, sparkly clip in her hair.

They were nothing more than a couple out for lunch at a popular VR bar.

"Let's take a look around," she said. "If Trent's here, don't kill him."

"Why not?" Nick's tone was dark.

She eyed him. "I can't tell if you're joking or not."

He met her gaze.

Not joking. "Okay, if Trent is responsible, I'm totally okay with him getting consequences, but I don't want to visit you in jail."

His scowl softened. "You'd visit me in jail?"

"Maybe. Once." Smiling, she pushed open the door of the VBar.

It was like an assault on the senses. Lots of pink, yellow, neon green, purple, and light blue. Neon signs glowed on the walls, spelling out words like, *Fun. Relax. Cruise. Vibe.*

There was a bar at the back in bright yellow. The crowd was fairly thick, and everyone at the bar and tables had VR goggles on. Lights strobed overhead.

"Well," Lainie said, looking at Nick.

He looked a mix of confused and vaguely horrified. "Let's get this done."

They walked to the bar. The advantage of having Nick with her was the crowd parted like warm butter.

He helped her onto a stool, then stood, leaning on the bar beside her. The servers were all dressed in hotpants and neon tank tops of different colors.

"It's so...gaudy," Lainie whispered.

The man sitting beside her had goggles on. He gasped, then let out raucous laughter. He was clearly enjoying his program.

"We'll order some food and drink." Nick snapped open the menu. "Blend in."

Lainie looked at her menu. It was just as tacky. There were cutesy named items. "I wonder what the Virtual Fantasy chicken is?"

"You want a drink?" Nick asked.

"What the hell, I'll try a cocktail. Help dull the pain of looking at all this neon."

Nick grunted.

"And I'll have the Metaverse salad." She wasn't up to risking the Virtual Fantasy.

He ordered a burger, along with a beer.

"I'll have the Simulation Sling," she told the twenty-something server eying Nick like he was candy.

He was too busy scanning the bar to notice the woman, a vague look of distaste on his face.

"This place is horrible," Lainie said. "I remember Trent having better taste."

"He's clearly changed."

"Clearly."

Her red drink arrived in a huge glass, letting off steam. She hoped she wasn't putting her life at risk. She took a sip. It was heavy on the pineapple goodness.

"Mmm, it's surprisingly not bad."

"I don't see Morton."

"Me neither." Her stomach was tight. She didn't really want to see him. Had he really tried to kill her? She looked blindly at her drink.

A big hand curled around her shoulder. "Lainie, we'll get him. I promise."

"I know."

"I'm going to the restroom. I want to see if there's an office or staff area back there."

She nodded. "I'll stay here." He hesitated and she took another sip. "Go. I'll wait for our food. If anything worries me, I'll scream."

He finally nodded and strode off. She watched a table of goggle-free women stare at his ass. She couldn't blame them, as it was definitely worth looking at.

The drink helped warm her belly. Nick was so solid and strong. And true. He'd never cheat. It was against his code.

What he'd done to her last night on the couch...

She shivered, letting the memory play back. She wanted him, and even knowing he might hurt her in the future, she wasn't sure she could hold back any longer.

She took another sip of her cocktail. Mmm, it was so good. She might get another one.

"You want to hire goggles?" a server asked her. The guy looked about twenty-one, with floppy hair and a square jaw. He shot her a flirty smile.

"Oh no. I had a bad experience recently."

He leaned closer. "I could help make it a better experience for you."

She gulped. "Um, thanks, but no."

With a wink, he left.

Then she sensed someone else behind her, but she knew instantly it wasn't Nick. Her throat tightened and she turned her head.

Thankfully it wasn't Trent, either.

Her eyes widened. "Keenan?"

Her ex gave her a small smile. "Hey, Lainie, I thought that was you."

Okay, objectively, she could see why she fell for his pretty face, lean body, and blond-tinged hair. He had a face that made women sigh, and he knew it. She also knew he spent a fortune on skin care. Probably whatever Rebecca Jade, the woman he'd cheated with, was pushing on her Instagram page.

"Hello, Keenan." Lainie looked past him. "What are you doing here?"

"Having lunch."

"Is Rebecca Jade with you?"

He shifted uncomfortably. "Actually, we broke up. She was caught in a hot tub with an actor in LA... Naked and testing out some new sex toys."

Oh man, thank you, karma. "I'm sorry." There, polite. No smugness at all.

Keenan moved closer. His cologne was so strong it made her eyes water. Funny, she'd forgotten about that.

"I miss you," he murmured.

What? She blinked. She realized her head was a little fuzzy and her insides were warm from her cocktail. Crap, the drink must be stronger than she'd guessed. She was feeling a bit tipsy. "Why?"

Keenan's brow creased. "We were good together, Lainie."

"No, we weren't."

He started. "We weren't bad."

"No, but even without you jumping into bed with

Rebecca Jade, who was most definitely not born with that name or those perky breasts of hers, we wouldn't have lasted."

"Lainie—" He reached for her.

"Back off." Nick appeared and stepped up behind her. He slid one arm around her while his other hand caught Keenan's wrist.

Keenan straightened. "Who the hell are you?"

"I'm Lainie's."

The heat inside her intensified at those words. And the feel of him, she wanted to snuggle back against him. *Hell, why not?* She leaned into Nick's chest.

"What?" Keenan said with a frown.

"Nick, this is my ex, Keenan Jonas. Keenan, my boyfriend, Nick Garrick." She looked up at Nick. Oh, that sexy beard. She loved it. "Nick, Keenan was the one who cheated on me with an influencer."

Mmm, his chest was so hard. She resisted the urge to slip her hand under his shirt.

"Boyfriend?" Keenan looked stunned.

What had he expected her to be doing? Pining for him?

"Sensory burger and Metaverse salad." The server put the food on the bar in front of them.

"Go now." Nick crowded Keenan until the man stepped back.

"Bye, Keenan." Lainie waved at him.

He shot her one more unhappy look, then stalked off. She giggled.

"Are you drunk?" Nick asked.

"No. Maybe a little tipsy." She tried for another sip,

but he moved the glass out of reach. "No fair, that's tasty, and enjoying Keenan getting an eyeful of his replacement was sensationally shallow of me, but I'm too tipsy to care."

Nick shook his head, a faint smile on his face. "Eat, so it soaks up some of the alcohol."

"Did you find Trent?"

He shook his head.

She leaned over the bar to catch the server's attention. "Hey, I heard an old college buddy of mine owns this place, Trent Morton."

"He does," the young man said.

"Oh, wow. Is he here? I'd love to say hi."

"No, sorry. He isn't in much at the moment. He's working on a big project."

Lainie's belly swirled. Like killing his ex-girlfriend?

"I need another cocktail," she muttered.

"No. Eat, and let's get out of here before our retinas get burned by the decor." Nick squeezed her knee.

CHAPTER ELEVEN

As they headed back to the car, Nick kept a tight grip on Lainie's elbow.

She wasn't exactly steady.

"So, Tacky Trent is off somewhere plotting to kill me." She threw her arms in the air, and almost tipped sideways. "I knew he was a waste of time, but killing me? That's insane."

Nick led her across the street. "Yeah, well I don't think killers have a firm grip on reality."

"Well, at least the Simulation Sling has made me not care quite so much. There was one good thing about that tacky excuse for a bar."

Nick fought back a laugh. Lainie was a bright light shining through all the dark. She didn't dwell, or let things keep her down for long.

And now she had him to lean on, to stand beside her when she needed the support.

When they reached his Aston Martin, she bumped

into him. He gripped her hip, then she shoved him, pressing him against the car. He raised a brow.

She ran her hands up his chest, then under his jacket. "I love the leather jacket look on you." She cocked her head. "I like you in the suit, too. I like you in anything, really."

"Lainie—"

"Did I tell you that I had a crush on you? A massive one."

He fought not to smile. "You mentioned it." She was killing him.

"Huge crush." She pressed against him, and he felt those beautiful breasts and the hard points of her nipples. "Massive. At first, I just thought you were gorgeous, then I was jealous of Nola. That she had a brother like you. Older, supportive. I'm still a little envious." There was a wistful note to her voice.

Nick knew she'd been tight with her brother, but he'd been younger.

"Then when I got older, I just flat-out wanted you. That kiss by the pool... Best kiss ever. Until the more recent ones you've given me." Then her nose wrinkled. "It gutted me, back then, when you ran off like I was toxic. I figured I was a really bad kisser."

Hell. Nick cupped her cheeks and spun them, so she was pinned against the car.

She gasped.

"I left, otherwise I would've been fucking you on a pool lounger by my parents' pool."

Her eyes went wide. "Really?"

"Really. I kissed you, and my cock was rock-hard

the entire time. You were so damn sweet and pretty. Meanwhile, I was older, had just had a rip-roaring fight with my stepfather, and I was dealing with stuff that I was doing in the Navy. I had missions coming up that were messing with my head. I had no right touching you."

She lifted her chin. "And now?"

"And now you're getting your gorgeous ass in the car. We're out in the open." He pulled her up, opened the door, and shoved her inside.

Traffic was slow as they headed back to Sentinel Security.

Lainie fidgeted in her seat.

"What's wrong?" he asked.

She bit her lip and shifted again.

"Lainie?"

She turned in the seat. "I really want you to fuck me on a pool lounger, now. I can't stop thinking about it."

Jesus. His hands clamped on the wheel, and he looked straight ahead.

"I'm bummed it's winter," she continued.

"Be quiet," he growled. Now, he shifted uncomfortably. His pants were tight. "Later, I'm going to make you pay for this." With his hands, mouth, and cock.

A hand touched his arm. He was so aware of her.

"Are you imagining it?" Her voice lowered. "Are you hard?"

"*Lainie.*" She was major trouble, especially now, with her inhibitions lowered thanks to an overpriced, badly named cocktail.

Her hand slipped lower, heading for his lap.

He caught her wrist and narrowly avoided slamming into the car in front of them.

He moved her hand back. "Behave. I'm driving, and I need to keep an eye out."

Her head tilted. "What do I get in return if I behave?"

He saw a glimmer of the tough CEO, well-practiced at negotiation. "When we get back, you'll get one kiss."

Her lips twitched. "Like that kiss last night?"

"Behave," he warned again.

"I'd like to give you a kiss."

Her tone left no doubt as to what she meant, and he growled.

Thankfully, she quit actively tormenting him. But Lainie just sitting there, her pretty scent in the air, was still a distraction.

They finally pulled into the underground parking at Sentinel Security. He shut off the engine and climbed out. Lainie was already out of the car, smiling at him.

She had no idea how crazy she drove him.

He strode to her, gripped her hips and then lifted her. He set her on the hood of his car.

She gasped. "I know this car is expensive."

He pushed her legs apart and stood between them. "I don't care. And it's made of carbon fiber. You're not going to break it." He tipped her chin up. "Still tipsy?"

"No."

"Good."

He sealed his mouth over hers.

With a moan, she wrapped her arms and legs around him, pulling him closer.

Nick parted her lips with his tongue, tasting her. Their tongues tangled, pressing against each other. The kiss became a battle for dominance, a race for more.

He groaned.

"I love that sound." Her voice was low, sexy, and husky.

Nick sucked in a breath. "What sound?"

"That sexy—" she wrapped one leg around his hip, her hot center pressed against his aching cock, and his fingers bit into her hips "—growl."

He set his mouth on her neck, nipping her skin. "Lainie."

"I love how you say my name, too." Her pretty eyes met his. "No one's wanted me like you do."

Desire twisted in his gut. He took her mouth again.

This kiss was hard, hot. Her sweet mouth drove him crazy, the need inside him ratcheting higher.

Pretty, smart Lainie Madden. In his arms. Hot, eager, and most of all, sweet. It was like holding sunshine.

"Nick." She undulated against him. "I love your body. So hard and strong." Her hands clamped on his ass, squeezed.

He slid a hand up to cup one of her breasts. The gentle squeeze made her moan.

"And you're so soft," he said.

"What in blazing hell?" a voice behind them squeaked.

It was like a spray of cold, icy water. In his arms, Lainie froze and blinked.

Nick pulled back and turned to look at his sister.

Nola was short and slim, dressed in fitted pants and a

filmy, cream-colored shirt with a tie at the neck. Her dark hair was cut pixie-short, and she had large blue eyes.

She was staring at them, her gaze moving between them like the ball at a tennis match.

His desire turned to concrete in his gut. "Nola—"

He'd dreaded this. He'd known touching his sister's best friend had complication stamped all over it.

But he hadn't been able to stop himself. Lainie had stopped being just Nola's best friend to him a long time ago.

"Nola." Lainie's voice was panicked and shaky. "God, look, we can explain. We...Nick's pretending to be my boyfriend to protect me."

Nola blinked. "It doesn't look very fake."

"Because it's not," Nick growled.

Lainie elbowed him. "Nick—"

"I love this!" Nola suddenly squealed, clapping her hands. "Oh my God, the two people I love most are going at each other like horny rabbits." Nola cocked her head. "Beautiful, sexy rabbits."

Nick stared at her.

"You guys." She sighed happily, then frowned. "This better be more than a hook up." She skewered him with a look. "Because Lainie is awesome." And she pointed at Lainie. "And you need some awesome, big bro. And Lainie, you need a man who isn't a weak, whiny asshole."

They both just stared at Nola.

"I'll be in the Sentinel Security office. I need a coffee, and Killian has a kickass machine. Oh, and Lainie, Hex got me access to your apartment. I'm not going to tell you what a mess it was. I have a suitcase for you full of what clothes I could salvage."

She disappeared with a click of heels.

Nick looked back at Lainie, still trying to digest what had happened. She giggled.

And that made him want to kiss her again.

Instead, he kissed her nose and lifted her down off the car.

"Let's go." He took her hand.

LAINIE TRIED NOT to blush as she and Nick walked into the Sentinel Security office. Nola was holding a coffee and chatting with Hex.

Her best friend looked at them and smiled. She didn't seem upset that she'd just busted her bestie and her brother going at it. On the hood of an expensive car.

Oh, boy, it had been hot.

Lainie's cheeks heated.

She'd never confessed to Nola that she'd kissed Nick years ago, and that she'd had a raging crush on him. It was the only secret she'd ever kept from her friend.

Now, her crush was a full-blown case of lust.

Except she already knew it was more than that. She released a breath. This was the last thing she needed, really. Her business kept her crazy busy, her luck with men was not so great, and someone was out to kill her.

Added to all that, he wouldn't stay. Not long term. Not a man like Nick.

Her fizzy mood plummeted.

"Wolf?" Killian appeared, looking sexy in his suit. "Can I talk to you for a second?"

With a nod, Nick disappeared into Killian's office.

Nola stared at Killian's ass. "That man. If he didn't scare me so much, I'd throw myself at him, naked."

Lainie giggled.

Hex just shook her head.

"I'd have his babies, but I think he's just a little too much man for me," Nola said. "I like a gooey center in my guys. And I'm not sure Killian has a gooey anything."

"So, the VR bar was a bust?" Hex asked Lainie.

"Trent wasn't there, and the place was horrible. Nick looked like he'd prefer to take on a bunch of terrorists or stab himself with a fork." Lainie sighed. "I don't want to think it's Trent. I mean, aside from being a cheater, he wasn't an evil person."

"Wait, Trent Morton?" Nola said. "Your loser ex from college?"

Lainie nodded. "Evidence is pointing to him as the person sending me these threats."

"People change," Hex said. "He might have graduated from cheater to killer."

"I am really terrible at picking men," Lainie moaned.

Nola smiled. "Seems your taste has improved." She leaned toward Hex conspiratorially. "Caught my brother and my best friend getting frisky on his car."

"What?" Hex grinned. "We have CCTV down there. Let me take a look."

"No!" Lainie cried, clapping her hands over her cheeks.

"Nick's one of the good ones." Nola's face turned

serious. "He's rough around the edges, bossy, sometimes rude..."

"Great sales pitch," Lainie muttered.

"But he's good. Honorable. When he loves you, he never lets go."

Lainie's heart did a huge flip-flop. The L word was...

Scary.

She swallowed, her throat suddenly dry. Every man she'd ever cared for had let her go. Why would Nick be any different?

Still, the idea of a man like Nick in love with her completely took her breath away.

"I...I've always liked him."

"I knew it." Nola snapped her fingers. "I could tell by the way you watched him, even when we were teenagers."

"The man is watchable," Hex conceded.

Lainie turned in her chair. "You're really okay about it, Nola?"

"Two of the best people I know into each other? Uh, yes."

"My life's a mess. My business leaves me zero time. I have cheating exes and a stalker/killer after me. I don't have room for a man."

"You're afraid," Nola said.

"Of course, I'm afraid." Lainie ran a shaky hand through her hair. "Guys don't stick around. I'm deficient or something. They move on, they leave..." She thought of Elliott. "They die."

"Elliott loved you like crazy," Nola said. "He didn't

want to leave you. The rest of them weren't good enough for you."

"What if Nick breaks my heart? He isn't going to stick around forever. He's...a lone wolf. Busy off saving the world, and I'm sure he has exposure to some beautiful, amazing women."

"You're a beautiful, amazing woman," Nola said fiercely. "And he's just a man. One who needs love, too." Her face twisted. "Our mother is hopeless in that department, his bio dad was bad news and never had anything to do with him, and my dad..." She looked away. Nola always had conflicted feelings about her father. "He never treated Nick like a son. He was mean to him." Nola gripped Lainie's hand. "Just...give it a chance."

There was no need for her friend to say that. Lainie was already so tangled up in Nick it would be impossible to walk away.

She nodded. "Whatever happens, I love you."

Nola's face turned soft. "Right back at you, my sparkly friend."

Lainie took a deep breath and looked at Hex. "So, a server at the bar said Trent is busy working on a big project."

"We'll find him," the hacker said. "We'll track him down. We always do."

Killian and Nick returned.

"We have to head out for another job," Nick said. "Killian needs my help."

"Okay," Lainie said.

"You stay here."

There was that bossiness. "Nola, your brother is very bossy."

"Oh, I know."

Nick scowled. "I'm not bossy."

Lainie rolled her eyes. "You're clearly in denial."

"I'm *not* bossy. I'm efficient, and good at giving orders."

"Another way of saying bossy."

He drew in a breath. "Stay. Don't go anywhere."

"Aye, aye, captain." She saluted.

Both Killian and Nick winced.

"No explosions while I'm not around." Nick closed the distance between them and cupped her cheek.

Tingles of electricity broke out over her skin. "Sure thing."

He stroked a thumb over her lips, then he swiveled and strode out with Killian. She stared after them.

"Think she knows what her face looks like right now?" Hex's voice.

"I think I like blue for my maid of honor dress."

Lainie shook her head. "I seem to be the only one without coffee around here."

Nola chatted to her while she made herself a latte on the sci-fi like machine in the kitchenette. Her friend didn't treat her any differently, even knowing Lainie and Nick were...whatever the hell they were. They wandered back to the command center.

"Hex, is there anything I can do to help search for my stalker?" she asked.

"Sure. Let's—"

Lainie's phone pinged. "Wait, it's a message from the

Pintura office." She read it, her heart sinking. "Oh no! We're under a massive cyber attack. There's a deluge of hits on the website, and some of the servers are down." She looked up. "My team is freaking out. I need to get to the office."

"Crap." Hex grabbed an earpiece and slipped it in. "Let me talk to Wolf."

Lainie couldn't hear his side of the conversation, but he didn't sound happy.

"I'll take her," Hex said. "Ha ha, yes, I do go in the sunlight sometimes. Of course I'm armed, Wolf. What the hell kind of question is that? I promise I won't leave her side." Hex spun. "Lainie, you get a short, pink-haired hacker bodyguard today."

"You're sure?"

"Let's roll." She gathered her things. "Besides, if I'm on-site at Pintura, I might be able to help your team with the cyber attack." Her smile sharpened. "I like teaching black-hat hackers a lesson."

"Well," Nola said. "Since I'm not a badass, I'd better get back to work." She hugged Lainie. "I just wanted to check on you. I didn't expect you to be making out with my brother—"

Lainie groaned.

"But clearly, I'm the only one not freaking out about that. Stay safe."

"I will. Thanks, Nola."

"Nick will take good care of you. Stay sparkly."

Once Nola had left, Hex and Lainie headed to the parking level.

"This is my ride." The locks on the blood-red, sporty Audi TT bleeped.

Lainie slid into the passenger seat, and Hex revved the engine. She sped out of the parking space fast enough to push Lainie back in the seat.

"I like to go fast," Hex pronounced.

Lainie gripped her seat. "Okay."

Thankfully, once they were on the street, there was too much traffic for Hex to speed.

Lainie pulled out her phone and quickly called her security team. From the noise and yelling in the background, they were frantically working to stop the cyber attack.

"I'll be there shortly. I'm bringing another cyber expert with me. Jet Adler. Organize for her to have full system access when I arrive."

After ending the call, Lainie turned her phone over and over in her hand, one foot bouncing. She'd had enough of this. Enough of waiting around to be the target. It was time to go on the offence.

They headed toward downtown, and ahead, Lainie saw the top of her building.

God, she hoped the attacker wasn't wreaking too much havoc. Her gut twisted. Trent had the skills to initiate these sorts of attacks, she knew that. She closed her eyes.

What had she done to deserve this? She turned to look out the window, staring blindly at a construction site outside where a new building was going up.

Suddenly, Hex wrenched the wheel. She changed lanes, and horns honked.

Lainie glanced at her. The woman's hands were clenched on the wheel, her eyes on the rearview mirror.

"Hex?"

"Hang on."

"What's wrong?"

"I was hoping nothing..."

"But?"

Hex met her gaze. "There are two motorcycles whipping through the traffic. In our direction."

Lainie's pulse skittered. She looked back and saw the two men. They were on black bikes, with black helmets.

"They could be going anywhere," Lainie said.

"My Spidey sense says no. And it's pretty finely tuned."

The traffic thickened and they slowed to barely a crawl. The men on the bikes were gaining on them.

As Lainie watched, one rider drew a huge handgun.

Oh, shit.

The man aimed at their car.

"Hex, get down!" Lainie ducked, as bullets peppered the Audi.

CHAPTER TWELVE

The brakes slammed on, tossing Lainie forward against her seat belt. Glass smashed. The thunk of bullets on metal was deafeningly loud.

She heard Hex talking to someone. Talking on her phone, but Lainie was too panicked to make out the words.

Air lodged in her chest so she couldn't even scream.

Hex cursed steadily. The woman reached over and opened the glove compartment. She pulled out a big handgun.

"We need to get out. The traffic's got us penned in." She undid Lainie's belt. "Crawl across and follow me." Hex pushed open the driver side door and slipped out.

Lainie sat frozen.

"Lainie!"

Pulling herself together, she nodded. There was a pause in the barrage of bullets, and she crawled over into the now-vacated driver's seat. Hex crouched outside behind the open door, her face calm, set, and focused.

Then the hacker raised her gun and returned fire.

The motorcycle riders were not expecting it.

As Lainie glanced back, she saw one rider jerk and swerve. He slammed into a stopped car.

"Come on!" Hex urged.

The hacker grabbed Lainie's hand. They sprinted across the street, dodging through cars that were thankfully mostly at a standstill.

As they dodged around one car, a female driver stared at Hex's weapon, her mouth hanging open.

There were more gunshots. Bullets peppered the cars nearby.

"Down." Hex yanked Lainie behind a cab.

The hacker popped up and returned fire. She was cool as a cucumber.

Hex was a pint-sized superhero.

"Lainie, we need to get off the street." Hex pressed her back to the car and scanned around. "Run through that temporary fencing and into the construction site."

Lainie looked at the half-constructed tower and nodded.

"Good. I'll lay down cover fire, you run. Don't look back. I've already alerted Killian and Wolf. They're coming."

Lainie nodded again. Her heart was pounding like a drum.

"Ready?" Hex asked.

Lainie swallowed. "I'm ready."

Hex popped up and fired.

Lainie sprinted for the construction site. Her lungs burned and fear boiled inside her. Any second, she expected a bullet to hit her. She slid through a gap in the wire fence and ran into the building.

There were no workers, but there was plenty of gear scattered everywhere. Rolls of wire and insulation sat in an untidy row by some huge, locked toolboxes. A wheelbarrow was stacked with trash. Lainie ran through a door, her blood pounding. The concrete floor was covered in a layer of grit and dust.

Ahead, lay a set of bare-concrete stairs, and she ran up them.

At the top, she paused, catching her breath. Gunfire continued to echo on the street below.

God, she hoped Hex was okay. If the woman got hurt protecting Lainie...

Her heart clenched into a hard ball. "Stay calm. Hex is trained..."

In the silence between gunshots, a sound came from below. Carefully, she peered down the stairs.

A big, muscular guy in a helmet was moving stealthily through the lower level, an ugly, black gun in his hand.

Shit.

Lainie turned. She moved as quietly as she could and darted up to the next level.

She needed somewhere really good to hide.

Chest tight, panic threatening, she shoved it all down and kept moving. She'd learned to conquer her nerves. A jittery CEO didn't inspire people. She took a few deep breaths.

Okay, calm was beyond her. She'd have to settle for not totally losing it.

She took another flight of stairs. The next level of the building wasn't as complete as the ones below. She swallowed. There were no walls.

She took a step and her foot hit something.

She watched in horror as an aerosol can of some sort rolled across the floor.

It sounded like a damn orchestra hitting the peak of a crescendo.

Running footsteps suddenly came from below.

No. No. No.

She raced across the concrete floor. There was some construction gear stacked in an unwieldy pile—steel, some rolls of...something. Lainie ducked down behind the pile, trying not to breathe too loudly.

Stay still. Stay calm.

She peered through a gap in the pile.

The guy crested the stairs, his helmet still on.

Oh, shit. The man's head turned slowly as he scanned the level.

Nothing to see here.

She willed the guy to keep going. Where was Hex? What if this guy had shot her?

Lainie bit down on her lip.

The man started across the floor in her direction.

Shit. Oh, shit.

She looked around and spotted a hammer. She snatched it up and swallowed.

The sad reality was she didn't think she could actually hit someone with a hammer.

She squeezed the rubber grip.

The man moved closer. He paused, then started to turn away.

Her heart leaped. *Yes, that's it...*

The man swiveled and kicked the pile of gear she was hiding behind. Metal frames crashed to the floor.

He spotted her and Lainie leaped to her feet.

"Back off, asshole." She brandished the hammer.

He advanced on her, not saying a word.

Lainie swung at him. He caught the hammer and wrenched it out of her hand.

Well, crap. She backed up, and he leveled the gun on her. Her breath caught in her throat.

"Come with me." His voice was muffled by the helmet.

"Um, no."

"That wasn't a question."

"It's still a no."

"I'll shoot you."

"If you want me to come with you, you clearly aren't planning to shoot me."

"I can shoot you in the arm," the man growled.

Lainie was sick of being afraid. He'd disarmed her, but she was a woman who lived in New York. She remembered Nick's lesson. *React fast, break their hold, and run for help. Poke the eyes, ram a palm to the nose, chop to the throat, and a kick to the knee.* She mentally smiled. *And the balls.*

She let her shoulders droop and shuffled toward him.

When she got close, she lifted her knee and swung her leg up. She kicked him right between his legs.

He made a strangled sound and staggered.

Damn, she'd aimed that perfectly.

Okay, run, Lainie.

She sprinted past him.

A gunshot echoed loudly. She saw a bullet hit the concrete near her feet. With a scream, she stopped and threw her arms up.

"Bitch." He limped toward her.

Lainie backed up and tripped over something. She fell on her butt. The man leaned over her, and she hated that the black helmet made him seem more menacing. He tried to grab her, but she slapped at him.

Then he hit her in the face.

Ears ringing, she fell heavily on her side. She lay there, blinking through the pain, and tasted blood on her lip.

He gripped her jacket and yanked her up.

Oh, God.

Suddenly, a big body rushed in from the side and tackled her attacker.

The sounds of grunts and scuffling echoed off the concrete walls.

Lainie sat up and watched Nick pin the helmeted asshole to the ground. He ripped the guy's helmet off, uncovering a hard face with a heavy brow and a large nose. Then Nick rained blows down on the man.

"You don't touch her," Nick growled, landing another punch. "Never again."

With a groan, the guy tried to fend Nick off. The next punch knocked the man out cold.

Lainie let out a shaky breath.

Nick's head whipped around, his hot, turbulent eyes meeting hers.

NICK LEVERED off the man who'd hit Lainie. The asshole was unconscious. Nick quickly flipped the man, turning him facedown, then pulled zip ties out of his pockets. He fastened the guy's hands and ankles.

He wasn't going anywhere.

Nick wanted to keep hitting the fucker, but they needed to question him. Nick got a very tenuous lock on his rage.

There was a nice holding room at Sentinel Security with this guy's name on it.

Nick had some questions he wanted answered.

He swiveled. Lainie was sitting up, and looked dazed. Dirt smeared on her hands and face, and her lip was swollen.

Fury ripped through him. He wanted to punch the guy all over again.

He strode over to help her up.

"Shit, Lainie." He touched the side of her mouth.

She winced. "Nick... I..." She threw herself at him.

He held her against his chest, felt her shaking. "You're safe now."

"There was shooting. Hex told me to run. I heard that guy coming. Then I was hiding. There was a hammer."

She was talking fast, her words a jumble.

"You're safe, kitten." He smoothed his hands up and down her back. "Just take a deep breath."

She drew one in. Shakily.

"Again."

The next breath was smoother. He looked down at her and the lock on his anger threatened to snap. She'd have some bruising on her jaw. He needed to make sure nothing was broken, but she seemed to be talking fine.

"Hex?" There was worry all over Lainie's face.

"Is fine. She's downstairs with Killian."

"I'm right here." Killian appeared at the top of the stairs.

Nick's boss looked at the trussed-up man on the ground, then Lainie's face, and Killian's features darkened.

"I'm all right," she said quietly, but she was still shaking.

"I'm taking her back to my place," Nick said.

"I have to get to Pintura," she said.

Over his dead body.

"Hex is on the way to Pintura," Killian said. "She'll help your team."

"She was amazing. Like Wonder Woman, just smaller, and with pinker hair."

Nick took Lainie's hands; they were cold. He rubbed them between his. "Come on, kitten. You need ice on your jaw."

Killian gave him a nod. His boss would deal with her attacker.

They exited the building, and Nick bundled Lainie

into his car. She sat quietly beside him, while inside, Nick raged.

When he'd gotten the call from Hex that she and Lainie were under fire...

The entire drive there, Killian had talked Nick down off the ledge. He'd worried every minute of the drive that he'd be too late.

Like he had been for Jennifer and Madison.

He tried to breathe through his tight chest. Lainie had fought back. She was alive.

He glanced over and his jaw tightened. Seeing the swelling and developing bruising on her face made his gut churn.

"Nick, this is *not* your fault," she said, like she could read his mind. "The person to blame is that asshole who hit me, and whoever gave him his orders."

Nick didn't reply.

"Nick?" She pressed a hand to his thigh, and her nails bit in, even through his pants. "Repeat after me, 'I'm not in charge of or responsible for the entire world.'"

"I'm in charge of you."

She crossed her arms. "You are not."

That got a smile out of him. "Fine. I'm in charge of your safety."

"This is a joint effort, Garrick. You're helping me."

They reached the warehouse. After he'd parked, he whisked her up to his apartment.

"Sit," he ordered, pointing at the kitchen stools.

She rolled her eyes at him. "I'm going to wash the dust off and change first."

He took a step to follow her.

She held a hand up like a traffic cop. "No. I can change myself, and no bad guy can get me in here."

She was right, but he stewed having her out of his sight. He pressed his hands to the kitchen counter.

Damn, he had it bad.

He busied himself getting an ice pack out of the freezer. He had a collection of them, in various sizes and types. He'd lost count of the bruises, black eyes, and sore ribs he'd had over the years.

Next, he pulled out a crystal glass and a bottle of his favorite Angel's Envy Cask Strength bourbon.

When she returned, in leggings and one of his business shirts, he felt his gut knot. Her hair was up in a loose, messy bun.

He cleared his throat. He shouldn't be sitting here lusting over a woman with a swollen face. "Sit."

She arched a brow.

He sighed and held up the ice pack. "Please."

His less gruff demand made her smile. She sat on the stool.

Nick gently probed her jawbone, then her cheekbone and temple.

"I'm not in that much pain," she said. "It just throbs a little."

Thankfully, nothing appeared broken. She was lucky. The guy had been far bigger than her. Nick pressed the ice pack to her jaw.

"Here." He nudged a shot of bourbon that he'd poured for her in her direction. "You're still a little shaken."

"I'm coming down now. It's a little scary to be

running from gunshots." Her gaze locked on his face. "But you know that already."

"I should've been there."

"Sorry, I didn't see your cape anywhere." She knocked back her shot and shuddered. Then she grabbed the bottle, poured another splash of bourbon, and nudged it to him. "You aren't a superhero."

He drank the bourbon. The warm burn, followed by a hit of sweetness, gave him something to focus on other than his anger. "It's what I'm good at. Fighting, protecting others."

"It's not all you're good at. What do you do when you aren't working?"

He looked at her. "Sleep."

Her nose wrinkled. "Nick. For fun."

"I... Work a lot. I spend time with the Sentinel guys."

"You must have a TV show you like? Places you visit? Do you cook? Or do something for fun and relaxation?"

He guessed she wasn't talking about the odd one-night stand with a woman from a bar.

She stared at him, her face turning serious. She lowered the ice pack. "You don't do anything fun?"

Feeling uncomfortable, he lifted his shoulder. "I enjoy my work. It's important. Like I said, I'm good at it." He paused. "From what I can see, this is a classic pot and kettle situation."

"What?"

"You don't have much fun. You're always working."

She took a breath. "Damn, you're right, but I at least know I work too hard and should relax more. You're in denial."

Again, Nick lifted his shoulder.

Her face twisted. "I blame that asshole stepfather of yours. He made you feel you had to earn your way to be accepted. He might be Nola's father, but he's still an asshole. He never deserved you."

Nick felt an unfamiliar shot of warmth. "I stopped letting him matter a long time ago."

"Bullshit." She leaped off the stool, waving the ice pack in the air. "He planted the seeds. Your father did, too, when he abandoned you and your mom. And your mom just checked out, married a new man to take care of her. And then you ran off to save the world." She turned to him. "I know it's not an easy job."

"How did this become about me? You're the one with the swollen lip and bruised jaw."

"Who did you lose, Nick? On that mission?"

Silence.

He looked past her, staring blindly at the windows.

"Nick?" she said softly. "If you can't talk about it...or don't want to share with me, I understand, I—"

"The mission was to evacuate the ambassador to Colombia. I was there with a team to evacuate him and his family." It felt like he was chewing glass. "I fucked up."

"I doubt that."

"I was juggling too much, and I took my eye off my main priority. Because of me, his wife and daughter died."

"I'm sorry." Sympathy swam in her eyes.

"Madison—" his muscles tensed, a rock settled in his chest "—was six."

Lainie gasped. She stepped toward him, but he waved her off with a hand.

"She was so little," he whispered. "She trusted me, and I let her down."

"I assume you were in a dangerous situation with a lot going on. Nick, you can't shoulder all that blame. I get feeling regret, but did you pull the trigger?"

"No, but—"

"Did you willfully put them in the line of fire?" She shook her head. "Of course not. You'd protect a woman or child you didn't know in an instant. I've known you practically all your life, and I know the man you are. I see it right now. I know you're upset I was attacked today, but it's not your fault. And that little girl's death wasn't your fault, either."

Nick just stared at her.

"Does the ambassador blame you?"

Nick swallowed. "He calls me. Checks in."

"So no." She eyed him, warmth on her face. "Can I come to you now?"

There was no disgust or horror in her eyes, just simple, quiet understanding, and sympathy.

He nodded.

She came to him, wrapped her arms around him, and held on. The quiet comfort was almost too much. He pulled her tightly against him and pressed his face to her hair. He drew in her vanilla scent and absorbed the moment.

"Well, we're both going to take it easy," Lainie announced. "That's how I survive my work schedule, by enjoying the small moments of downtime. A movie, a glass of wine, a bubble bath."

Nick made a face. The thought of soaking in a bath of bubbles did not entice him.

She laughed. "I'm going to help you relax, Nick Garrick. And have some fun and enjoy yourself."

"As long as you're resting, I don't care." He pressed the ice pack back on her face.

"I'll only rest if you do, too. With me."

His gut cramped. *Shit.* The more time he spent with her, the more he wasn't sure he could say no to her. He cleared his throat. "Deal."

CHAPTER THIRTEEN

Hearing Lainie laugh loosened up things in Nick.

They were on his couch, watching a movie. They'd fought playfully over the choice of viewing. He'd won, vetoing a boring drama about a bunch of self-absorbed beautiful people.

Lainie laughed again, tears in her eyes. Good ones.

She was lying on his couch, her feet in his lap.

Despite what had happened today, she was relaxed. She'd checked in with Hex, who along with Lainie's security team, had stopped the cyber attack. Hex was also sending a couple of her Sentinel Security cyber guys to help add more security to the Pintura site. She'd also talked with her management team as they'd be in charge while Lainie attended the conference in Las Vegas. Tomorrow morning, she and Nick were flying out.

Nick had also traded several messages with Killian. They had the one motorcycle attacker in a holding cell. So far, the guy hadn't said anything useful. They'd been hired anonymously through a now-closed email account.

But if anyone could get the guy to talk, it was Killian.

"This movie is ridiculous."

"Ridiculous fun," he said.

"Nick, there's not just one giant megalodon, there are two."

"Yep." He smiled. "Twice the fun."

She cocked a brow. "At least the leading man keeps losing his shirt."

Nick looked back at the screen. The guy was shirtless again. He frowned.

Lainie nudged Nick with her foot. "Don't worry, your chest is still way better."

And just like that, his cock, which had been half hard all evening, stiffened. He shifted his feet a little, so she didn't notice.

He swallowed, staring at the screen.

Lainie had been chased by gunmen and hurt. Now was not the time to be thinking about touching her, tasting her...

"Nick, you're as tense as a board." She sat up. "You're supposed to be relaxing."

"I told you, I don't relax."

She shook her head. "Sit on the floor in front of me."

He eyed her warily. "Why?"

She huffed out a breath. "I'm not going to hurt you."

He slid to the floor, his back against the couch. She moved so her legs were on either side of him. He tensed even more, keeping his gaze glued to the television.

Then her fingers hit his shoulders, and she started kneading.

Hell. He tried to relax, but Lainie's hands were on him. "You shouldn't do that with your injured hands."

"I've taken the bandages off, and my hands are fine. Healing up well." She dug her fingers in. "God, you're really tense. I did a massage course in college. I used to give sports massages for extra money. I have strong fingers."

He tilted his neck. She was good, but there was no way he would relax with her touching him like this, and so close, his senses filled with her freshly showered scent.

He'd vowed not to touch her again tonight. She'd been so shaken after the attack. She'd been hit. He wasn't going to be an asshole and take advantage of that.

"Nick." Frustration welled in her tone. "You're getting even tenser. You're supposed to *relax*."

"I can't with you touching me," he growled.

Her hands went still.

"When your hands are on me, the last thing I want to do is relax."

She paused, the silence dragging out. "What do you want to do?"

His hands flexed. "Things I'm not going to do because you need to relax and take it easy."

"I am relaxed...and I want to hear what you want to do to me."

He growled, his chin dropping to his chest. "I'm trying to do the right thing here, Lainie. You were hurt today—"

Her fingers dug into his skin. "I'm fine. I'm not letting a few bruises get me down. And I'm not letting Tacky

Trent dictate what I do." She slid a hand into Nick's hair. "Tell me."

Nick's control snapped like a rusty chain. He practically heard the crack in his head. He spun on his knees. Her cheeks were flushed, her voice a little breathless.

He gripped her knees. "You want to know?"

Her lips parted. "*Yes.*"

"I want that mouth of yours." He pushed her knees apart and pulled her closer.

She dropped back on the couch with a gasp, her gaze locked on him.

"I want my mouth back on your sweet pussy. I can still taste you. That sweet honey is all I think about."

She squirmed. "Nick—"

Because he needed it, he leaned over and kissed her. Her warm lips parted for him instantly. As his tongue met hers, stroke for stroke, she curled a hand around his neck, pulling him closer.

Groaning, he was careful not to put too much pressure on her sore lip. He couldn't get enough of her.

Then she wrapped her legs around him, pressing herself against him, rubbing. "*Nick,*" she moaned.

Such a sweet, sweet sound. He pulled back and straightened.

"No, don't stop," she said breathlessly.

"I'm not stopping, kitten." He ran his hands up her leggings, gripped the waistband, then slowly pulled them down her legs, taking her panties along with them, as well.

Lainie's chest was rising and falling fast, her heated gaze locked on his hands.

"I'm going to put my mouth on you again. You're going to let me."

She swallowed. "Yes. *Please.* Yes."

"Say it, kitten." His gut twisted with need. He had to know that this gorgeous woman was with him all the way.

The way she was watching him, it made him realize just how badly he wanted her.

"Nick, please put your mouth on me." She lifted her hips, and helped him so he could drag her leggings off, leaving her bare.

Heat shot through him. She was so damn pretty.

"I want to feel your beard on my skin," she said. "Your tongue on my clit."

Fuck. "You like talking dirty, kitten?" He dragged her closer to the edge of the couch.

"I never have before," she said.

He slid his palms under the curves of her ass and pulled her to his hungry mouth.

Nick licked her pussy, the taste of her filling him. *Damn.* So good. He growled against her skin.

As he dragged his tongue over her, she cried out, making sweet, desperate sounds.

He kept licking, his thumb finding her clit. The sounds she made turned inarticulate. Her body arched and she pressed one foot to his shoulder blade.

Then she cried out his name.

Nick moved his mouth to her clit and sucked. She pulsed against his mouth, coming hard.

His desire had a stranglehold on him. He was shaking from it.

Panting, she lay on the couch, beautiful and wrecked.

His hot blood pounded through him. It was time to claim his woman.

He scooped her up and tossed her over his shoulder.

"Nick!"

He pressed a hand to her bare, curvy butt, and headed for his bedroom.

"You're mine now, kitten."

He dropped her on the bed, his hunger tearing at him.

"I need to fuck you, Lainie. Hard and deep."

She moaned.

"Lose the shirt."

She pulled it over her head and ditched her bra as well.

Her gorgeous, full breasts were free. He drank her in, his cock rock-hard in his trousers. He kept his gaze on hers as he started shedding his own clothes. Lainie bit her lip, watching him.

Shirt gone, he shoved his pants off, then his boxer shorts. His swollen cock sprang free.

"*Nick.*" She licked her lips.

Fuck. He strode to the bed and straddled her. He walked up her body on his knees.

Her eyes were wide, filled with scorching hunger.

"Suck me, pretty Lainie."

God, he was saying this to sweet Lainie Madden.

But then, she did.

She licked the head of his cock, lapping hungrily. Her hand gripped his thighs, then she sucked him deep.

Nick groaned. Her mouth—all wet heat and suction —was perfect.

She moved her hand, sliding her mouth on his hard length.

God. Pleasure was hot and burning. It pulsed down his spine.

He was going to come in a second. But he didn't want to come in her mouth.

He pulled free. "Need you, kitten."

LAINIE WAS ABOUT TO SELF-COMBUST.

She'd already come thanks to Nick's talented mouth between her legs. But she already felt the desire building again.

It helped having that hard, rough male body on top of hers.

That cock in her mouth.

The man was gorgeous all over.

She lay back and cupped her breasts. Fire flared in his eyes, and it made her feel so desired.

"So take me, Nick. I'm all yours."

He shifted, then reached over and opened the drawer on the nightstand. She watched him tear open the condom package with the edge of his teeth. She loved watching the way he gripped his cock. He stroked it a few times, then rolled the condom on.

Lainie squirmed. Oh boy, she needed that inside her. Needed Nick moving inside her, filling her. *Yes, please.*

She rolled over, desperate. Had she ever needed someone, needed a man, like this before?

On her hands and knees, she looked back. "Hurry."

Nick groaned, gripping her hips.

"This pretty ass on offer, and all mine." He dragged her to the edge of the bed. "You're beautiful, Lainie."

"Nick—" She was trembling.

Then he rubbed his cock between her folds. The feeling was electric. She was panting with need.

"*Please.*"

His fingers tightened on her hip, and he thrust inside her.

Lainie moaned, throwing her head back.

Finally. Nick Garrick inside her. Filling her. It felt so right.

"Kitten." His voice was thick. She looked back over her shoulder and her belly clenched.

The look on his face...

Like he'd come home.

"Nick, please. *Move.*"

He pulled back, then slammed back inside her.

"Yes." The pleasure was outrageous. She arched her back, then he powered inside her. She pressed her cheek to the bed, taking his powerful thrusts.

"So slick, so tight," he said through gritted teeth. "So beautiful, my Lainie."

He slid a hand under her and found her clit.

Oh. *God.* Everything inside her was coiling tight. She pushed back against him, and he fucked her harder, faster.

"Fuck, kitten."

She wanted to see his face. She wanted to watch him come. "Nick—"

"What is it, baby?"

"I need to see you. I want to watch you come."

With a low growl, he pulled out.

Lainie moaned, missing him instantly.

Then he flipped her over. She was flat on her back, staring up at him breathlessly.

God. His face. It was rugged, brutal desire stamped all over it.

"Look at you." His gaze raked over her, settling on her chest. "So pretty. Pretty Lainie Madden, all mine to ruin."

He knelt on the bed, that big cock jutting out. Her belly clenched. She needed him back inside her.

He cupped her breasts and stroked her nipples, then lowered his head. He pressed kisses to the curves of her breasts, then sucked one nipple until she cried out.

She gripped his arms. "I need you back inside me. *Now.*"

He flashed her a sexy grin. "Whatever my kitten needs."

When he gripped his cock, she whimpered. She let her legs fall open and enjoyed his deep groan.

Nick covered her, using a knee to keep her thighs spread for him.

She felt the swollen head of his cock between her legs.

Their gazes meshed.

"Nick," she breathed.

A muscle ticked in his jaw, then he pushed inside her, slowly. He stretched her, making her feel every inch.

She moaned. She slid her arms around him, her nails digging into his sweat-slicked back.

"You feel so good, Lainie. Perfect." His voice sounded like grit.

She couldn't form words anymore. It was beyond her. She managed a whimper.

"I shouldn't be touching you," he said. "I shouldn't be between these pretty thighs, inside this gorgeous body."

"Shut up, Nick. You should."

"Nothing could drag me away now."

He started to move. It wasn't slow. It was fast, furious, deep.

There was no restraint, just relentless need. She drank Nick in, enjoying the picture of that hard muscled body thrusting inside her.

"Look at me, Lainie."

She lifted her gaze to meet his. God, the look on his face.

He surged deeper. "I want you to come, kitten. I want to watch you come on my cock. Fuck, Lainie Madden taking my cock. You fit me just right."

God, every word drove her closer. Every slide of his cock brought her orgasm nearer.

She ran her hands over his back.

"Come now, Lainie," he gritted out.

On his next heavy stroke, she did.

She gasped his name, pleasure a wild rush filling her.

"That's it, kitten," he growled. "I can feel you clenching on me."

She trembled, arching into him, pleasure shuddering through her. She heard his grunts as he kept thrusting.

On his next deep thrust, he gripped her tight and groaned her name.

She watched him find his release. God, he was beautiful.

Finally, Nick rolled to the side, pulling her against his body.

"Kitten." He kissed her, then nuzzled her hair. "So sweet and sexy."

She smiled. "That was...nice."

"Nice?" He pinched her ass.

"Oh, you don't like that? Okay, it was really good." Another pinch. "Fine. Magnificent. Glorious. Earth-shattering."

"Cheeky." He dropped a kiss on her shoulder.

Her smile faded, and she stared at his rugged face. "It's the best I've ever had, Nick."

She saw an unreadable look cross his face. He cupped her jaw, careful not to touch her bruises.

"Lainie." He kissed her again. "Now I want to fuck you again."

She gripped his wrist. "I'm on board with that." She swallowed. "Regrets?"

"No. Never, kitten. I just hope you don't—"

She pressed her mouth to his.

He slid a hand into her hair, then he rolled over, and she straddled him.

CHAPTER FOURTEEN

Nick woke up with a weight on top of him.

It took him a second, then he smiled.

He was in his bed, with Lainie sprawled on top of him.

He ran a hand down her sleek back. Mmm, he could get used to her using him as her bed.

Damn. They'd gone at each other several times throughout the night. She'd been an enthusiastic and uninhibited lover. She didn't hide how much she liked taking his cock.

How much she liked him.

He felt a very unfamiliar fear grip him. She still wasn't safe.

He couldn't lose her.

He needed to use every bit of his focus and skills to make sure she didn't get hurt.

She stirred, made a cute sound, and lifted her head.

She saw him and blinked. Color filled her cheeks. "Why am I on top of you?"

"You must've climbed on during the night."

"Really?"

He stroked his fingers down her spine, enjoying her shiver. "I don't mind."

She smiled. God, she was beautiful. Then she wriggled her hips against his morning erection. Nick was just starting to make some naughty plans, when her gaze shifted to the clock on his nightstand.

She sat up, her hair flying everywhere. "My God, we need to get to the airport. Our flight to Las Vegas is scheduled to leave in two hours."

Nick's gaze was on her breasts. "It's a private jet. It won't leave without us."

She scrambled off him. "The pilots will be waiting. There's a cocktail party to open the conference tonight. We can't be late just because I want to have sex with you." Her gaze moved to his body, traveling downward and she seemed to lose track of her thoughts.

He smiled. "You sure?"

She licked her lips. "The pilots would know."

"They won't." He sat up.

"I'm going to shower." She disappeared into the bathroom.

Hmm. He rose. Maybe it was time to introduce Lainie to the shower quickie.

When they arrived at Teterboro Airport, just over an hour and a half later, Lainie was still flushed from being thoroughly fucked against the wall in his shower.

The sleek jet was waiting for them.

Nick scanned around, then pulled their suitcases out of the car. Lainie was tapping on her phone and had her laptop bag on her shoulder. She'd already been sucked into work.

He wished they weren't going on this trip. A part of him just wanted to lock her up so he could keep her safe.

He blew out a breath. He knew this conference was important to her, to her company.

He'd be her shield. He'd keep her safe.

He was very quickly realizing just how much he'd do for this woman.

They checked in and a smiling man in work gear took their suitcases. Nick had ensured the jet company Lainie used was thoroughly vetted before today's flight.

As they boarded, a smiling flight attendant greeted them. "Good morning." She shot Nick a professional smile. "Ms. Madden, your coffee is ready. I've added a fresh croissant, as well."

Lainie looked up. "Thanks, Shauna. Oh, this is my boyfriend, Nick."

"Would you like a drink, Nick?" Shauna asked.

"Black coffee, one sugar. Thanks."

Soon, they were settled in the plush seats. Lainie opened her laptop and got busy with work. Nick opened his own laptop to check the casino schematics Hex had sent him.

He'd already called ahead and had spoken with the casino's head of security. Craig Miller was a former Marine. Nick liked the older man, especially since Miller had promised whatever resources he could spare to keep Lainie safe.

Nick and Lainie would be staying in the penthouse at the Aurora Casino. The FutureTech conference was being held in the attached conference center. The first event was this cocktail party tonight, then Lainie had a small presentation tomorrow, followed by her big keynote.

He flexed his hands. He would keep her safe. Best case, Trent Morton wouldn't follow them to Las Vegas. But Nick wasn't taking any chances.

Hades and Hex had flown into Vegas this morning ahead of them on the Sentinel Security jet. Hades would check out the penthouse and venue. Hex would already be hunkered down in a hotel room, tapped into the casino security feed and facial-recognition database.

If Morton made an appearance, they'd know.

A few hours later, they landed, and a black SUV driven by a trusted Sentinel Security contractor met them. Nick pressed a hand to Lainie's lower back and led her off the plane to the vehicle.

"Tom." Nick lifted his chin at the man.

"Wolf." The man was almost as wide as he was tall, but all solid muscle. He looked like a bruiser and had a deep, rumbling voice.

"I'm Lainie." She held out her hand.

Tom stared at her for a beat, then gently shook her hand. "Ma'am."

Nick loaded Lainie into the vehicle while Tom dealt with their bags. Soon, they were driving down the Las Vegas Strip.

Lights glittered and danced. Buildings and casinos of all shapes and sizes rose up around them. It was an assault on the senses.

"I have a love-hate thing for Las Vegas," Lainie said.

"A part of me loves the glitz, the energy, the sense of show. But I wouldn't want to be a part of it all the time."

"New York has a lot of that."

"But it's less in-your-face. I love New York, although I sometimes think I'd like a quiet place upstate. Somewhere in the country."

"Surrounded by trees, with a pond where you can do some decent fishing."

She smiled. "Ah, not so much the fishing bit." She cocked her head. "I never pictured you as a fisherman."

"Don't get a chance to do it much."

"I could swim in this pond in the summer, then cozy up by the fire in the winter."

"You could always buy one of those mansions in the Hamptons," he said.

Her nose wrinkled. "It's not really my thing." She grabbed his hand. "Would you come with me and fish in my pond, if I buy one?"

"I feel like that's a dirty metaphor for something else."

She giggled and kissed him.

Nick had an instant image of a naked Lainie rising up out of a lake, then another of her spread out on a rug in front of a roaring fire.

He squeezed her fingers. "Yes, Lainie. I'd like to fish in your pond."

She was still staring at him when they pulled up into the curved driveway at the Aurora Casino. Nick pulled himself away and made himself open the door.

The Aurora was a newer casino and was housed in a huge, glass spire of a building. Inside the lobby, massive chandeliers hung overhead, light glittering off them.

"Wow." She arched her head back. "This place is incredible."

Nick spotted a grizzled man in a suit waiting for them. Craig Miller.

He shook hands with the man. "Nick Garrick. Thanks for the assistance."

The head of security nodded. "My team is busy with conference security, but whatever you need, we'll do our best to help." He looked at Lainie. "We want to ensure Ms. Madden is safe during her stay."

"Thank you," she said.

"Here are your key cards for the penthouse elevator. Access has been restricted. Your teammate has been through it an hour ago."

"Thanks," Nick said.

He wasted no time whisking Lainie through the busy lobby, barely letting her glimpse the main casino floor, with its giant, glass roof. He wanted her safely upstairs. He didn't want her exposed.

"Oh, wow." She stepped off the elevator and into their suite. She didn't waste any time kicking off her shoes.

The place was light and airy, but also had Las Vegas glitz. Two long, narrow chandeliers made of crystal dripped from the ceiling in the living area. Outside, a plunge pool was set into the terrace, balanced on the very edge to give an unimpeded view of the Strip below.

Lainie drank it all in like an excited schoolgirl. There was nothing jaded about her. Her wealth and success hadn't changed her. She peered around with interest and shed her jacket. Then she looked out the huge windows. The Strip spread out below like a gaudy slash of color, drawn by an excited toddler using all their crayons. Beyond that lay the mountains.

Nick felt a violent need for her. To possess her. To capture that goodness and wonder.

She turned. "You want to grab a snack before—?" She caught the look on his face and her chest hitched. "Nick?"

"I'm hungry, but not for food." He stalked toward her.

When he grabbed her, she came eagerly. His mouth took hers, and she kissed him back with a moan.

He speared a hand into her hair, pulling her head back roughly so he could take everything.

But it wasn't taking when she was giving it.

He swung them around, desire an urgent beat inside him. Then he bent her over the back of the leather couch.

"Oh," she gasped, gripping the cushions.

He yanked her jeans and panties down. Damn, that ass. He caressed her.

She squirmed. "Nick... Please..."

He slid a hand between her legs and stroked. She was wet for him.

"You with me?" he asked.

"Yes. Yes," she chanted.

With a frantic tug, he ripped his pants open. He needed her.

Shit. "I don't have a condom handy."

"It's safe. I'm safe." She looked back over her shoulder. "I'm on the Pill. After my ex cheated, I got tested and I haven't been with anyone since. You?"

She wanted him bare. "Yeah. We're tested regularly at work. I'm clean." He'd never fucked anyone without a condom before. A shudder went through him.

Her cheeks were flushed. "Do it, Nick."

He bent over her and fit his cock against her, then surged inside.

Her neck arched. "Yes, God, yes."

He was inside her. Nothing between them. "Fuck, Lainie." She felt like heaven. Wet, tight. "It's going to be rough, kitten."

"Good, I—"

He thrust hard. She cried out.

"Hang on, Lainie."

Nick pounded into her. He tried to hold on, but he was losing the battle. He felt Lainie come, spasming on his cock. She cried out as her climax ravaged her.

With a groan, he sank a hand in her hair, pulling her head up so he could kiss her, while his cock was lodged deep inside her.

He came, pleasure like fire down his spine, as he poured himself inside her.

———

LAINIE FINISHED TOUCHING up her makeup.

She was ready for the cocktail party. She'd kept her hair in a sleek ponytail and had dangly diamonds in her ears. Her dress was black. She needed to keep it professional.

Well, professional with an edge. She had a hot guy to impress.

She shifted and felt the throb between her legs. *God.* The things she let Nick do to her. The dark, delicious things. She closed her eyes, smiling. The way he made her feel...

Nick was every secret fantasy come to life. In bed and outside of it.

He made her feel beautiful. Special.

Fear tried to well up, but she stomped on it. Nick would never cheat on her. He'd never betray her. She needed to stop judging everyone based on the men who'd hurt her in the past.

She ran her hands down her dress. She was hoping this dress made Nick want to fuck her over the couch again.

Or in the giant, king-size bed in the master bedroom.

She strode out. He was on the phone, barking orders about security to someone. He was in a dark-blue suit, and her belly clenched. She loved how he looked, the smooth contrast of his clothes to the rough edge of his rugged face and beard.

He looked up and saw her. His blue gaze roamed over her, and his lips tipped up in a smile.

"Thanks, Hades. Yeah. We'll be there soon." Nick slipped the phone away. "You look gorgeous."

"Thanks."

"I'm grateful that while that dress hugs your curves, it has a high neck. I don't have to scare off as many idiots drooling all over you."

She rolled her eyes, but her belly fluttered. It was a compliment, Nick-style. "Ready?"

"Yes. Hex has eyes on the party. Hades is pretending to be a guest. Miller and his security team have been briefed."

She turned to grab her small evening bag. "Then let's go."

She turned back, and saw Nick staring at her, frozen.

"Wait." On a growl, he strode toward her, and her belly jumped.

He spun her and ran his hand down her bare spine.

Her dress had no back.

He growled again. "Are you trying to kill me?"

She tossed her hair back. "I dress for myself, Nick Garrick."

He tickled her lower back with his callused fingers, and she shivered. "I think you're lying."

She met his burning, blue gaze. "Maybe. Maybe what's under this is for you. Later."

"Witch." He dropped a quick kiss to her mouth. "Let's go before I tear that dress off you, and we miss the party." He held her hand and led her into the elevator.

When they entered the party, it was in full swing. A curved, glass wall made an impact, and the glass chandeliers in this room were all fun, funky shapes that glowed with different colors.

As soon as she entered, people she knew mobbed her —other tech entrepreneurs, journalists, conference attendees.

Nick stayed close, his face set and serious. Whenever she looked at him, he was scanning the room. Lainie chatted and smiled, and every now and then, looked his way.

His quiet nod fizzed inside her. It was so intoxicating to have his full attention. She wasn't sure she'd ever had anyone's full attention. Her parents loved her, but they'd considered their job done once she become an adult. Elliott had been the best little brother, but busy with his own life, and later with his battle with cancer.

No boyfriend had ever made her feel so seen, so right.

She chatted with more partygoers. Lots of people peppered her with questions on Pintura or the Bloom acquisition. There were tons of influential people in attendance.

Nick brought her a glass of wine, and she thanked him with a smile.

"I'd ask if that fabulous hunk of a man is single," Hillary Evans said. The older woman ran a cloud storage company and Lainie had always liked her. Hillary sipped her own flute of champagne, her eyes were bright behind her huge, funky, red-framed glasses. "But the way he looks at you is giving me a hot flush."

Lainie blushed. "He's my boyfriend."

"Good for you, Lainie. Hold on to that one."

She sipped her drink, but her belly bubbled. Could she keep Nick's interest? After only a few days, Lainie knew what she felt for Nick was so much bigger than anything she'd ever felt before.

She could fall in love with him. Hell, she was already half in love with him.

Her heart thumped. Realizing her glass was empty, she set it aside.

She glanced his way and saw tall, dark, bad-boy Hades stride up to him. The other Sentinel Security man looked like a sexy Mafia don. Whatever Hades said had both men frowning.

Nick looked her way and gave her a pointed look. *Stay there.*

She nodded. God, she hoped nothing was wrong.

Nick and Hades turned, and she saw the grizzled head of security, Craig Miller, appear. A shiver slid down her spine.

"Ms. Madden?"

She turned to see a nervous woman with frizzy, blonde hair, wearing a blue dress on her thin frame.

"Yes?"

"I'm Deb. I'm a *huge* fan." The woman gave a nervous laugh. Her voice was breathy and high-pitched. "I've read up on all your success. It's amazing what you've achieved all on your own."

"Thank you, but I have a great team, and it involves a lot of hard work and some luck."

"I *love* using Pintura. It's so easy. I run a blog and have lots of social media channels."

"That's fabulous," Lainie said. "I designed Pintura for people like you." She laughed. "Or like me. I had a blog, too, in college. I used to complain about how long graphics took to make. My brother was an artist and used to help me out. He urged me to start Pintura."

"Well, you've done a wonderful job. Here." Deb held out a glass of champagne. "Here's to Pintura's future. Can I get a picture?" She lifted her phone.

"Sure."

Lainie posed with the woman, and they lifted their champagne flutes. Deb was wearing so much Chanel No. 5 that Lainie fought the urge to sneeze. She'd worn the perfume in college, mostly because Trent had loved it, but now she found it overpowering.

"To Pintura," Deb said.

"Cheers." They clinked glasses, then sipped.

A man and woman came into view, hovering close by, trying to get Lainie's attention.

"I'd better keep doing the rounds," Lainie said. "It was nice to meet you."

Deb smiled. "You, too."

"Hi." Lainie greeted the couple. When she looked back, Deb had slipped into the party crowd.

Lainie talked some more, taking a few more sips of her drink. The champagne was sweet and fizzy, but she didn't want to drink too much. She tried to keep a limit on the alcohol when she was at work functions.

She looked for Nick, and spotted him by the wall, still talking with Hades. Except now, the men were suddenly a little blurry. A shot of nerves made her stomach clench. She set her glass down.

What the hell?

She hadn't had that much to drink. She took a step, unsteady on her feet. She gripped the edge of a nearby table.

Someone was talking to her, but the sound was muffled. She felt like her senses were overloaded, and she couldn't focus.

She blinked. Her chest tightened and she felt a flush of heat.

Something was wrong.

She staggered and pressed a hand to her chest. Her pulse was racing. She held a hand out. She needed Nick.

"Lainie?" A face swam into view, along with blonde hair. "Are you okay?"

She frowned at the woman. She looked a bit familiar. Diane? No, Deb.

Lainie's vision blurred again, and her stomach turned to a hard point. "I... I..." She couldn't talk. *Nick.* She wanted Nick.

"Let me help you." Deb took her arm.

No. Lainie wanted Nick.

She staggered and nearly fell. When she looked up, Nick turned her way. She saw his brow crease, and then he was shoving people aside to get to her.

With a gasp, Lainie's knees gave out. She heard people crying out in surprise.

Then arms caught her.

"Kitten?"

Nick. "Something's wrong..." Her eyes fluttered closed.

"Hades!" Nick roared. "Get a doctor."

"On it."

Nick laid her flat on her back, bellowing at bystanders to back up.

She closed her eyes. Everything was spinning.

"I've got you, Lainie."

She gripped his arm. She wasn't so afraid now.

She knew he would take care of her.

CHAPTER FIFTEEN

Lainie woke up with a dry mouth and her head a little fuzzy.

The morning light made a rectangle around the heavy curtains over the windows. She blinked. This wasn't her bedroom.

That's right, they were in Las Vegas.

She registered a heavy arm across her waist and a hot body pressed against her back.

She turned her head and met with bronze flesh covered in a smattering of dark hair.

Mmm. Still the best chest in the world.

Nick's eyes were closed, dark shadows smudged under them.

Lainie had a pressing urge to pee. As soon as she shifted, his eyes popped open.

"Lainie, you okay?" His voice was a deep rumble.

"Yes, I..." He was watching her like a hawk. "Oh, God." Memories rushed in like clothes falling out of an overstuffed closet. "The cocktail party."

He sat up, cupping her face, his gaze like a laser moving over her face.

"What happened?" she whispered. "I remember feeling woozy. I wanted you...then nothing."

Emotion rippled across his rugged face. "You were poisoned."

Her heart felt like claws clamped on it. "Poisoned?"

"It was my fucking fault. Miller needed to talk to me about a breach in hotel security, and I looked away for a few minutes."

Of course Nick would blame himself.

"Nick." She gripped his wrists. "It was *not* your fault. I took a glass of champagne from a woman without thinking. I was in the middle of a damn party, surrounded by people."

A muscled worked in his tight jaw. "The champagne was laced with a synthetic poison. If you'd taken more than a few sips..."

She blew out a breath and stroked the pulse point on his wrist. "I'm fine. You got to me in time."

His big body shuddered.

"Nick Garrick, repeat after me, 'this was not my fault.'"

His blue eyes bored into hers. "I can't lose you, Lainie."

Oh. Her belly filled with pleasant, warm tingles. This man was ruining her for anyone else. She stroked her fingers up to the corner of his eyes, across the dark shadows beneath them. "Did you get any sleep?"

"I had to watch over you. Make sure you were safe. Make sure you had no further reaction to the poison. The hotel doctor said you'd be fine once the poison cleared your system."

And her own protective wolf had watched over her all night.

"So you didn't sleep at all?"

"I dozed. I'm used to it. I don't need much sleep."

Screw that. In the future, she was going to make sure her man got enough sleep.

Her pulse skipped. *Her man.*

That sounded so right. Nick was hers. A part of her had always known that, had always been drawn to him. She wasn't going to let her fears of being hurt stop her from being with him.

"I really need the bathroom," she said. "I'll be right back." She slipped out of bed. All she had on was a large T-shirt that had to be Nick's. She fingered the soft cotton and glanced at him.

From the bed, he watched her carefully, like he expected her to collapse or disappear. Dull color filled his cheeks. "I wanted you in my shirt."

Lainie hid her smile. Her inner cave girl liked the possessive move. She quickly slipped into the bathroom, relieved her full bladder, then washed her hands and face. Next, she brushed her teeth. She felt surprisingly good for someone who'd been poisoned.

Her belly knotted. She still couldn't believe someone, likely directed by her ex-boyfriend, had tried to kill her.

And Nick felt responsible.

She stared at herself in the mirror. She needed to distract him and talk him out of that nonsense.

When she walked out, he was propped up against the

headboard. He was only wearing dark blue boxer shorts. God, he was built.

She walked toward him, desire firing in her belly.

"You have your big keynote talk today," he said.

Jeez, she'd forgotten about it. But right in that moment, she didn't really care about it.

Right now, Nick was more important. She crawled onto the bed.

"You need to eat something, shower, practice your speech. We released a story that you had an allergic reaction to something in the champagne, but you were fine and resting."

"Good thinking." She straddled him.

He gripped her hips. "I'll order breakfast, then I need to go over security again. In light of what happened, I've called in more people. You'll be covered today."

"More people?"

"I called Vander Norcross. He runs Norcross Security out of San Francisco. It's a good outfit. Vander's ex-military."

"A Navy SEAL like you?"

"No. Former black ops. He's coming with his brother Rhys, who's also former black ops."

She barely resisted the urge to roll her eyes. Of course Nick would call in total badasses to protect her.

"And Killian made some calls. He has some local contacts. There are three additional people coming in to help."

"And what do they do? Invade small nations? Take down dictators?"

"It's classified."

"Nick—"

"They're current black ops. That's all I can say. I don't even know."

Her eyes widened. "You have any assassins or air support organized as well?"

Nick slid a hand into her hair. "I'm not fucking around when it comes to keeping you breathing."

She saw the darkness bleeding into his eyes. "I'm okay, Nick." She undulated against him and felt his growing cock beneath her. "I'm very much alive."

His nostrils flared, and his hand clenched in her hair.

She rested her hands on his chest, scratching her nails over his flat nipples. "I think you need me to prove it to you."

"Lainie—"

She gripped the T-shirt she was wearing and whipped it over her head. Then she leaned down and kissed him.

Of course, he took control of the kiss. It was hard, needy. Yes, her man needed some soothing, some reassurance.

She rocked against him and moaned into his mouth.

Things escalated quickly.

Lainie reached between them and shoved his boxer shorts down enough to free his cock.

"Fuck." His voice was pure grit.

She made him like this. Geek at heart, Lainie Madden, drove a man like Nick Garrick to the edge. It made her feel powerful.

She gripped his cock and stroked. As she found a rhythm, his hips bucked up, pushing into her fist.

With a husky moan, she pressed her mouth to his. "When I'm with you, Nick, you make me feel safe, protected." Her lips moved across his cheekbone. "I know you'll be there for me, no matter what."

He shuddered, his cock throbbing in her hand.

"Lainie, you're all I think about." His hot gaze collided with hers. "All I've ever wanted."

Emotions filled her chest. She rose up and moved his cock between her legs. The thick mushroom head nestled in her slick folds. They both groaned.

"Kitten, you feel so good," he groaned.

Lainie slowly sank down, taking every inch of him inside her. Nick made a hoarse sound.

"You're so deep," she panted.

His breathing was labored. "You fit me so well. *Perfect.*"

"And you stretch me just enough to make it feel so, so good," she moaned.

"Lainie. My Lainie. Made for my cock."

"*Yes.*" She gripped his shoulders, threw her head back, and moved. She rocked fast, riding his cock, driving both of them wild.

"I love your sweet pussy, kitten. Don't stop."

"Nick. Yes. God, *yes.*"

His hand squeezed her breast, then slid lower. He found her clit, rubbing it faster and faster.

The lightning sensations made her gasp. She couldn't breathe. She dug her nails into his shoulders and knew she was drawing blood.

His gaze locked on hers. "I love everything about you, Lainie."

His words set her off. She thrust her hips down, coming hard.

Nick's hands gripped her ass, squeezing. He worked her up and down on his cock. Then he shouted her name. His hips bucked, and she felt him shoot deep inside her.

Lainie collapsed forward. She was totally spent. Nick's chest was heaving, and he ran a hand up to grip the nape of her neck.

"I could stay here forever," she murmured.

A second later, there was a sound from out in the suite's living room.

"Okay, you two, sexy time is over." It was Hex's unrepentant voice.

Lainie and Nick both froze.

"We brought breakfast," Hadley said.

"And coffee." Hades' amused voice.

"Oh, God." Lainie gripped Nick tighter.

He cupped her ass and squeezed. "They're nosy and unapologetic about it. They won't leave."

"I am kind of hungry," she said.

He pressed a quick kiss to her lips. "Let's hit the shower, then eat." His face turned serious. "Then let's get this keynote presentation over and done with."

So he could get her safe. She heard his unspoken words.

EDGILY, Nick paced the suite's living area. He'd gone over the security plans for the keynote presentation three times.

He still wasn't happy.

The pleasant feelings from sex with Lainie had worn off. Today, she'd be on stage in an auditorium filled with strangers.

The perfect target.

He'd almost lost her. The sight of her unconscious and poisoned tormented him.

"She's okay, *amico mio*."

Nick looked at Hades.

"You just had the doctor here to check on her. He gave her a clean bill of health," Hades said.

"Could've ended differently," Nick muttered.

"It didn't. And today, we'll all keep her safe. Norcross just called and is on his way from the airport. Lachlan Hunter and his guys should be here any minute now."

Nick nodded. They'd have some supercharged backup. He knew Killian had pulled a lot of strings to make it happen because Nick had asked.

He heard Lainie's laugh from the bedroom. Hex and Hadley were with her. The three of them were fussing over what Lainie would wear for the keynote. His friends were taking her mind off her nerves.

Hades gripped Nick's shoulder. "You've got this. We've got your girl covered."

Nick nodded.

"Did Miller say anything more on the system security breach?" Hades asked.

Nick shook his head. "All we know is that someone hacked the Aurora Casino's computer system and downloaded detailed schematics of the hotel." He released a sharp breath. "We have to assume it's Morton, and that he's going to make a play."

"Then we'll be ready," Hades said darkly.

There was a sound from behind them. Nick turned, just as Lainie stepped out of the bedroom, her arms spread.

"Well, what do you think of this one?" she asked.

Nick stared at her.

She ran her hands down the dark blue trousers of the jumpsuit thing she was wearing. The trousers nipped in at the waist, and the top finished at a band around her neck, leaving her arms and shoulders bare. Her brown hair was loose, styled in gentle waves.

She looked gorgeous and fresh. Professional, but fun. Like her company.

"She looks perfect." Hadley strode out of the bedroom. "I knew this halter-neck jumpsuit was just the thing."

"Hadley, your shopping game is strong," Hex said.

Hadley buffed her nails on her shirt. "It's a God-given talent."

"You look great," Nick said to Lainie.

Hades made an amused sound.

"Great?" Hadley put a hand on her hip and shook her head. "That's the best you can do?"

Hex grinned. "I think he prefers her naked."

Lainie gasped, then giggled.

Fuck, he loved that sound. He moved over to her and pressed a gentle kiss to her lips. "You look beautiful. You'll knock this out of the park." He took her hand. "If you're ready to go, let's get down there. I want to do another walk-through, and we need to meet Norcross and Hunter."

She lifted her chin. "I'm ready."

They made it to the auditorium quickly. Hex set up her laptop in the back of the large room. Hades and Hadley stuck close to Lainie as she set up on the stage.

"Wolf," a deep voice said.

Nick turned and clocked Vander Norcross and his brother Rhys striding toward him.

Both men had dark hair and faces that showed their Italian-American heritage. Their suits did little to hide their fit, muscular bodies. Neither of them had gone soft since leaving the military.

Rhys' hair was a little longer and shaggier, and he was smiling. Vander was the opposite. As always, Vander Norcross radiated a lethal intensity, his face blank. Wolf knew Vander would have already assessed the threat potential of all the people in the room and clocked all the exits. He reminded Wolf a lot of Killian. A thin layer of civilized covering a whole lot of dangerous.

Both of the Norcross brothers were former Ghost Ops—made up of the best of the best of special forces. Vander had been a hell of a commander, and now kept busy running Norcross Security and keeping his pulse on what went on in San Francisco.

He also kept busy with his ballsy police detective fiancée.

"Vander. Rhys." Nick shook Vander's hand, then Rhys'. "How's Saskia?"

Rhys grinned. "She and Cam are still in the honeymoon phase. They have 'lunch' together a lot." The younger Norcross winked. "We all know what that means."

"I'm not sure my boss wants to hear that about his sister," Nick said.

"She's happy," Vander said. "And safe."

"I appreciate you coming to help," Nick said. "We're expecting a capacity crowd, and this fucker isn't going to get Lainie again." He knew he didn't manage to keep his anger in check.

Vander's gaze moved to the stage, and Rhys' did too.

"So, our charge is both rich and beautiful," Rhys said.

Nick scowled at the man. He knew that Rhys was in love with his own woman, but still.

"And she's taken by the looks of things." Vander had a faint smile lurking on his mouth.

Nick nodded. "She's mine."

"We'll help you keep her safe," Vander said.

"I need you two to blend into the crowd. Keep an eye out for anything that looks off. I'll have Hex text you pictures of Trent Morton and the woman we think is his accomplice. The woman tried to poison Lainie last night."

"She okay?" Rhys asked.

"Yeah." *Thank fuck.*

Vander nodded. "We're on it."

The doors of the auditorium opened. A man strode in flanked by a man and woman.

"Badass hottie alert," Hex murmured in Nick's earpiece.

Nick stared at the newcomers. The man in front had to be Lachlan Hunter. He had a big body, rugged face, and flat, golden eyes. Like a tiger heading in for the kill. He wore dark jeans and a brown suede jacket.

The man on his left was leaner, sharper, with dark hair. One side of his face was movie-star handsome, while the other was covered in scars. Not someone to mess with. The woman on Hunter's right at first glance just looked like a fit, attractive blonde in jeans and a black leather jacket. But a closer look at her face and Nick knew she'd be a tough opponent in a fight.

"Garrick?" The golden-eyed man said.

"Yeah. Hunter?"

The man nodded and held out a hand. Then his gaze shifted. "Hey, Vander. Rhys."

"Lachlan," Vander said.

"You guys know each other," Nick said.

"Yeah," Vander said. "Lachlan's team is good at appearing out of nowhere and confiscating expensive things."

Lachlan Hunter just smiled.

Pieces clicked in Nick's brain. "You're Team 52."

A highly covert team that agents around the world whispered about. What was known about them was more rumor than fact.

Lachlan inclined his head. "We're off duty today. Lynch here owed Killian a favor."

Nick studied the dark-haired man. "Seth Lynch? You were CIA. I entered Special Activities about the time you left."

"Thought you looked familiar," Seth said.

Nick hadn't crossed paths with Lynch at the CIA, but he'd heard about the man.

"Seth dragged himself away from his wife and baby," the blonde woman said. "And I'm only missing out on cupcakes in bed with my husband because he got called into the station." She looked around. "So I hope we at least get a good fight out of this."

Nick would prefer things stayed boring, but with these five backing them up, he was feeling a little better.

"This is my second in command, Blair Mason," Lachlan introduced her.

Nick nodded. "Thanks for coming. I'll get Hex—" he pointed to the hacker, who waved "—to get you set up with earpieces and images of our suspects. Whatever happens, we protect Lainie." He glanced her way.

She was watching them and shot them all a nervous smile.

"We've got your and your woman's back, Wolf," Vander said.

Seth looked around. "Haven't been here for a while. Lachlan hates the Aurora."

The leader of Team 52 just grunted.

"His wife fell off the casino roof into the pool once," Seth said. "She was being chased by bad guys."

Blair nodded, her ponytail bouncing. "Rowan has a bad habit of falling off high places."

"Can we not talk about this?" Lachlan growled.

"It's almost time," Hadley called out from the stage.

Nick finished introducing everyone and watched as Hex handed out earpieces. His muscles were still tight with nerves. No mission had ever been more important to him.

216

That's when Nick saw Hex look at her laptop and stiffen. He hurried over to her.

"Problem?"

"There are conference goers *everywhere*, and it's taking forever to run all the facial recognition, but we just got a hit." Her blue-green eyes met his. "On Trent Morton."

Nick stiffened. "You're sure?"

"An eighty-six percent match. He had a hat on, so it's only a partial shot. He was in the main event hall."

Nick felt a tickle across the back of his neck. He touched his ear. "Lachlan, can you send Seth to look for Morton in the main hall. Facial rec picked him up."

He saw Seth peel away and jog to the door.

"We're ready," Hex said. "Even if he's here, he isn't getting to her."

"You get another ping, you let me know." Nick moved to the stage. Lainie was pacing, her lips moving as she practiced her speech. He climbed up the steps. "It's almost time to open the doors." He decided not to mention that Morton might be there. He didn't want to throw her off. Not when he knew how important this speech was.

She pressed a hand to her stomach. "I'm so nervous. Between my talk and worrying if Tacky Trent and the frizzy blonde are going to storm the stage..."

He touched her silky hair. "Don't worry, I'll take care of Trent."

"Knowing you're here helps," she said.

"And I know that you'll smash it up here. You're so damn smart, I think you could do anything."

Her eyes warmed. "Oh, now I want to kiss you, but I can't ruin my lipstick."

He pressed a kiss to the side of her neck. She made a cute, needy sound.

"Kick ass, and then I'll fuck you over the couch after."

She sucked in a breath, excitement lighting her eyes. "Really?"

"Oh, God," Hex said in Nick's ear. "I can hear you guys. Dying of jealousy, here."

Nick squeezed Lainie's arm. "Go and be amazing, kitten."

CHAPTER SIXTEEN

"As we continue to innovate and make designing easier and more fun, Pintura wants to empower *you* to design and create. To help your business, your website, your social media shine. We want you to have the power to design anything you want, to share your story with the world, and look good doing it."

Applause broke out, filling the auditorium.

Lainie glanced across the crowd. Her gaze shifted toward the edge of the stage until she found Nick.

He was watching her, smiling.

God. She could feel how proud he was of her.

Her parents had never told her they were proud. But she realized that she was proud of herself. All her hard work had been worth it.

And sharing this with Nick, made it extra special.

Hope you're watching, El.

She knew her brother would be smiling all the way.

She looked at Nick again. God, she felt safe. She

hadn't worried about Trent at all while she'd been on the stage talking.

Nick and his team of badasses—who were all prowling the crowd—meant she hadn't felt scared or unsafe.

She waved and headed to the edge of the stage.

Her keynote had been a huge success, which should help the Bloom acquisition proceed without a hitch.

Once Trent was caught, life would be sparkly again. She had a growing, thriving company, and a hot guy she was falling in love with. Her heart squeezed.

Nick was there to greet her.

"I'm going to mess up your lipstick now." He lifted her off her feet for a kiss. "You were brilliant, Lainie."

"Thanks. And thanks for making me feel safe while I did it."

He touched her jaw. "My honor."

"Lainie!"

Hadley and Hex rushed in for hugs.

"You were ah–mazing," Hex said.

"And you look a million bucks," Hadley added.

Nick's phone dinged and he pulled it out. He frowned. "I need a second. You two, stay with her." He strode through a doorway.

"So," Lainie said. "The Aurora has a brilliant day spa. I booked in for a few treatments, and I booked you both in as well. As my bodyguards."

The women grinned.

"A full-body massage?" Hex said. "I'm in."

"You're not taking Wolf?" Hadley asked.

Lainie snorted. "The man doesn't know the meaning

of the word relax. Can you imagine him sitting still for a pedicure?"

They all looked at each other for a second, then burst out laughing.

"Our appointments are in two hours," Lainie said.

"Oh boy, a massage." Hex's dual-colored eyes rolled back. "It's the closest I'll get to an orgasm of late. Unlike some other lucky bitch." She eyed Lainie.

"Nick is good at giving plenty of those," Lainie said.

"Total bitch," Hex whined.

Hadley laughed.

"Don't rub it in," Hex said. "I haven't had time to date for months, even if I could find a man I found remotely interesting. Anyway, a full-body massage is a close second to orgasms."

"I'm going to grab Nick and drag him upstairs for a... rest," Lainie said.

"Oh my God, you just keep rubbing it in." Hex patted her arm. "You did good out there. You've earned a hot couch quickie."

Lainie blushed. She could hear the rumble of Nick's deep voice out in the hall, talking to someone.

"He said...he said he loved everything about me," she said quietly.

"Wolf?" Hadley said. "He said the L word?"

"Well, he didn't say 'I love you' exactly." Her stomach felt jittery.

"That man is head over heels for you," Hadley said.

Lainie's smile was so wide it was a wonder her mouth didn't hurt. "I'm head over heels for him to."

God, it felt good to admit it.

"Go, get your orgasms," Hex said. "Before you're mobbed by conference geeks wanting to talk tech."

"I'll see you guys at the spa." Lainie strode out into the corridor with a wave.

She wasn't expecting the emotional gut punch that followed.

Nick was standing in the hall, kissing a beautiful woman.

They hadn't noticed her. Didn't appear to notice anything but each other. Lainie stared, time seeming to freeze. Her insides crumpled.

The woman was tall, elegant, and impossibly slender. She wore chic, fitted, black pants, a crisp white shirt, and spiked black heels. Her black hair was swept up in an effortless twist, and the profile of her face was perfect.

Lainie took a step back. She couldn't breathe. Couldn't think.

The woman was pressed up against Nick like she belonged there. Like she'd been there numerous times before.

Lainie felt like she was going to vomit.

Suddenly, Nick disengaged. His head snapped up, gaze colliding with hers over the woman's head.

For once, Lainie couldn't read the emotion that crossed his face. Pain? Guilt?

She turned and ran.

"Lainie!" Nick yelled.

She didn't stop. There were too many things rattling around in her head. Too many emotions tearing her open. Too many old memories.

Trent naked in bed with another girl.

Keenan and Rebecca Jade's locked lips splashed all over the tabloids.

That beautiful woman kissing Nick.

Lainie saw one of the men from earlier. The dark, dangerous one with the good-looking face and dark-blue eyes.

"I need to get to my suite. Um, I can't remember your name, sorry."

"Norcross. Vander Norcross." He glanced behind her. "Where's Wolf?"

"He's busy. *Please.*" She was barely holding on. "I need to go, now." She pulled in a shaky breath.

Vander assessed her, then nodded.

He pressed a hand to her lower back and hurried her through a side door, then into the elevator.

Once the elevator doors closed, Lainie sagged against the wall. "Thank you."

Now she really focused on him, and the hairs on the back of her neck rose. If she thought Nick was a wolf, this man was a sleek, deadly shark.

And those dark eyes looked like they saw too much. He nodded.

Then Lainie closed her eyes and shut everything out.

"FUCK." Nick watched Lainie run, and his gut tied in knots.

He took a step away from Gisele. He knew that Lainie was running from her worst nightmare.

Panic felt slick and hot inside him. He had to make this right.

Hurting his kitten, even if it was him doing it, was intolerable.

"Ah, now I know why you didn't kiss me back," Gisele said in her lilting French accent. "I didn't realize you already had a diversion while you were here."

"She's not a diversion. She's mine."

Gisele's pale-blue eyes widened. "Wolf is off the market? I never believed that I'd see the day."

"Gisele, why are you here?"

"I was passing through for work." She tossed her head back. "I called your office and they said you were here." She gave an elegant shrug. "I figured I'd give you the additional intel on the Cardoza Cartel in person."

Hearing that name, thinking of Martinez, didn't hit quite so hard.

He still wanted justice for Jennifer and Madison but —he took a deep breath—he knew he couldn't keep living in the past.

"Thanks, Gisele. Send it through to my email. Now, I have to go." He prayed Lainie hadn't run off on her own. He needed to get to her.

Gisele sighed. "I'll miss our times together." She rose up and pressed a kiss to his cheek. "Go find your woman, Wolf."

With a nod, he strode down the hall. He turned a corner and nearly ran into Vander. The other man looked past Nick, eying the departing Interpol agent.

"Lainie?" Nick said. "Have you seen—?"

"I escorted her to her suite."

Nick released a breath and stepped toward the elevator. But Vander sidestepped, blocking his way.

Nick scowled. "Move, Vander. I need to get to Lainie."

"She was upset, and now I see why. She's not the kind of woman you toy with, Garrick."

Nick growled. "I'm not toying with her."

"For years I never got tangled up. I kept things with women brief and unemotional. I didn't think relationships were for a man like me." Vander was quiet for a moment. "You and me, Wolf, we've got blood on our hands. We've waded into life's shit too many times to count."

Nick's gut tightened, he met Vander's gaze head on.

"Falling in love with Brynn—" Vander shook his head. "I never expected her, and she never gave up on me. She's the best thing that ever happened to me. She makes it all worth it. Every dark, dirty thing I've ever done, I'd do it again as long as it means I get her."

"Vander—" Nick's chest was tight "—I get it. Lainie and I...*fuck.*"

A smile broke out on Vander's face. "You're in love with her."

Nick huffed out a breath. "Yes. I am. Can I go to my woman now?"

Vander stepped aside and waved a hand. "Better have a good grovel ready."

With a growl, Nick held his card up to the reader.

When he entered the suite, nerves prickled across his skin like he was heading out on an important mission.

He spotted her straight away. She was still in her

jumpsuit, but had no shoes on, and was standing silhouetted at the windows. She had her arms wrapped around her middle.

His heart was pounding hard as he took several steps toward her.

She turned.

Her face was pale, her eyes dark and wide.

"Lainie—"

She held up a hand.

Nick's gut dropped.

Then she shot across the space toward him. "I'm sorry. I'm sorry I panicked and ran."

Relief hit him like a sledgehammer. She rammed into him, and he wrapped his arms around her. She buried her face against his chest.

"For a second—" her voice wavered, "—all I saw were the assholes who'd hurt me before. I know you're nothing like them, Nick."

"Kitten, I'm sorry. She took me by surprise and kissed me. I didn't kiss her back."

Lainie swallowed and looked up. He hated the uncertainty on her face.

"But she felt she had the right to kiss you," Lainie said.

His hands flexed on Lainie's arms. "I know her."

"She's very beautiful. Chic. She's your ex?"

"God, no. A colleague, sort of. She works for Interpol. What we had...it was extremely casual. Not a relationship."

Lainie nodded, her gaze dropped, and she still looked troubled.

He gripped her chin. "I would never cheat on you. That's not who I am. And I couldn't, not when you're the only woman I see. The only woman I want."

She pressed her cheek into his palm, and her eyes closed for a second. Then she stepped back.

Nick bit back a growl. He hated the distance between them.

"I know you're too honorable to cheat, but this made something clear to me." She swallowed. "Maybe I'm not ready. Maybe I have too many scars to truly trust someone."

"No." Nick shook his head.

"I think it's for the best if we—"

He felt like he'd swallowed lead. "You aren't running from me, Lainie."

"Nick, I—" Her face twisted.

"You're afraid, because you feel things for me."

Her eyes looked huge. "I'm terrified."

"I know, because I feel it too." He closed the gap between them and cupped both her cheeks. "I'm fucking falling for you, Lainie Madden. Hell, I think it started with a moonlight kiss by the pool. No, before that. When a sweet girl talked to me, made me laugh and feel better."

Her mouth formed an O, and she stared at him.

He nuzzled her ear, her cheek. "I'm falling for my sweet, smart, sexy kitten."

She moaned. "*Nick.*"

He pulled her closer and claimed her mouth.

God, if she pushed him away, if she left him, he'd be broken.

She. Was. His.

He wasn't letting her go.

A rush of possessive desire hit him. He pulled her up on her toes, bending her head back with the force of his kiss.

She didn't protest or push him away.

No, Lainie pulled him closer and met his kiss, hot and eager.

"Need you," he growled. He couldn't think. He couldn't be gentle.

"Take me," she panted.

They staggered across the living area to the couch. Nick yanked at the zipper on her jumpsuit with growing impatience.

He got it free, and the fabric slithered off her, leaving her in tiny black panties and a bra.

His blood was pounding, making him dizzy. He gripped the side of her panties and tore them off.

She gasped, heat flaring in her eyes.

"Fuck, you're so beautiful, Lainie." He skimmed a hand down her side. "I can't go slow. I can't be gentle."

"I don't want gentle. I want you."

He scooped her up and laid her on the couch. He spread her legs, roughly stroking through her folds.

"*Nick.*" She arched into him.

"My kitten's already wet for me." She was perfect.

He spread her thighs wide and settled his weight on top of her. Desperately, he yanked at his pants.

Lainie reached her arms above her head, gripping the cushions. "Hurry, Nick."

Finally, he freed his cock and gripped her thigh. He thrust deep.

Oh, yeah, perfect. Right where he needed to be.

"Mine. *Lainie.*" He thrust heavily, pinning her down. "You are not leaving me. I'm not going to let you be afraid."

"Don't stop," she begged.

"You need this. You need me. You need my cock inside you."

"*Yes.*" She writhed against him.

He took one of her hands. He leaned back enough to move her fingers down to where she was stretched around him, where he was sliding into her.

"Feel that, Lainie? Where we're joined? One."

"Nick." Her eyes locked with his.

"Give it to me, kitten. Now."

She came, her thighs tucked against his rib cage, his name ripped from her lips.

Nick had never felt anything better or heard anything better.

On his next thrust, he felt his own release close in, his body coiling.

"Come on me," she said breathlessly.

He jerked.

"Mark me," she murmured.

Fuck. He pulled out, pleasure a hot fire in his gut. He came, ropes of semen hitting her belly.

Nick groaned, long and loud. He slumped down, totally spent, pressing one palm to the couch to keep the bulk of his weight off her.

She smiled. Her cheeks were pink, and her belly was coated in his come. Damn, Lainie Madden had ruined him for anyone else. She reached down and ran her fingers through the fluid on her belly.

Yes, he was totally in love with this woman.

"Lainie—" His cell phone rang, and he groaned. "That's Hex's ringtone." He tucked his cock away. "Go and clean up."

She nodded. He watched her sweet ass as she walked naked and a little unsteadily toward the bedroom.

He pressed the phone to his ear. "Hex?"

"Wolf." Hex sounded hyper alert.

He straightened. "What is it?"

"I got a hit on Trent Morton. He flew into Vegas on a redeye commercial flight and landed this morning."

Nick's fingers clenched on the phone. "He didn't hide it?"

"No. And...I just got a hit on a hotel room at the Flamingo Casino in his name."

Damn. That was just over a block away from the Aurora.

"Call Hades and tell him and Vander to meet me out front."

Lainie appeared in a robe, her face concerned.

"I need you and Hadley on Lainie, Hex," Nick said.

"On it. We're going to the spa anyway."

"Don't take your eyes off her."

"You know we won't. We'll take care of your girl."

"What is it?" Lainie asked as he slid the phone away.

"Hex found Trent. He booked a hotel room not far from here."

"He's here." She pressed a hand to her throat.

Nick hugged her. "I'm not letting him anywhere near you."

"I know." She leaned into him. "But I don't want you to get hurt either."

"Not happening. Stay with Hex and Hadley."

She nodded. "Go. So this can be over and you can come back to me safely."

He kissed her again, drawing in her scent. Nick would walk through hell to make it back to this woman.

CHAPTER SEVENTEEN

Nick lifted a boot and kicked down the door.

As he charged into the hotel room, Hades was right behind him. Vander stayed in the doorway.

Hades and Nick both held SIG Sauer P229s in their hands.

"What the fuck?" The man resting on the bed in his boxer shorts watching TV scrambled up.

"Don't move, asshole." Nick leaped forward. He dragged Trent Morton off the bed and forced him face-down on the patterned carpet. "Stay down. Hands behind your head."

The guy complied, shaking, and Nick kept his SIG aimed at him.

"Hades?"

Nick's friend jerked his chin up. He checked the small bathroom and opened all the closet doors. The room wasn't very big, and a little dated. It was also empty.

"Clear," Hades said.

Vander slipped inside and closed the door. He leaned against the wall and watched impassively.

"Who the hell are you?" Trent spluttered.

"Get up." Nick pulled the guy to his feet.

Morton sat on the edge of the bed. He was slender, with pale skin and covered in freckles. His light brown hair was thinning a little, and he was swallowing hard.

He wouldn't cause them any trouble.

"We're here, asshole, because you've been threatening Elaine Madden," Nick said.

Morton frowned. "Lainie? I haven't threatened her. I haven't seen her in years."

"Really?" Nick reached inside his jacket and pulled out some printouts. "Here are some of the sick threats you've been sending her." He tossed them on the bed beside the guy.

Morton snatched one up.

"You've also been bombarding Pintura with cyber attacks," Nick added.

"What? No!" Morton read the first threat, then another. His face drained of color. "Fuck me." He looked at Nick. "I didn't do this. I wouldn't."

Fucking hell. Nick stared at the man, then looked at Hades. The other man shook his head.

Morton was either the world's best liar, or he was telling them the truth.

"I fucked up with Lainie in college. I was a first-rate asshole, but I'd never hurt her. I'd never threaten to kill her." Morton scrunched up the papers.

"So you've never felt envious, like you're entitled to some of her Pintura success?" Nick asked.

Morton flinched, then sighed. "Ah, can I put some pants on?"

Nick ran his tongue over his teeth. He tucked his gun away and waved at the man.

Morton went to an open suitcase and yanked out some jeans. Nick watched like a hawk as he pulled them on, followed by a gray T-shirt. Then Morton ran a hand through his sandy hair.

"Look, have I been envious of what Lainie did with Pintura? Sure. She bounced early ideas off me, and I gave her some advice." He shook his head. "Get me sloshed, and I'll go on and on about how I let her get away, about how I—"

"Cheated on her?"

"Yeah." Morton's face twisted. "If I'd stayed with her, maybe we would have launched Pintura together, but Pintura is all Lainie. I tried once, when I was younger and cockier, for a cut, but I was wrong. I have my own business now. A VR bar. It's doing well, and I've been working on a plan to expand. We're going to open more bars in LA, Denver, Houston, and Chicago."

That was Morton's big project?

Shit. Nick glanced at Hades and Vander. Morton wasn't the guy. Nick wanted him to be, but his gut was telling him that Trent Morton wasn't the one.

"You're not behind the death threats or attacks on Lainie?"

"No!"

"Last night, a woman tried to poison Lainie at the FutureTech cocktail party. She was blonde, frizzy hair."

"What?" Morton's mouth open and closed. "Is Lainie all right?"

"She's fine. The woman? Do you know her?"

"*No*. God, I'd never hurt Lainie."

"Do you have a sister?" Nick pressed. "A girlfriend?"

"My girlfriend is blonde, but she has straight hair. And Claire, she'd never..." Morton drifted off.

"Morton?" Nick prompted.

"No, it's not possible." He scraped a shaky hand over his face.

"Wolf?" Hades said.

Nick glanced over and Hades nodded his head at a second suitcase on the floor in the room. It was filled with female clothes.

"I'm here with my girlfriend," Trent said. "She's... pretty intense. Very supportive. She's banged on at me about how I should've had some credit for Pintura." Color filled his cheeks. "I might've ranted a few times when I'd had too many beers, about hearing the early ideas. I've told her to back off, but—" he shrugged "—she's full on."

"Enough to threaten Lainie?" Nick asked. "To try and kill her?"

"No. Jesus, no."

Nick pulled out the picture of the woman who tried to poison Lainie. It wasn't a great shot, but it was the best they had. The woman was in profile.

"Take a look at this. She called herself Deb."

Morton grabbed the photo. "No. It can't be."

Nick stilled. "You know her?"

The man just stared at the photo, shaking his head.

"Morton," Nick snapped.

He looked up, his face pale. He swallowed, his Adam's apple bobbing. "It's Claire. My girlfriend. Her name is Claire Deborah Hall."

Nick stiffened. "Hall?"

Morton nodded. "She came into my bar. That's how we met. She's good with computers."

"Wolf?" Hades was watching with a narrow stare. "What is it?"

"Lainie had a disgruntled Pintura employee," Nick said. "She was a bully, was difficult to work with, then tried to hack company files. She went off the radar. But her name is Clara. Clara Hall."

Morton jolted. "No. They can't be the same woman. Claire's smart, dedicated."

Nick pulled out his phone and scrolled through his photos. "Here. An employee photo of Clara Hall."

Morton startled and frowned. "Claire's really thin."

And Clara Hall was plumper, curvier.

Then Morton cursed. "Jesus, that's Claire. With a few more pounds on. *Shit*."

"Claire, your girlfriend, is Clara Hall," Nick confirmed.

"A woman with an axe to grind with Lainie," Hades said.

"No. She wouldn't kill anyone," Morton pleaded.

"You sure?" Nick felt sick. "You said she was obsessed with Lainie."

"*Shit*. She said I deserved my share. That Lainie was greedy." Morton scraped a hand through his hair. "This can't be happening."

"Hall targeted you to help her with her revenge against Lainie," Nick said.

Morton closed his eyes.

"Clara Hall is after Lainie." Nick pressed the button to call Hex. The phone rang and rang. He tried Hadley, but her phone rang and rang too. His gut tightened. "Fuck," he spat. "Hadley and Hex aren't answering."

He saw Vander straighten.

"They were going to the spa," Hades said. "They might not have their phones with them."

"Hex and Hadley wouldn't leave their phones behind. They don't know that Clara Hall is after Lainie. That she might be disguised. We need to get back to the Aurora Casino. Now!"

"NOW, THIS IS MORE LIKE IT," Hadley drawled.

Lainie smiled and turned her head. Hadley and Hex rested beside her, all of them wearing thick, white robes. Hadley still somehow managed to look like an elegant queen. Hex looked like a little girl playing dress-up. The hacker was munching on some grapes and sipping some fancy herbal tea.

They were all stretched out on comfy loungers, their feet soaking in warm water.

There was a candle burning on a side table—the scent of ylang ylang and...well, Lainie had no idea what it was, but it smelled like a spa should.

She was trying to stay relaxed and not think of Nick, Matteo and Vander confronting Trent.

"She's thinking," Hex said. "And stressing."

Lainie blew out a breath. "I'm worried. Do you think they're okay?"

Hadley snorted. Elegantly. "It's Wolf and Hades, and add in Vander Norcross. Those three could take on a warlord's small army and not break a sweat."

Lainie shifted. "Yes, well, I finally have Nick." God, the idea still shocked her and made her giddy. "I don't want to lose him."

"Look at her face," Hex said. "I'm burning up with jealousy." She threw a grape at Lainie.

Lainie tried to catch it and missed. "I caught a woman kissing him earlier." It still gave her a bit of a sour feeling.

"What?" Hex squawked.

Hadley sat up, a brow arched.

"She kissed him, but he didn't kiss her back. She's an ex of his. She's French."

Hex's nose wrinkled. "Gisele. Interpol."

Gisele. Such a glamorous name. "I don't want to know her name, or any more details. She was thin, beautiful." Lainie waved a hand. "When I saw them, I sort of... freaked out. I've been cheated on before."

"Wolf would never cheat," Hadley said forcefully. "That man has an inner core of loyalty that he would never break."

"I know," Lainie said. "I realized once I'd calmed down."

"Did you two sort things out?" Hex asked. "The guy is all sorts of crazy about you."

"We did. Um, on the couch." She still throbbed in

some sensitive places.

The women burst into laughter.

Hadley nodded. "That's exactly how I expect an alpha male like Wolf to sort things out."

"He's falling in love with me." The words tumbled out of Lainie.

Both women gasped.

"That's huge," Hadley said.

Hex nodded. "Love is something Wolf has always avoided."

Hadley tilted her head. "Do you love him, Lainie? He deserves it. So much."

Lainie's heart was pounding. "I've been in love with him since I was eighteen. Or at least the spark was there. Looking at him, I knew there was a chance for more." She pulled in a breath. "The chance to feel how I feel now." She pressed a hand to her belly. "God, falling in love is scary. It's like diving off a cliff."

The women smiled at her.

"All right, let's get ourselves beautified and massaged," Hadley said. "And Lainie, you should get a Brazilian wax. Rock your man's world."

Lainie giggled. She really, really liked Nick's friends. She thought of Nola. She hoped her best friend would be happy for her and Nick too.

Another woman entered the room, also wearing a robe. She had straight blonde hair pulled back in a messy bun, and her face was free of makeup. She was very thin, the belt cinched tightly at her waist.

Lainie looked at the woman's face, the sharp slashes of her cheekbones. There was something familiar about her, but Lainie couldn't think where she'd seen her. Maybe at the conference?

The woman sat on a lounger and picked up a magazine.

"I think we should hit the shops after this." Hadley waggled her eyebrows. "Lainie, you should get some lingerie and celebrate with your man once this situation is sorted out."

"I'm hoping to have a 'my unhinged, douche bag college ex-boyfriend is locked away' celebration soon," Lainie said.

The blonde woman snapped her magazine closed.

Lainie cleared her throat. "Lingerie shopping sounds good." She was pretty sure it would be a wasted effort, as Nick seemed to yank hers off her very quickly. "I can't wait for this nightmare to be over."

Hadley leaned over and patted her arm. "Soon. You're almost there."

Suddenly, the blonde woman leaped up. She tossed her robe off, and Lainie saw she was dressed underneath in black pants and a black, long-sleeved T-shirt. She whipped some device out from the back of her waistband.

Hadley was already moving, but the blonde jammed the device against Hadley's side.

The Sentinel Security woman shuddered, then collapsed to the floor.

Lainie gasped. *A stun gun.*

It felt like time slowed, and Lainie couldn't get enough air into her constricted lungs.

Hex moved, but the blonde threw herself across the

lounge chair and rammed the crackling stun gun into Hex's belly.

The hacker collapsed onto the lounger, then slid bonelessly to the floor.

Lainie just stood there, frozen. *Move. Move, you idiot.*

The blonde turned, brandishing the stun gun.

"It is going to end today, Lainie. The way it should."

That voice. Lainie frowned. "Clara?"

"That's right." She lifted her chin. "The employee you unfairly dismissed. You thought you were so perfect, so wonderful. The great Lainie Madden."

Clara had lost so much weight that Lainie barely recognized her. Another image popped into Lainie's head. She pictured this version of Clara with frizzy blonde hair and a high-pitched voice. She gasped. "It was you at the cocktail party. You tried to poison me."

"I wasn't planning to kill you, just get you disoriented enough to come with me. I needed to get you away from that brawny guard dog of yours."

"It's been you doing this? All the threats? The cyber attacks? All for some sick revenge?"

"Yes! Because you took what was mine. My career. You ruined it. I should have been in senior management at Pintura, but you were threatened by me."

"Hardly. You ruined it yourself with your unprofessional behavior."

Clara made a scoffing sound. "Like you can talk. You stole Pintura from Trent."

Lainie frowned. Was Clara behind everything all on her own, or was Trent involved too?

241

"I have Trent you know." Clara smirked, looking smug. "You couldn't keep him, but I can."

"You hooked up with Trent?"

"Yes. I know Pintura was his idea, and you stole it."

Anger burned some of Lainie's fear away. "That's bullshit."

"I've been with him, talking with him, fucking him, helping him run his VR bar. But now, I'm gonna give him everything."

Lainie swallowed. The woman was delusional. And dangerous.

Clara tucked the stun gun away and pulled out a deadly-looking handgun.

Lainie just stared at it. *Oh, shit.*

"We're heading out," Clara said. "Somewhere private, where before I kill you, you can sign over owner-ship of Pintura to Trent."

Hell. Lainie's mouth went dry. "Clara—"

"No talking!" She waved the gun and strode closer. She grabbed Lainie's robe and pulled hard. "Now, let's go. Move!"

Lainie cast one last glance at Hadley and Hex collapsed on the floor before Clara dragged her out of the room.

CHAPTER EIGHTEEN

Lainie stumbled, trying to keep up as Clara pulled her out of the elevator and onto the rooftop of the Aurora Casino.

The sun was shining, but it wasn't exactly warm. And since she was only in a robe and bare feet, chill air swept around her legs.

"Clara, look, can we talk—?"

"*No.*" The woman prodded Lainie with the gun.

Jesus. Lainie's throat was so tight. The concrete was cold under her feet and the breeze whipped at her hair.

She'd heard about the casino's rooftop glass sculpture collection. As she stumbled in front of Clara, she took in some of the amazing fantasy-like art pieces. There were huge twists and curls of glass, bigger than Lainie, all in different colors. One looked like a wave made of blue-green glass. Another was twin flames curling around each other. A third one stood higher than the others, made of a deep pink glass, with a thick base and the top seeming to break apart.

She really wanted to come back and look at the sculptures. Without the would-be killer with the gun.

Heart pounding, fueled by fear, Lainie walked across the rooftop. Were Hadley and Hex all right? She prayed they were.

Nick would come.

The man she loved—her big, bossy protector—would come for her.

She just had to hold on until then.

A sense of calm infused her. She knew she could count on Nick.

"So Trent didn't have anything to do with this?" Lainie asked.

Clara's eyes flashed. "No. He never thinks about you."

O-kay.

"You stole his success—"

"I did *not*," Lainie snapped. "I hadn't even started Pintura when Trent and I dated. It was just some nebulous ideas."

"Lies! He deserves to run the company. He's brilliant, humble. He deserves to bask in the success."

There was no point arguing with her, but Lainie needed to stall for more time.

Nick, I hope you're on the way.

"So, what's your plan, Clara?"

The woman pulled some paperwork out of her pocket and unfolded it. The paper rustled in the breeze.

"First, you sign this contract transferring your interest in Pintura to Trent."

Lainie wrapped her arms around herself. "Then

what? Then you kill me? I don't think your contract will stand if I'm found with a bullet in my head."

"Oh, I'm not going to shoot you." A slow, calculated smile curled Clara's lips. "You're going to jump." She jerked her head toward the edge of the roof.

Lainie's belly curdled, her skin going cold before it flushed hot. She stared at the circular, empty helicopter landing pad attached to the building, jutting out into the air.

Now her stomach did an unhappy somersault. She didn't mind heights—when she was safely behind glass or a sturdy railing.

"Clara—"

"Shut up! I don't want to hear your whining or pleading."

Lainie crossed her arms. "Good, because I wasn't going to whine or plead. This isn't going to end the way you'd hoped." Lainie had way too much to live for—her company, her friends, and Nick.

The man she loved so much.

Oh God, if something happened to her, he'd blame himself. Like he did about Jennifer and Madison.

No, Lainie wasn't going to let Clara destroy her and Nick.

"You're going to end up in jail, Clara."

The blonde shook the papers. "You *will* sign these. I *will* have my revenge. Trent will have what he deserves, and the man I love will be happy."

Lainie shook her head.

"Yes." Clara stepped closer. "You'll also sign a nice little suicide note I've typed up for you before you jump. Saying that you can't live with the guilt any longer."

"No way."

Clara's face twisted. She rammed the gun barrel into Lainie's chest. "Move on to the landing pad."

Lainie shuffled backward slowly, her brain whirling. She needed to buy more time.

Nick would come.

She stepped onto the circular pad and the wind picked up, the robe flapping around her legs.

Clara pulled out a pen. "Take it." She held it out.

Lainie took it and threw it over the edge.

With a choked noise, Clara rushed her and slammed the butt of the gun against Lainie's temple.

Ow. Pain exploded and Lainie took a step back. She cradled her throbbing face.

Clara handed her another pen. "Enough, Lainie. Just sign the papers." She shoved them at Lainie.

Swallowing, Lainie glanced at the words, but they swam before her eyes.

She saw the line at the bottom, waiting for her signature.

She quickly scribbled.

Clara smiled, her face glowing. "Excellent. I knew I was smarter than you." She snatched the contract. "I knew—" Her face changed, and she let out an angry squawk.

Lainie had written *fuck you* on the line.

"I'm not giving up my company. I'm not giving up my life!" Lainie charged.

React fast. Nick's deep voice in her head. *Poke the*

eyes, ram a palm to the nose, chop to the throat, and a kick to the knee.

She rammed into Clara, landing a chop to the woman's throat.

The gun flew through the air and hit the concrete several feet away. The papers were caught by the wind, fluttering over the side of the building.

Clara screamed. She grabbed Lainie's hair and yanked.

Ow. Ow. Lainie spun, and poked Clara's eyes. The woman yelped.

Next, Lainie slammed the palm of her hand into Clara's nose.

With a pained grunt, the woman's head flew back, blood pouring down her mouth and chin.

"Did you think I'd be an easy victim?" Lainie spat.

Clara growled and slammed into Lainie. They turned in an unwieldy circle, fighting for control. The lucky bitch got a hit in, her knuckles grinding into Lainie's ribs, driving the air out of her.

They scuffled, moving across the platform. Clara grabbed Lainie's hair again, pulling hard enough to have tears springing into her eyes. She shoved the woman, but Clara shoved back. She was stronger than she looked.

Lainie turned her head and sucked in a sharp breath.

Her foot was only inches away from the edge.

She had a gut-churning view of the Strip, far, far below.

Her heart leaped and lodged into her throat.

No.

She wasn't dying here.

She wanted to make love with Nick again—slow and steady, or hard and fast and rough on the couch.

She wanted to fall asleep on top of him. She wanted to make him laugh. She wanted to come home to him after a long day.

She wanted to have his babies.

Her chest hitched. She was *not* letting this woman steal that from her.

Lainie shoved against Clara, moving away from the edge.

She just had to hold on until Nick got there.

NICK, Hades, and Vander just pulled into the front of the Aurora Casino when all their phones went off.

Still brooding over the fact that Trent was not the perpetrator, Nick yanked his phone out. He was hoping Lainie and the women were busy in the spa.

It was Hex.

He pressed it to his ear. "Hex—"

"Fuck, Nick." The hacker's voice was hoarse. "A woman took Lainie."

His chest locked. "What?"

"A blonde. She came into the spa. She stun-gunned me and Hadley. Hadley's still out but just starting to come around. I'm so sorry, Nick." Hex coughed a little. "I'm on my laptop now, pulling up security feeds."

"It's Clara Hall," he said. "She was the woman with the frizzy hair at the party. She's lost weight, and has been calling herself Claire, and fucking Trent Morton."

"Shit. Okay. I sent alerts to Lachlan, Rhys, and the others to meet you."

"This woman can't have left the casino with Lainie. Someone would've noticed." Nick looked up at Hades and Vander. "Hall's got Lainie. We've got to find them."

"Come on." Hades strode into the lobby.

As Nick passed through the glass doors, his chest tightened. The blood in his veins turned to ice.

What if he was too late? What if he failed her?

Images of Jennifer and Madison's bodies shifted through his head. He shut his eyes.

Then he opened them. *No.*

Vander was watching him. "Your woman needs you, Wolf."

Nick nodded. "Let's find her."

As they crossed the lobby, he saw Craig Miller and two security guards heading in their direction.

"Miller, a blonde woman has taken Lainie," Nick said. "The woman's Clara Hall, and she's armed."

The older man nodded. "Had a guard report in. The elevator to the rooftop has been hacked. We don't have control of it."

Nick's gut clenched. "The rooftop." He lifted his phone and called Hex. "They're on the roof."

"Okay, pulling CCTV up now," Hex said. "Shit. They're up there! They're on the helo landing pad. Nick, they're fighting, and there's a handgun on the ground. Get up there!"

He saw Lachlan, Seth, and Blair jogging toward them with Rhys.

"Miller, is there another way onto the roof?" Nick barked.

Miller nodded. "We have a service elevator. Come on, I'll show you."

Nick was barely keeping his shit together. It was hard, but he dragged in air.

He had to save Lainie.

As he entered the unadorned service elevator, Hades, Vander, Lachlan, and the others filed in with him. His chest loosened. He wasn't alone. He had good people at his back to help him.

"We go in fast," he said. "We need to neutralize Hall. She's armed with at least one handgun. I'll secure Lainie."

"We've got this," Hades said.

The others all nodded, checking their weapons.

"Your woman's smart, Wolf," Vander said. "She'll do what she can to hold on until you get there."

"I...can't lose her."

The elevator slowed.

"You won't," Vander said.

The doors opened.

Nick charged out first. He paid no attention to the weird-ass glass sculptures. He heard a woman scream.

His pulse spiked, adrenaline charging through his system.

He raced out of the artwork and saw Lainie and Clara Hall shoving at each other on the helo pad.

Lainie was only wearing a thick, white robe, while Hall's nose was swollen and stained with blood. The blonde had several inches on Lainie but was several pounds lighter. She swung at Lainie.

Lainie ducked, then rammed her fist into Hall's stomach. She followed through with a sharp kick to the knee. The woman let out another enraged scream.

Nick kept his SIG up and aimed. He saw the rest of the team in his peripheral vision, fanning out.

"Hall, back up," Nick roared. "Hands in the air!"

The woman didn't react. She was lost in the heat of the fight.

But Lainie's head whipped around. She saw him and a beautiful smile broke out on her face.

Fuck. His Lainie.

Then, with a wild shout, Hall rammed herself into Lainie.

The women fell, hitting the ground, wrestling...and rolling dangerously close to the edge of the helo platform.

No. Throat tight, Nick advanced.

But he didn't have a clear shot. The way the women were rolling, he was just as likely to hit Lainie.

"Hades!" Nick yelled.

"Here," his friend answered.

"Get ready to take Hall down."

"They're too close to the edge," Rhys called out.

"Go!" Nick roared.

He charged in, trusting Hades and the others to pin Hall down.

Hades raced in, face set in harsh lines. Blair Mason sprinted, her arms pumping and ponytail whipping behind her. Vander moved, fast and lethal, Rhys at his side. Lachlan and Seth circled around the edge of the landing pad.

Nick heard Lainie and Hall grunting. The women rolled wildly.

Then he watched Lainie roll right to the edge.

No. No. No.

Big brown eyes met his, then she tipped over the edge of the platform.

Nick lunged. He saw Hades and Blair leap on Hall, pinning her down.

"Lainie!" Nick yelled hoarsely. He threw himself forward. As he hit the platform on his stomach, Lainie disappeared from view.

Fuck. No. The words were a roar in his head. His stomach felt shredded.

Then he looked over the edge and saw Lainie clinging to the metal struts holding up the platform, her legs swinging wildly.

"Lainie. Jesus fucking Christ." He could barely speak. His heart was pounding in his chest. He grabbed her wrists. "Hold on, kitten. I've got you."

"*Nick.*" Her eyes were wide, panicked.

"I've got you." He used his strength to haul her up.

The second he had her clear of the edge, he pulled her into his arms and scrambled back.

"Oh, God." She shuddered and clamped her arms around his neck. She pressed her face to his skin. "Nick."

"It's okay now." He ran his hands over her, reassuring himself that she was all right.

He rocked a little. *Christ.* The image of her going over

the edge—hanging hundreds of feet over the Strip—would play in his head for the rest of his life.

He heard sobbing. He saw Vander and Hades yank Clara Hall up, while Lachlan zip tied her hands behind her back.

Then Lachlan swiveled and crouched in front of Nick and Lainie.

"She okay?" the man asked.

"Yeah," Nick said. "Thanks for the assist."

Lachlan nodded, looking at the edge of the roof. "I hate this casino." He shot Nick a faint smile. "I'm glad she's fine."

Lainie pressed a hand to Nick's cheek. "I knew you'd come for me. Knowing that kept me from losing it and letting the fear take over." She stroked his beard. "I knew I just had to hold on until you came for me."

"Always, kitten. You're mine, and I won't let anyone hurt you, or take you from me."

She smiled, then gasped. "My God, Nick. I think I flashed the whole of Las Vegas. I have nothing on under this robe."

A laugh broke out of him, and he pulled her against him and kissed her.

"I love you, Lainie. So damn much."

She gasped, her hands tightening on his cheeks. "You do?"

"I do. Think I always have."

Her smile was blinding. "I love you too, Nick Garrick. And I think I always have as well."

CHAPTER NINETEEN

Lainie snuggled against Nick. They were back in their suite, and she was sitting on Nick's lap on the couch.

He'd been reluctant to let her go, but she'd managed to put some underwear on and change into black leggings and a cream sweater.

Nick nuzzled her hair, and she smiled. Her gorgeous bulldozer could be gentle.

People bustled in and out. Hex and Hadley, much to Lainie's relief, were all right. Hadley was sprawled in an armchair nearby, still looking a little pale. Hex was sitting cross-legged on the floor, her laptop open on the coffee table. Vander was currently on the terrace, phone pressed to his ear.

Lachlan, Seth, and Blair had said their goodbyes and left. Before she'd headed out, Blair had given Lainie a container of six delicious cupcakes.

"I think you've earned these," Blair had said with a small smile.

She totally had. Lainie had eaten two of them already.

The door of the suite opened, and Hades strode in with Rhys.

"Clara Hall is in custody and has been charged," Hades said.

Lainie blew out a breath. Nick's hands tightened on her.

"It's over," she said. "This whole ordeal is finally over."

Hades nodded. "Hall won't get out until she's a very old lady." Then he cleared his throat and slid his hands into his pockets. "There's someone who'd like to see you, Lainie." The man's gaze flicked to Nick.

Lainie frowned. "Who?"

"Trent Morton," Hades said.

Nick stiffened.

Lainie pressed a palm to his chest. "It's all right, Nick. I think this will bring some closure."

A muscle ticked in his jaw. "Fine."

Hades disappeared into the hall. Vander stepped back inside from the terrace and stood against the wall with his brother.

Hades ushered Trent in.

Lainie eyed her former boyfriend objectively. He looked like a normal guy, who was really nervous. His gaze snagged on Rhys and Vander. He missed a step, then his gaze moved away from the pair, and he gave them a wide berth.

He stopped, looking at Lainie sitting on Nick's lap, and his eyes widened.

"You guys are together?" He glanced at Nick. "No wonder that guy nearly killed me."

"Clara Hall nearly killed Lainie." Nick's voice was cutting.

Trent clenched his hands together in front of him. "Lainie, I'm so sorry. I had no idea. I knew Claire, Clara, was obsessed with you, but I never suspected this."

"It's okay, Trent," Lainie said.

Nick was tense beneath her, and she touched his arm and squeezed.

"She used you," Lainie said. "She was manipulative. She needs help."

Trent looked at the floor. "She flattered me. Said nice things about my work." He swallowed. "I was an idiot. I..." He looked straight at Lainie. "I'm sorry. I was an ass in college, and I was an ass again by not seeing through Clara. I'm sorry I played any part in her plan to hurt you."

Lainie nodded. "It's over now."

"Good luck, Lainie," Trent said. "Be happy."

Hades led Trent out.

"We're off," Vander announced. "Our jet is headed back to San Francisco shortly."

Nick set Lainie down on the couch and rose. He shook hands with Vander and Rhys. "Thanks, to both of you. For everything. I'll let you get back to your women."

Vander's lips quirked. "And we'll let you get back to yours. Take care of her."

Lainie got kisses on the cheek, and a saucy wink from Rhys, then the Norcross men left.

"Right, we're off too." Hadley rose and tugged on Hex's arm.

Hex frowned. "I still want to—"

"Go. You want to go. We'll grab Hades and get some dinner."

"No, I still—" Hex looked at Nick with his arm around Lainie. "Oh, yeah, I'm *really* hungry."

With hugs and kisses, the women left.

"Finally." Nick tilted Lainie's face up. He pressed gentle kisses to the bruises on her temple from the butt of Clara's gun.

Oh, yes, her man could be gentle.

But right now, she didn't want gentle.

She nipped his strong jaw. "I'm very, very happy to be alive."

"I'm very, very happy you're alive too. Lainie—"

She heard the dark tone in his voice. "No." She made him look at her. "You saved me. I know you haven't been able to save everyone, but it's impossible to do that. You're not a superhero and you can't save everyone. But I'm very glad you saved me today, Nick." She nudged him back a few steps to the couch. "Now I need something else from the rough, bossy man I love."

He arched a brow. "What's that?"

"I want you to fuck me over the couch again."

His eyes flashed, and he slid a hand down her body and cupped her ass.

"Guess I'd better get to work giving my kitten what she wants." He pulled her in for a hard kiss.

AS THE PRIVATE jet touched down in New York, Nick glanced at Lainie.

She was smiling, practically bouncing in the seat across from him. Happy to be home.

God, just looking at her warmed things inside him. She filled all the cracks and shone a light on old shadows.

He knew now that he wanted Lainie Madden in his life, in his bed, in his arms, for a very long time.

He wasn't going to let her go.

He'd be a greedy asshole and keep all that light for himself.

"We're finally home." Lainie bounded out of her seat.

Nick stood and ran a hand over her hair. "Home." For the first time in a long time, he was excited by the idea of home.

As Lainie headed down the jet stairs, Hex, Hadley, and Hades rose from their seats.

He met Hades' gaze.

"You are so gone for her." His friend shook his head.

"Yep. And believe me, I wouldn't change it for anything. You'll know how it feels one day."

Hades shook his head again. "I like variety, *amico mio*. There will never be just one lovely lady for me."

"We'll see," Nick replied.

Outside the jet, Nick saw Killian standing by a town car. And at the base of the stairs, Lainie and Nola were hugging wildly.

"God, Lainie, I'm *so* glad they stopped that woman," Nola said.

"Me too." Lainie smiled. "Your brother took very good care of me."

Nola snorted and reached over to hug Nick. "I bet he did." Then her gaze moved past Nick's shoulder. "Hello, handsome Matteo. Hi, ladies."

"Hello, *bella*." Hades shot Nick's sister a panty-melting smile.

Nick elbowed the man, before he nodded at Killian.

"Well done," Killian said.

"I'm just glad it's over," Lainie said. "It doesn't feel real."

Nick slipped an arm around her shoulders, and she leaned into him.

Killian's lips quirked. "It will soon."

"So, you two are officially dating," Nola said, with a gleeful smile.

"I don't date," Nick said.

His sister and his woman frowned.

Lainie put her hands on her hips. "What the hell are we doing then?"

"You're moving in with me."

She blinked. "Huh?"

"I'm planning to talk to Killian." He met his boss' dark gaze. "See if we can get a bigger place in the Sentinel Security warehouse. Make it ours."

Lainie's eyes filled with tears. "You are so bossy."

He pulled her to him and saw the happiness on her face.

"When the time is right, Lainie, I'll find the right ring and propose." Fuck, Lainie Madden as his wife. He wanted that.

A single tear slipped down her cheek. "I want that too."

He wiped the tear away.

"My bossy bulldozer of a brother." Nola's voice was thick with emotion.

"The bossiness has grown on me," Lainie murmured, pulling his head down for a kiss. "A lot."

BACK AT THE Sentinel Security warehouse, Lainie along with Nola, Hadley, and Hex disappeared up to Nick's apartment. They planned to make celebratory "the killer is in jail" cocktails. He still didn't like Lainie out of his sight, but he knew he'd get used to it. Eventually.

He might not tell her about the tracker he'd put on her cell phone, though.

He checked his messages and went through the mail on his desk.

"Wolf, I go away on a mission, then come back to hear you're in love and moving in with a woman." Bram "Excalibur" O'Donovan appeared in the arched doorway.

The Irishman was all muscle, with broad shoulders and a head full of dark red hair. His usual scowl was in place.

"Bram, wait until you meet her. She's my sister's best friend. She's a CEO, smart as hell. Beautiful."

Bram shook his head. "I was sure you'd had too much whiskey and hit your head."

"You know I prefer a good bourbon to that Irish whiskey you drink like water. How did it go in Cuba?"

"Fine. Too humid." He grunted. "I didn't fall in love, thank fuck."

"Well, make some time to have dinner with me and Lainie."

"She sounds too good for the likes of you."

"Totally."

"Lucky bastard." With a shake of his head, Bram stalked out.

A second later, Killian appeared. "Wolf?"

His head snapped up at Killian's tone. "Problem?"

"The info Gisele sent through paid off."

Nick raised his brows. He didn't want to think about Gisele.

"The intel you passed along, because of that, the feds busted the Cardoza Cartel's operations in Florida."

Nick felt a fierce sense of satisfaction. "Good."

"There's more," Killian said. "Martinez was there."

Nick stiffened.

"He was shot in the raid. He's not dead, but he's in jail. And with the amount of drugs seized, he's not wriggling out of the charges anytime soon."

Nick dropped his butt back onto his desk. Martinez behind bars. Something he'd dreamed about for years.

He was damn happy, but he realized something.

The poison he'd felt for so long had already leached. Being with Lainie had made him let go of some of the rotten, acidic anger.

He cleared his throat, his voice still thick. "I want to be the one to tell James."

Killian nodded.

Now Hades appeared, smiling. "You two done? I'm thinking we should join the ladies for cocktails."

"Sorry, Hades," Killian said. "No cocktails for you. I have a job for you."

Hades groaned. "I just got home."

"It's a simple one. I need you to meet a CIA contact in D.C. to get some important files. They can't be transferred electronically."

Hades tipped his head back and muttered in Italian.

Killian smiled. "I've reserved you a room at the Hay-Adams."

At the name of the exclusive hotel near the White House, Hades perked up. "I'm charging dinner at Lafayette and the best bottle of Valpolicella I can find on my company card."

"Deal," Killian said.

Hades headed for the doorway and gave them a salute. "Duty calls. Enjoy the cocktails."

"Stay out of trouble, Matteo," Killian called out.

"*Certo.*"

Nick shook his head. "That man couldn't stay out of trouble if he tried."

"It's only one night in D.C. to collect a file. Should be simple enough." Killian slapped Wolf's arm. "Now, how about a cocktail?"

"BYE. SEE YOU TOMORROW." Lainie was a little tipsy as she waved to Hadley, Hex, and Nola as Killian walked them toward the elevator.

"Bye, Nick. Bye, Lainie." Nola executed a graceful pirouette for someone who'd consumed a lot of cocktails. "Stay sparkly. OMG, we're going to be sisters for real soon!"

Nola was catching a cab home, while Hadley and Hex only lived one floor away. It was going to be so great to live in the same building with them.

Strong arms wrapped around her from behind.

"Happy, kitten?"

"So happy I could burst."

She pressed into Nick and wiggled her butt. "I own a billion-dollar company. I have a great team, good friends, and now a hot boyfriend I love."

He nuzzled her neck, and her legs turned liquid.

"And he loves you back."

"And I really like knowing that the man responsible for Jennifer and Madison's deaths is behind bars." Nick had told her earlier, and she'd had to sneak to the bathroom to cry a little. She knew how much this meant to him.

His hands clenched. "Yeah." He spun her, his face turning serious. He stroked her jaw. "Apart from Nola, I've never told anyone that I love them."

She stilled. "Nick—" Knowing his father, stepfather, and mother, she knew it was true. Her heart squeezed for him.

"And apart from Nola," he continued, "no one's loved me."

Lainie's heart squeezed even harder. She cupped his cheeks. "Nick 'Wolf' Garrick, I'm going to love you forever. Until I'm old and gray and can't remember my name." She nibbled at his lips. "I'm going to show you how much I love you every day of our lives. So you never doubt it. Ever."

"Lainie. Sweet Lainie Madden, all mine."

"All yours."

They lost themselves in the kiss, and it quickly turned heated. On a moan, she bit his bottom lip.

Nick started walking her toward the bedroom. "When we move into our new place, we're moving your bed in."

She grinned. "You like it?"

"Oh, yeah. I want your fingers holding onto the metal while I go down on you."

She let out a quick breath. "Okay."

"And soon, I want you to take some time off. I want to visit James in Tennessee."

Her face softened. "I'd like that."

She knew in her heart that this man would always be there for her. Through the tough times and the easy times. The good and the bad. He'd hold her hand. She'd never be alone.

Tears welled. Happy ones.

He'd be proud of her for her wins. He'd commiserate with her for her losses. He'd protect her. He'd boss her around. He'd never cheat, lie, or leave her.

And she'd do as she promised—she'd love Nick Garrick so much that he'd never, ever doubted that he deserved it.

Never doubted that he was a good guy.

She backed away from him and unzipped her skirt, then shimmied out of it.

At the sight of her lace thong, desire ignited in his blue eyes.

He started toward her, hunting her. Her wolf.

Desire curled in her belly.

"I see why they call you Wolf."

He slid his arms around her.

"I'm not Wolf to you, I'm Nick. You reminded me that I'm Nick too. The man. He can't always save everyone, but he can save you. I can be your man, your protector, your lover. Making sure you're happy and safe and loved, it means I have enough light in my life to keep me out of the shadows when I can't save others."

She bit her lip to keep the tears back. "I think Wolf's pretty hot, but I love Nick so much."

He lifted her off her feet and headed for the bedroom.

"Now I need to hear my woman scream my name."

She laughed and held on tight to the man who'd never let her go.

EPILOGUE

A few weeks later

Lainie bounced into the Sentinel Security office with a smile and two bottles in her hands. One was a bottle of champagne, and the other was a bottle of the Angel's Envy Cask Strength bourbon that Nick loved.

The Bloom acquisition was done. Her smile was so wide it hurt, but she didn't care.

Now, she wanted to celebrate with her man.

She saw Hex in her lair and waved. The woman had a headset on, barking at someone, but she waved back.

The Sentinel Security office had been in an uproar the last few weeks with Hades in danger and on the run with a woman, but things had settled down.

Life was awesome.

Killian had given Lainie and Nick a larger apartment in the Sentinel Security warehouse, and she'd rented out her newly renovated Tribeca apartment. Their new place had an amazing terrace with views of the water, and she planned to fill it with pots in the spring. In honor of Christmas coming soon, she'd had Nick string up lights. Next, they were going to get a tree and decorate it. He'd grumbled about it, but she could tell he was secretly excited.

Giving him a home, love, all the things that had been lacking in his life, made her happy.

Nola came around for dinner a lot and continued to express her extreme happiness that her best friend and brother were in love. Every day, Lainie woke up with a smile.

That wasn't to say that Nick didn't drive her crazy sometimes. Her inner cavegirl might love the tough, growly protector, but he could often let the bossiness go wild. She smiled. The makeup sex after a fight rocked, though.

As she neared his office, she heard the rumble of his deep voice and shivered. She was pretty sure when she was old, gray, and wrinkled, that man's voice would still give her shivers.

She paused in the brick archway to his office.

He was standing, wearing the killer suit that he'd put on that morning, with his cell phone pressed to his ear. He was facing away from her, giving her time to admire the view.

"Got it. Thanks, Turner. Yeah, of course, call me if there's any follow-up." Nick ended the call, turned, and spotted her. His lips curled. "Hello, kitten."

"Hi." She walked in and plonked the bottles down on his desk.

His lips quirked. "I take it that we're celebrating?"

"In a second." She wound her arms around his neck.

He pulled her flush against his body and kissed her.

Every kiss felt like a possession. Like a claiming. She couldn't get enough of it. Of him.

"Mmm." She nipped his bottom lip. "I missed you."

He squeezed her ass through her skirt. "It all went okay?"

She beamed at him. "Yes. Bloom is mine. The acquisition papers are all signed, sealed, and delivered. As of next week, we'll start integrating Bloom and its employees into the Pintura structure."

He toyed with her hair. "Proud of you."

It shone from his blue eyes, filling her chest with warmth. "Thanks."

He lowered his head and kissed her again.

As it often did, the kiss got a little wild. With a deep groan, he picked her up and set her on his desk. Luckily her skirt was a flirty, A-line style, so she easily parted her legs to let him step between them.

His mouth traveled down the side of her neck, and she arched into him, desire a hot wave inside her.

"My smart, sexy Lainie."

"*God.*" She slid her hands into his hair. "I wish your office had a door that could be closed and locked." She brought his mouth back to hers for another hungry kiss. "Then we could have sex on your desk."

Nick's hands clenched on her hips. "Damn. Now I'm hard...and picturing you naked on my desk."

Lainie grinned. Anytime she saw how much this man wanted her, loved her, it never failed to leave her happy and a little in awe.

For the first time in her life, she had someone who she truly meant the world to. A strong, solid partner who she could always depend on.

She smacked a kiss on his lips, then grabbed the bottle of champagne, and slid off the desk.

"You can fuck me on the desk at home when you're done here. I'll take this—" she lifted the bottle "—and put it on ice." She headed for the door. "You bring your bourbon."

"Oh, I'll bring it." He stood there with his hands on his hips, smiling.

God, he was gorgeous.

"You'd better be ready to celebrate, kitten. *Hard.*" There was a growl in his voice.

"Oh, I am. I didn't just get champagne and bourbon to celebrate with."

He raised a brow.

With her free hand, she gripped the hem of her skirt and lifted it, showing off the tops of her stockings and garters. "I bought some new lingerie to celebrate as well."

His blue eyes narrowed, and he took a step toward her.

"No door, remember?" she warned him.

"I love you, Lainie."

Those words always made her insides melt. "I know. I love you right back." She slipped out the doorway and blew him a kiss. "See you at home, Nick."

"Very soon, kitten. Very soon."

I hope you enjoyed Lainie and Nick's story!

Sentinel Security continues with *Hades*, starring Matteo "Hades" Mancini and a quick trip to Washington D.C. that doesn't go according to plan. Coming 20th September 2022.

For more action-packed romance, check out the first book in **Norcross Security**, *The Investigator* (Rhys Norcross' story). **Read on for a preview of the first chapter.**

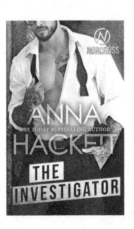

Don't miss out! For updates about new releases, free books, and other fun stuff, sign up for my VIP mailing list and get your *free box set* containing three action-packed romances.

Visit here to get started: www.annahackett.com

Would you like a FREE BOX SET of my books?

PREVIEW: THE INVESTIGATOR

There was a glass of chardonnay with her name on it waiting for her at home.

Haven McKinney smiled. The museum was closed, and she was *done* for the day.

As she walked across the East gallery of the Hutton Museum, her heels clicked on the marble floor.

God, she loved the place. The creamy marble that

made up the flooring and wrapped around the grand pillars was gorgeous. It had that hushed air of grandeur that made her heart squeeze a little every time she stepped inside. But more than that, the amazing art the Hutton housed sang to the art lover in her blood.

Snagging a job here as the curator six months ago had been a dream come true. She'd been at a low point in her life. Very low. Haven swallowed a snort and circled a stunning white-marble sculpture of a naked, reclining woman with the most perfect resting bitch face. She'd never guessed that her life would come crashing down at age twenty-nine.

She lifted her chin. Miami was her past. The Hutton and San Francisco were her future. No more throwing caution to the wind. She had a plan, and she was sticking to it.

She paused in front of a stunning exhibit of traditional Chinese painting and calligraphy. It was one of their newer exhibits, and had been Haven's brainchild. Nearby, an interactive display was partially assembled. Over the next few days, her staff would finish the installation. Excitement zipped through Haven. She couldn't wait to have the touchscreens operational. It was her passion to make art more accessible, especially to children. To help them be a part of it, not just look at it. To learn, to feel, to enjoy.

Art had helped her through some of the toughest times in her life, and she wanted to share that with others.

She looked at the gorgeous old paintings again. One portrayed a mountainous landscape with beautiful maple trees. It soothed her nerves.

Wine would soothe her nerves, as well. *Right*. She needed to get upstairs to her office and grab her handbag, then get an Uber home.

Her cell phone rang and she unclipped it from the lanyard she wore at the museum. "Hello?"

"Change of plans, girlfriend," a smoky female voice said. "Let's go out and celebrate being gorgeous, successful, and single. I'm done at the office, and believe me, it has been a *grueling* day."

Haven smiled at her new best friend. She'd met Gia Norcross when she joined the Hutton. Gia's wealthy brother, Easton Norcross, owned the museum, and was Haven's boss. The museum was just a small asset in the businessman's empire. Haven suspected Easton owned at least a third of San Francisco. Maybe half.

She liked and respected her boss. Easton could be tough, but he valued her opinions. And she loved his bossy, take-charge, energetic sister. Gia ran a highly successful PR firm in the city, and did all the PR and advertising for the Hutton. They'd met not long after Haven had started work at the museum.

After their first meeting, Gia had dragged Haven out to her favorite restaurant and bar, and the rest was history.

"I guess making people's Instagram look pretty and not staged is hard work," Haven said with a grin.

"Bitch." Gia laughed. "God, I had a meeting with a businessman caught in...well, let's just say he and his assistant were *not* taking notes on the boardroom table."

Haven felt an old, unwelcome memory rise up. She mentally stomped it down. "I don't feel sorry for the cheating asshole, I feel sorry for whatever poor shmuck got more than they were paid for when they walked into the boardroom."

"Actually, it was the cheating businessman's wife."

"Uh-oh."

"And the assistant was male," Gia added.

"Double uh-oh."

"Then said cheater comes to my PR firm, telling me to clean up his mess, because he's thinking he might run for governor one day. I mean, I'm good, but I can't wrangle miracles."

Haven suspected that Gia had verbally eviscerated the man and sent him on his way. Gia Norcross had a sharp tongue, and wasn't afraid to use it.

"So, grueling day and I need alcohol. I'll meet you at ONE65, and the first drink is on me."

"I'm pretty wiped, Gia—"

"Uh-uh, no excuses. I'll see you in an hour." And with that, Gia was gone.

Haven clipped her phone to her lanyard. Well, it looked like she was having that chardonnay at ONE65, the six-story, French dining experience Gia loved. Each level offered something different, from patisserie, to bistro and grill, to bar and lounge.

Haven walked into the museum's main gallery, and her blood pressure dropped to a more normal level. It was her favorite space in the museum. The smell of wood, the gorgeous lights gleaming overhead, and the amazing paintings combined to create a soothing room. She smoothed her hands down her fitted, black skirt. Haven was tall, at five foot eight, and curvy, just like her mom had been. Her boobs, currently covered by a cute, white blouse with a tie around her neck, weren't much to write home about, but she had to buy her skirts one size bigger. She sighed. No matter how much she walked or jogged —*blergh*, okay, she didn't jog much—she still had an ass.

Even in her last couple of months in Miami, when stress had caused her to lose a bunch of weight due to everything going on, her ass hadn't budged.

Memories of Miami—and her douchebag-of-epic-proportions-ex—threatened, churning like storm clouds on the horizon.

Nope. She locked those thoughts down. She was *not* going there.

She had a plan, and the number one thing for taking back and rebuilding her life was *no* men. She'd sworn off anyone with a Y chromosome.

She didn't need one, didn't want one, she was D-O-N-E, done.

She stopped in front of the museum's star attraction. Claude Monet's *Water Lilies.*

Haven loved the impressionist's work. She loved the colors, the delicate strokes. This one depicted water lilies and lily pads floating on a gentle pond. His paintings always made an impact, and had a haunting, yet soothing feel to them.

It was also worth just over a hundred million dollars.

The price tag still made her heart flutter. She'd put a business case to Easton, and they'd purchased the painting three weeks ago at auction. Haven had planned out the display down to the rivets used on the wood. She'd thrown herself into the project.

Gia had put together a killer marketing campaign, and Haven had reluctantly been interviewed by the local paper. But it had paid off. Ticket sales to the museum were up, and everyone wanted to see *Water Lilies*.

Footsteps echoed through the empty museum, and she turned to see a uniformed security guard appear in the doorway.

"Ms. McKinney?"

"Yes, David? I was just getting ready to leave."

"Sorry to delay you. There's a delivery truck at the back entrance. They say they have a delivery of a Zadkine bronze."

Haven frowned, running through the next day's schedule in her head. "That's due tomorrow."

"It sounds like they had some other deliveries nearby and thought they'd squeeze it in."

She glanced at her slim, silver wristwatch, fighting back annoyance. She'd had a long day, and now she'd be late to meet Gia. "Fine. Have them bring it in."

With a nod, David disappeared. Haven pulled out her phone and quickly fired off a text to warn Gia that she'd be late. Then Haven headed up to her office, and checked her notes for tomorrow. She had several calls to make to chase down some pieces for a new exhibit she wanted to launch in the winter. There were some restoration quotes to go over, and a charity gala for her art charity to plan. She needed to get down into the storage rooms and see if there was anything they could cycle out and put on display.

God, she loved her job. Not many people would get

excited about digging around in dusty storage rooms, but Haven couldn't wait.

She made sure her laptop was off and grabbed her handbag. She slipped her lanyard off and stuffed her phone in her bag.

When she reached the bottom of the stairs, she heard a strange noise from the gallery. A muffled pop, then a thump.

Frowning, she took one step toward the gallery.

Suddenly, David staggered through the doorway, a splotch of red on his shirt.

Haven's pulse spiked. *Oh God, was that blood?* "David—"

"Run." He collapsed to the floor.

Fear choking her, she kicked off her heels and spun. She had to get help.

But she'd only taken two steps when a hand sank into her hair, pulling her neat twist loose, and sending her brown hair cascading over her shoulders.

"Let me go!"

She was dragged into the main gallery, and when she lifted her head, her gut churned.

Five men dressed in black, all wearing balaclavas, stood in a small group.

No...oh, no.

Their other guard, Gus, stood with his hands in the air. He was older, former military. She was shoved closer toward him.

"Ms. McKinney, you okay?" Gus asked.

She managed a nod. "They shot David."

"I kn—"

"No talking," one man growled.

Haven lifted her chin. "What do you want?" There was a slight quaver in her voice.

The man who'd grabbed her glared. His cold, blue eyes glittered through the slits in his balaclava. Then he ignored her, and with the others, they turned to face the *Water Lilies*.

Haven's stomach dropped. *No*. This couldn't be happening.

A thin man moved forward, studying the painting's gilt frame with gloved hands. "It's wired to an alarm."

Blue Eyes, clearly the group's leader, turned and aimed the gun at Gus' barrel chest. "Disconnect it."

"No," the guard said belligerently.

"I'm not asking."

Haven held up her hands. "Please—"

The gun fired. Gus dropped to one knee, pressing a hand to his shoulder.

"No!" she cried.

The leader stepped forward and pressed the gun to the older man's head.

"No." Haven fought back her fear and panic. "Don't hurt him. I'll disconnect it."

Slowly, she inched toward the painting, carefully avoiding the thin man still standing close to it. She touched the security panel built in beside the frame, pressing her palm to the small pad.

A second later, there was a discreet beep.

Two other men came forward and grabbed the frame.

She glanced around at them. "You're making a mistake. If you know who owns this museum, then you know you won't get away with this." Who would go up against the Norcross family? Easton, rich as sin, had a lot of connections, but his brother, Vander... Haven suppressed a shiver. Gia's middle brother might be hot, but he scared the bejesus out of Haven.

Vander Norcross, former military badass, owned Norcross Security and Investigations. His team had put in the high-tech security for the museum.

No one in their right mind wanted to go up against Vander, or the third Norcross brother who also worked with Vander, or the rest of Vander's team of badasses.

"Look, if you just—"

The blow to her head made her stagger. She blinked, pain radiating through her face. Blue Eyes had back-handed her.

He moved in and hit her again, and Haven cried out, clutching her face. It wasn't the first time she'd been hit. Her douchebag ex had hit her once. That was the day she'd left him for good.

But this was worse. Way worse.

"Shut up, you stupid bitch."

The next blow sent her to the floor. She thought she heard someone chuckle. He followed with a kick to her ribs, and Haven curled into a ball, a sob in her throat.

Her vision wavered and she blinked. Blue Eyes crouched down, putting his hand to the tiles right in front of her. Dizziness hit her, and she vaguely took in the freckles on the man's hand. They formed a spiral pattern.

"No one talks back to me," the man growled. "Especially a woman." He moved away.

She saw the men were busy maneuvering the

painting off the wall. It was easy for two people to move. She knew its exact dimensions—eighty by one hundred centimeters.

No one was paying any attention to her. Fighting through the nausea and dizziness, she dragged herself a few inches across the floor, closer to the nearby pillar. A pillar that had one of several hidden, high-tech panic buttons built into it.

When the men were turned away, she reached up and pressed the button.

Then blackness sucked her under.

Haven sat on one of the lovely wooden benches she'd had installed around the museum. She'd wanted somewhere for guests to sit and take in the art.

She'd never expected to be sitting on one, holding a melting ice pack to her throbbing face, and staring at the empty wall where a multi-million-dollar masterpiece should be hanging. And she definitely didn't expect to be doing it with police dusting black powder all over the museum's walls.

Tears pricked her eyes. She was alive, her guards were hurt but alive, and that was what mattered. The police had questioned her and she'd told them everything she could remember. The paramedics had checked her over and given her the ice pack. Nothing was broken, but she'd been told to expect swelling and bruising.

David and Gus had been taken to the hospital. She'd

been assured the men would be okay. Last she'd heard, David was in surgery. Her throat tightened. *Oh, God.*

What was she going to tell Easton?

Haven bit her lip and a tear fell down her cheek. She hadn't cried in months. She'd shed more than enough tears over Leo after he'd gone crazy and hit her. She'd left Miami the next day. She'd needed to get away from her ex and, unfortunately, despite loving her job at a classy Miami art gallery, Leo's cousin had owned it. Alyssa had been the one who had introduced them.

Haven had learned a painful lesson to not mix business and pleasure.

She'd been done with Leo's growing moodiness, outbursts, and cheating on her and hitting her had been the last straw. *Asshole.*

She wiped the tear away. San Francisco was as far from Miami as she could get and still be in the continental US. This was supposed to be her fresh new start.

She heard footsteps—solid, quick, and purposeful. Easton strode in.

He was a tall man, with dark hair that curled at the collar of his perfectly fitted suit. Haven had sworn off men, but she was still woman enough to appreciate her boss' good looks. His mother was Italian-American, and she'd passed down her very good genes to her children.

Like his brothers, Easton had been in the military, too, although he'd joined the Army Rangers. It showed in his muscled body. Once, she'd seen his shirt sleeves rolled up when they'd had a late meeting. He had some interesting ink that was totally at odds with his sophisticated-businessman persona.

His gaze swept the room, his jaw tight. It settled on her and he strode over.

"Haven—"

"Oh God, Easton. I'm so sorry."

He sat beside her and took her free hand. He squeezed her cold fingers, then he looked at her face and cursed.

She hadn't been brave enough to look in the mirror, but she guessed it was bad.

"They took the *Water Lilies*," she said.

"Okay, don't worry about it just now."

She gave a hiccupping laugh. "Don't worry? It's worth a hundred and ten *million* dollars."

A muscle ticked in his jaw. "You're okay, and that's the main thing. And the guards are in serious but stable condition at the hospital."

She nodded numbly. "It's all my fault."

Easton's gaze went to the police, and then moved back to her. "That's not true."

"I let them in." Her voice broke. God, she wanted the marble floor to crack and swallow her.

"Don't worry." Easton's face turned very serious. "Vander and Rhys will find the painting."

Her boss' tone made her shiver. Something made her suspect that Easton wanted his brothers to find the men who'd stolen the painting more than recovering the price-less piece of art.

She licked her lips, and felt the skin on her cheek tug. She'd have some spectacular bruises later. *Great. Thanks, universe.*

Then Easton's head jerked up, and Haven followed his gaze.

A man stood in the doorway. She hadn't heard him coming. Nope, Vander Norcross moved silently, like a ghost.

He was a few inches over six feet, had a powerful body, and radiated authority. His suit didn't do much to tone down the sense that a predator had stalked into the room. While Easton was handsome, Vander wasn't. His face was too rugged, and while both he and Easton had blue eyes, Vander's were dark indigo, and as cold as the deepest ocean depths.

He didn't look happy. She fought back a shiver.

Then another man stepped up beside Vander.

Haven's chest locked. *Oh, no. No, no, no.*

She should have known. He was Vander's top investigator. Rhys Matteo Norcross, the youngest of the Norcross brothers.

At first glance, he looked like his brothers—similar build, muscular body, dark hair and bronze skin. But Rhys was the youngest, and he had a charming edge his brothers didn't share. He smiled more frequently, and his shaggy, thick hair always made her imagine him as a rock star, holding a guitar and making girls scream.

Haven was also totally, one hundred percent in lust with him. Any time he got near, he made her body flare to life, her heart beat faster, and made her brain freeze up. She could barely talk around the man.

She did *not* want Rhys Norcross to notice her. Or talk to her. Or turn his soulful, brown eyes her way.

Nuh-uh. No way. She'd sworn off men. This one

should have a giant warning sign hanging on him. *Watch out, heartbreak waiting to happen.*

Rhys had been in the military with Vander. Some hush-hush special unit that no one talked about. Now he worked at Norcross Security—apparently finding anything and anyone.

He also raced cars and boats in his free time. The man liked to go fast. Oh, and he bedded women. His reputation was legendary. Rhys liked a variety of adventures and experiences.

It was lucky Haven had sworn off men.

Especially when they happened to be her boss' brother.

And especially, especially when they were also her best friend's brother.

Off limits.

She saw the pair turn to look her and Easton's way.

Crap. Pulse racing, she looked at her bare feet and red toenails, which made her realize she hadn't recovered her shoes yet. They were her favorites.

She felt the men looking at her, and like she was drawn by a magnet, she looked up. Vander was scowling. Rhys' dark gaze was locked on her.

Haven's traitorous heart did a little tango in her chest.

Before she knew what was happening, Rhys went down on one knee in front of her.

She saw rage twist his handsome features. Then he shocked her by cupping her jaw, and pushing the ice pack away.

They'd never talked much. At Gia's parties, Haven

purposely avoided him. He'd never touched her before, and she felt the warmth of him singe through her.

His eyes flashed. "It's going to be okay, baby."

Baby?

He stroked her cheekbone, those long fingers gentle.

Fighting for some control, Haven closed her hand over his wrist. She swallowed. "I—"

"Don't worry, Haven. I'm going to find the man who did this to you and make him regret it."

Her belly tightened. *Oh, God.* When was the last time anyone had looked out for her like this? She was certain no one had ever promised to hunt anyone down for her. Her gaze dropped to his lips.

He had amazingly shaped lips, a little fuller than such a tough man should have, framed by dark stubble.

There was a shift in his eyes and his face warmed. His fingers kept stroking her skin and she felt that caress all over.

Then she heard the click of heels moving at speed. Gia burst into the room.

"What the hell is going on?"

Haven jerked back from Rhys and his hypnotic touch. Damn, she'd been proven right—she was so weak where this man was concerned.

Gia hurried toward them. She was five-foot-four, with a curvy, little body, and a mass of dark, curly hair. As usual, she wore one of her power suits—short skirt, fitted jacket, and sky-high heels.

"Out of my way." Gia shouldered Rhys aside. When her friend got a look at Haven, her mouth twisted. "I'm going to *kill* them."

"Gia," Vander said. "The place is filled with cops. Maybe keep your plans for murder and vengeance quiet."

"Fix this." She pointed at Vander's chest, then at Rhys. Then she turned and hugged Haven. "You're coming home with me."

"Gia—"

"No. No arguments." Gia held up her palm like a traffic cop. Haven had seen "the hand" before. It was pointless arguing.

Besides, she realized she didn't want to be alone. And the quicker she got away from Rhys' dark, far-too-perceptive gaze, the better.

Norcross Security

The Investigator

The Troubleshooter

The Specialist

The Bodyguard

The Hacker

The Powerbroker

The Detective

The Medic

The Protector

W ant to learn more about the mysterious, covert *Team 52*? Check out the first book in the series, *Mission: Her Protection.*

When Rowan's Arctic research team pulls

a strange object out of the ice in Northern Canada, things start to go wrong...very, very wrong. Rescued by a covert, black ops team, she finds herself in the powerful arms of a man with scary gold eyes. A man who vows to do everything and anything to protect her...

Dr. Rowan Schafer has learned it's best to do things herself and not depend on anyone else. Her cold, academic parents taught her that lesson. She loves the challenge of running a research base, until the day her scientists discover the object in a retreating glacier. Under attack, Rowan finds herself fighting to survive... until the mysterious Team 52 arrives.

Former special forces Marine Lachlan Hunter's military career ended in blood and screams, until he was recruited to lead a special team. A team tasked with a top-secret mission—to secure and safeguard pieces of powerful ancient technology. Married to his job, he's done too much and seen too much to risk inflicting his demons on a woman. But when his team arrives in the Arctic, he uncovers both an unexplained artifact, and a young girl from his past, now all grown up. A woman who ignites emotions inside him like never before.

But as Team 52 heads back to their base in Nevada, other hostile forces are after the artifact. Rowan finds herself under attack, and as the bullets fly, Lachlan vows to protect her at all costs. But in the face of danger like they've never seen before, will it be enough to keep her alive.

Team 52

Mission: Her Protection
Mission: Her Rescue
Mission: Her Security
Mission: Her Defense
Mission: Her Safety
Mission: Her Freedom
Mission: Her Shield
Also Available as Audiobooks!

Want to learn more about *Treasure Hunter Security*?
Check out the first book in the series, *Undiscovered*,
Declan Ward's action-packed story.

**One former Navy SEAL. One dedicated
archeologist. One secret map to a fabulous
lost oasis.**

Finding undiscovered treasures is always daring, dangerous, and deadly. Perfect for the men of Treasure Hunter Security. Former Navy SEAL Declan Ward is haunted by the demons of his past and throws everything he has into his security business—Treasure Hunter Security. Dangerous archeological digs – no problem. Daring expeditions – sure thing. Museum security for invaluable exhibits – easy. But on a simple dig in the Egyptian desert, he collides with a stubborn, smart archeologist, Dr. Layne Rush, and together they get swept into a deadly treasure hunt for a mythical lost oasis. When an evil from his past reappears, Declan vows to do anything to protect Layne.

Dr. Layne Rush is dedicated to building a successful career—a promise to the parents she lost far too young. But when her dig is plagued by strange accidents, targeted by a lethal black market antiquities ring, and artifacts are stolen, she is forced to turn to Treasure Hunter Security, and to the tough, sexy, and too-used-to-giving-orders Declan. Soon her organized dig morphs into a wild treasure hunt across the desert dunes.

Danger is hunting them every step of the way, and Layne and Declan must find a way to work together...to not only find the treasure but to survive.

Treasure Hunter Security
Undiscovered
Uncharted
Unexplored
Unfathomed

Untraveled
Unmapped
Unidentified
Undetected
Also Available as Audiobooks!

ALSO BY ANNA HACKETT

Mark of Eon

Claim of Eon

Storm of Eon

Soul of Eon

King of Eon

Also Available as Audiobooks!

Galactic Gladiators: House of Rone

Sentinel

Defender

Centurion

Paladin

Guard

Weapons Master

Also Available as Audiobooks!

Galactic Gladiators

Gladiator

Warrior

Hero

Protector

Champion

Barbarian

Beast

Rogue

Guardian

Cyborg

Imperator

Hunter

Also Available as Audiobooks!

Hell Squad

Marcus

Cruz

Gabe

Reed

Roth

Noah

Shaw

Holmes

Niko

Finn

Devlin

Theron

Hemi

Ash

Levi

Manu

Griff

Dom

Survivors

Tane

Also Available as Audiobooks!

The Anomaly Series

Time Thief

Mind Raider

Soul Stealer

Salvation

Anomaly Series Box Set

The Phoenix Adventures

Among Galactic Ruins

At Star's End

In the Devil's Nebula

On a Rogue Planet

Beneath a Trojan Moon

Beyond Galaxy's Edge

On a Cyborg Planet

Return to Dark Earth

On a Barbarian World

Lost in Barbarian Space

Through Uncharted Space

Crashed on an Ice World

Perma Series

Winter Fusion

A Galactic Holiday

Warriors of the Wind

Tempest

Storm & Seduction

Fury & Darkness

Standalone Titles

Savage Dragon

Hunter's Surrender

One Night with the Wolf

For more information visit www.annahackett.com

ABOUT THE AUTHOR

I'm a USA Today bestselling romance author who's passionate about *fast-paced, emotion-filled* contemporary romantic suspense and science fiction romance. I love writing about people overcoming unbeatable odds and achieving seemingly impossible goals. I like to believe it's possible for all of us to do the same.

I live in Australia with my own personal hero and two very busy, always-on-the-move sons.

For release dates, behind-the-scenes info, free books, and other fun stuff, sign up for the latest news here:

Website: www.annahackett.com